ROSES
IN THE
TEMPEST

Roses in the Tempest

A Tale of Tudor England

JERI WESTERSON

Old London Press

www.JeriWesterson.com

Cover design by Jeri Westerson. Images by Thinkstockphotos.com and Canstockphoto.com. Priory plan illustration created by Jeri Westerson and inspired by plan provided by David Bywater.

ISBN-10: 1505895723
ISBN-13: 978-1505895728

First Edition: April 2015

For Craig, the hero of all my tales

ACKNOWLEDGMENTS

This novel would have been impossible to write without the generous help of all those helpful strangers across the Atlantic who gave of their free time: To webmaven Cathy Knight who found me struggling to get information on Brewood from its website, and who befriended me and gathered for me documents and maps so hard to attain; to David Horovitz who literally wrote the book on Brewood (an invaluable resource), and who also offered his time and suggestions; to David Bywater, the former owner of Blackladies for providing floor plans and photographs of the buildings; to Jane Rogers who gave helpful advice and clarification; to the Staffordshire Archive Service for their kind and prompt help; for the beta help of Rebecca Farnbach, Mark Redfern, Carol Thomas, and copy editing from Lisa Edwards; to my ever patient husband Craig; and last but not least, to a family friend who asked the question in the first place, "Whatever happened to all those poor nuns?"

INTRODUCTION

For a moment the lie becomes truth. –Fëdor Dostoevski

Way back in 2001, I wrote this book when I was still thinking of writing historical fiction before I turned to medieval mysteries and my Crispin Guest series. It is unusual in that the main events in this novel were true, with every person mentioned real and factual. Even the waifs Jane and Mary existed, though we do not know their names or their fates.

I have called this a "tale" of Tudor England for a very good reason. In my initial research into this era and to this particular priory, and into the people who inhabited it, I began to form an opinion as to who the people were and their relationships to each other. It is a common practice amongst authors of historical fiction to extrapolate the facts as they know them and form their fiction around it, staying as close to the truth as they can, but naturally making up those scenes and dialogue that no one ever could have written down.

So as I began to research, it occurred to me as the bits and pieces of their lives fell into place, and the more I delved into their histories and wondered about them and their motivation for certain events, it seemed to speak to me of an unlikely love story between Thomas Giffard and Isabella Launder. After all, it is the job of the writer to ask "What if?" and to cobble together a pleasing narrative.

But in the end, it is *only* a pleasing story. There is no *concrete* evidence to suggest that there was such a relationship between these two people.

So, dear Reader, take the story for what it is. All the other events transpired as they did some five hundred years ago.

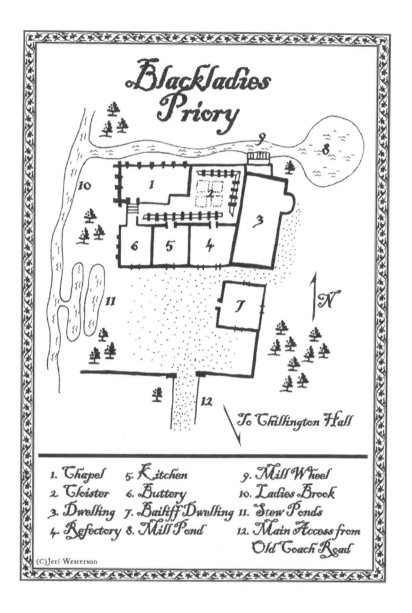

Blackladies
Priory

1. Chapel   5. Kitchen   9. Mill Wheel
2. Cloister   6. Buttery   10. Ladies Brook
3. Dwelling   7. Bailiff Dwelling 11. Stew Ponds
4. Refectory   8. Mill Pond   12. Main Access from
                                           Old Coach Road

(C) Jeri Westerson

To Chillington Hall

PROLOGUE

24 MARCH, 1551
Swynnerton, Staffordshire England

What would the rose with all her pride be worth
were there no sun to call her brightness forth?
                                        —Thomas More

I have ridden this road in my mind too many times to count, dreading its eventuality. And now that my horse has trod that bleak ribbon, I felt nothing but numbness. It wasn't only the cold, though today was a winter wearing its deepest mantle. There was no movement from the frosted shrubs along the verges. No breeze, no breath, no reminder of life. The only movement was a crest of dark trees along the horizon, throbbing from a distant wind.

Looking up I saw the house, a darker gray against a slate sky laid out broad behind it. With winter still misting the hedgerows, we cantered along. The stallion's breath huffed in cloudy gusts through his bridle until we finally thumped up the long lane through the open stone gate and entered the empty courtyard.

The old house was not cared for. Not as she had cared for Blackladies, for there, even in its poverty, disrepair was worn about its timbered shoulders with all the dignity of a patched cloak.

But in this place, a place she never expected to be, tiles had vanished from the roof, and the stone foundations never saw the points of a bristle brush or soap. A broken pane of glass, like a dour eye, was gouged and replaced with a rag flapping in the breeze, beckoning me to a duty I dreaded most.

Which was her window? Was it that one with the rag?

Stiffly I dismounted, feeling every one of my sixty years, and entered the house without waiting for a groom. A servant brushed past me before jerking to a halt in surprised horror, bending almost double in belated courtesy when his eyes scoured my velvet doublet and mud-splattered jerkin—surely the richest gentleman to cross this mean threshold.

"Where?" I said. He knew what I meant. Who else could I be, even to his mill wheel brain?

"This way, Lord Giffard," he said, and led me up a staircase whose balusters were dull and cloudy from old, unpolished beeswax. My heart pounded as I followed him down a long, dim gallery until coming upon a door. I would rather be walking into a French prison than through that sealed portal, yet my feet moved on without my willing them to that place, to that which I knew I must see.

The servant opened the door and stepped aside, allowing me to enter alone. The room smelled of mildew with a precious hint of lavender clouding the stench of decay. Heavy curtains secured the casement lest vital sunshine intrude. Instead, a candle burned at the head of the bed, its flame sputtering indignantly, issuing its own incense of smoky tallow.

I could not look at the figure reposing on the bed. Not yet. Only with my vision's periphery did I see, taking in bedstead and shadowy bed curtains. When I finally gathered the courage to look, I gasped as I becrossed myself. How many years was it since she wore her nun's weeds? It was as if I viewed the past through a glass, seeing her as she was, and not as she finally became. Suddenly I was grateful. Surely this was Isabella's last request. Or

2

perhaps one of them. With my optimist's heart, I hoped also that a final wish might have been to see me.

Her face was lined and waxy in death, as white as the wimple that gathered about her cheeks. Never a beauty in life, her face now radiated a luminous quality. Long fingers lay gently on a rosary upon her breast. This woman who was always my twin in height seemed now shrunken within the cloud of feather ticking.

I moved to stand beside her, shaking my head as our shared history unfolded in my mind.

Then, slowly, I knelt.

"Oh, Isabella. What wonders are you at last privy to? How trivial are the matters in this little kingdom, for you now reside in the greatest of kingdoms. I have no doubt you sit at the feet of the Almighty." My elbows sank into the mattress and I interlaced my fingers to a single upraised fist, resting it against my whiskered chin. The flat plates of my thumbnails caressed my lower lip and I considered. "It is Thomas Giffard, in case you have forgotten."

Almost, I thought her composed lips turned up with indulgence. I smiled. "You knew I would come. Late, of course. Too late." I chuckled, for it was only then that I could allow tears to flow. Without it I should lose all control. "And you would not want that," I told her corpse. "I am glad to see you so garbed. It is you who has the last laugh, then. I would tell you to give old King Hal a tweak, but I know he is not with you in that place, but in some other." I sighed and lowered my hands, idly smoothing the rough coverlet with a callused palm before wiping the wet from my cheek.

"Isabella. Who would have thought they could take our religion from us? I saw it happening and barely understood, as powerless as the best of them to stop it. Even poor Thomas More." I recalled them all; those who had stood against the king when he strove to put aside his good queen in favor of the whore Boleyn. If they only knew what mummery was to come of it, I wonder how many would have been the king's man then? Of course there was

Thomas Cromwell and his lackeys, but the headsman has since made shorter men of them.

And now there is sickly King Edward. If only he would die.

I glanced at her still countenance. "Forgive me, Lady Prioress. You would have scolded me for that uncharitable thought." Watching her silent, unmoving features, I could stand it no more, and I leapt to my feet, casting aside the heavy curtains allowing the gray light of afternoon to tumble into the deadened room. I inhaled fresh air from a draughty window before turning back to her, my shoulder blades couched against the diamond panes. "And so, you are at your end, my dear Lady Prioress. Worries are done. Old sentiments set aside. Everything resolved at last."

The feeling of a bodkin twisting in my gut was one of old, and I could not help but stare at her face and wonder, as I had wondered for so many years.

She was silent. As silent as always. No more words now. "Isabella," I whispered. "Sweet Isabella, if we could change but one summer, which would it be?"

ISABELLA LAUNDER
SUMMER, 1515
Beech, Staffordshire England

I

"Worst of all wounds is that of the heart..."
—Sirach 25:12

I was grateful for the sun, its warmth nudging my shoulders even through the brown-dyed wool. I was happily in the only quiet place on the entire grange where I could be alone with my thoughts. My garden, my secret and solitary pleasure amid the acres of Father's land. It was safe amongst the broad cabbage leaves gesturing like supplicating hands. These and my roses served to hide me from my family, a noisy lot full of gossip and chatter.

I looked out beyond the little square of burgeoning rows where there stood a long, low wall of stone, and beyond that the vast green countryside of Beech, whose hills darkened under the languid ramble of low-slung clouds.

"How I daydream," I murmured to myself, shaking my head for the hundredth time that day. "These weeds will not uproot themselves." I leaned into the hoe at last, yet even as the rhythm of my thoughts tilled along with the hoe, I naturally drifted into a reverie as aimless as the buzzing midges encircling my head, until my reflections lit, as they always somehow managed, on Thomas Giffard.

Thomas Giffard. I slowed tilling once again, thinking of him. Thomas Giffard. Such unusual society. I was nothing like him, in temperament or in looks. Framed willowy and tall, I was as tall as most men, though not graced with their form. Possessed of uninspired brown locks, I kept them tucked under a linen kerchief, not out of any modesty but embarrassment at such unruly strands. In the glass, I saw only the semblance of a sheep's face with its long nose and bruise-lidded eyes, and a small mouth curving over a hint of chin. No beauty I, surely. A face I should characterize as forgettable.

Hoof falls closing fast upon the garden wall snapped me out of my daydream, and all at once, the rusty hide of the beast arced over the wall, sheared a flurry of hedge, and scrabbled in an unsettling turn near the edge of my sprouting vegetables. The horse circled, gnawing the bit with frothed lips while Thomas Giffard himself, calf-high boots covered in mud and cloak hanging precariously from a shoulder, eyed me with a dark scowl.

I blushed, believing he could read my thoughts from my face. But his fitful expression brought me firmly back to earth. Straightening, I dropped the hoe, gathered myself, and smoothed the wrinkles out of my gown with a dirty hand.

Jangling the bridle, the horse toed the earth and bobbed its head. Thomas threw his leg over the saddle and slid at last to the ground. He wore no hat and his collar was untidily knotted. His lips, usually curled upward at some jest, hung downward, dragging the dark beard and mustache with it. He strode forward without ceremony and stared at me with dark-rimmed eyes.

"Damn!"

"Thomas," I whispered, shamed by his oath.

"Isabella! My father. My *wretched* father! He has ruined me!"

Like cogwheels in a mill, my mind slowly grew to life again, with etiquette yanking at the hem of my thoughts. "Come into the house, Thomas. Let us not speak in the mud like tradesmen."

He leaned an arm across his sturdy thigh, measuring the stone wall, the window, and finally the roof. "No," he grumbled.

Why am I trembling? I stared at my hands, willing them to stop, slowly closing one over the other, resting them against the dingy napron. "But Father would be pleased to meet you at last…"

He shook his head and ran a hand across his dark beard. Neatly trimmed and warmly familiar, the beard ran close to the jaw, making a noble profile. "No. Oh, Isabella." He reached for my hands and dragged them into his own, the soft leather of the gloves pillowing my callused fingers. He held them awkwardly a long time, bowing his head toward them, and inhaling deeply to calm himself.

I looked down upon his uncovered hair, so much like a little boy's, shining with sweat and emanating an honest, musky scent. Were my hands not captured by his, I might have been tempted to reach out and stroke that head. "Whatever it is, Thomas…"

He chuckled, its low rumble almost more tangible than his touch. It reverberated under my skin. "Mistress Launder, your keen words of advice and wisdom cannot salvage the situation this time. My father," he said with a strained breath, "whom of late betrothed himself to the king's young ward Dorothy Montgomery, decided against the match and betrothed himself to her mother, the rich widow."

Such nonsense. I cooled my concern. "But this is a better match, Thomas. They are closer in age and it appears to be more economically practical. Lady Montgomery has use of the lands and—"

"Economically practical," he spat. "Yes, that is my father, right enough. Why marry the daughter when the young widow is willing? You are a keen observer, Isabella. Always you have been." I regretted an immodest and uncontrollable blush warming my cheek. "The things you must be privy to," he went on, "and yet I know how solemn you keep your secrets. Better than a priest in the confessional."

"Then what is the matter, Thomas? Is it that you do not like your father's choice?"

"My father's *choice*! Dammit, Isabella!" Fiercely, he threw my hands away.

"Thomas! I have told you countless times you must not make oaths in my presence and with my name! I beg you to calm yourself."

"You do not understand!" he cried, pounding his chest with gloved knuckles. "He has betrothed *me* to Dorothy Montgomery!"

My breath caught. Similar words I had long expected, yet to hear them actually uttered stabbed something deep within me. Thomas continued talking, but I could not discern the words.

I knew of his father, Sir John Giffard. He was a knight and well liked in King Henry's court. He owned estates in Caverswall and distant Brewood and many others, and was appointed sheriff twice. The Giffards and Montgomerys were courtiers, while the Launders only farmers. It was merely more of Thomas' foolishness and his wish to jibe his father that he spent time with me. I endured it as I always did, for there were no suitors to fill my vacant hours. Rafe Launder made little effort to seek a marriage for his eldest daughter, though my brother Robert and sister Agnes had made fine matches.

"Do not be foolish, Thomas," I muttered under his exclamations.

"Isabella! Did you hear me?"

He took my hands again and shook them before I gently freed myself. My steps sank into the soft earth until I reached the haven of a fence post and slowly leaned against it. I raised my face but not my eyes, feeling his hard breath upon me. "Do you fear it?"

"I fear nothing," he said, posturing.

Dry mouthed, I asked, "Is it…that you love another?"

"Isabella! My heart!" His shadow fell across me and I was overwhelmed momentarily with the masculine presence of him. "I am a lusty man. It is not in my nature to settle for one. And in truth, I would not yet have it so."

His words urged an ache in my chest. "We both know a man in your position has responsibilities."

"I will not have it! I will not take Father's leavings!" He postured with a deep scowl, until it eventually softened. He stared at me a long time before something of his former self became visible in his eyes, and he rose up the incline to stand over me, resting his warm hand on my shoulder. He smiled, and all at once we were young again with no dark pall hanging over our heads, no drear future hazing our sight. Then it was gone, as fleeting as its recovery. The world rushed in again and Thomas' face reflected all the burden of responsibilities he had always denied. The dark bronze on his cheeks now seemed more like ruddy smudges. He sighed. "What are we to do, Isabella?"

I could not help it. I blushed from such sudden intimacy, and lowered my eyes. "We are only friends, Thomas. I can offer little." Rolling my shoulder along the post, I stepped lightly away, running my hand over the stubbled nose of his horse. The stallion's lips nuzzled my palm, but found only dirt and sweat. "All I have is advice. And the only advice I have for you is to do as your father wishes."

Stunned, Thomas stood in the mud, his palms open and fingers outstretched. "Isabella!"

I whirled on him then. How dare he come riding here in his indignation wrapped in that velvet cloak of nobility! How dare he announce what I always knew would be. "Why do you continue to deceive yourself? You are a fool!"

Thomas rushed forward, his hands ready to capture, but I turned to escape. His brows converged, brooding. "So you *want* me to marry her. Is that it?"

These were all the wrong protests, and I would have had him say a script full of any other courtly avowals.

But snatching a glimpse at my dusty wooden shoes and frayed gown, I knew I would not hear such.

Thomas' fingers closed unexpectedly on my arm, yanking me toward him. "Tell me, Mistress Launder! Do you tire of me? And after I gave you my friendship all these years!"

"Have I not given you mine?"

Searching my face, he surrendered and released me. With curled fingers, he raked his glistening hair. Then, pegging his fists into his hips, he stared deeply into the countryside. The sky directly above had changed again. The deep summer blue was painted now with transparent brushstrokes of white. He seemed to be contemplating it, deciding. Was it only now he realized the world did not spin on the pin he held? Poor Thomas. Perhaps to be too wealthy was as burdensome as being too poor.

"You must have known this day would come," I said aloud.

He dropped his head. The back of his neck was red from the sun. No doubt, he had ridden all the way from Caverswall. "I...I only..." When he swiveled toward me, his face wore all the passion of a child being disciplined. "I thought I could marry for love. We are rich enough...Oh, Isabella! Be my friend in this. If it were not for you and our long friendship..."

My face tightened. "How could I stand against your father's decision? Who am I, after all?" I shook my head at the enormity of it. "Friends! This friendship of ours. It could be misinterpreted... by someone."

"Isabella," he said, waving his hand dismissively. "It is not as if we are lovers. You are, and have ever been, like a sister to me. Surely all know that! There are many other women in this shire for lovers. Friends are harder come by."

"Shame on you for those thoughts, Thomas!" I cried, too loudly. "Lovers! A betrothal is a promise made before God. Would you break a promise made to God?"

He scowled. "You do not understand at all, do you, with your quaint ways and rustic traditions?"

I did not much like his tone and opened my mouth to object when he interrupted. "The Giffards go back to William the Conqueror. We marry who is profitable. We do not have to love them...but we *do* have to love."

"And the idea of fidelity is rustic to your mind? I pity you, Thomas. Oh not because of some marriage contract which is suitable for your position and even your temperament—though you are unwilling to recognize it. But because you have all the advantages of a name and a heritage and they mean nothing to you."

"But I would share these things with you, Isabella," he said with his Giffard's petulance. "You have been more to me than any wife could be."

"You could never share them with me. I know my place. These things are for your betrothed. I would never take them."

"Then you would be a fool!"

His face—so often cheerful and charming—took on an unpleasant demeanor.

"Then I *am* a fool," I admitted softly. "A practical fool." Suddenly all our days together fell away. He was Thomas Giffard the nobleman, and I...and I...only Isabella Launder.

I did not want his anger just now. Perhaps he used it as a shield. I knew not. But there was little left to say. Turning away from his indignant scowl I trudged back toward the house when I spied the broken rose bush nearest the wall. His horse stood on them still. The sight of it assailed me so sharply that I was unprepared for the onrush of emotion welling up. I fell to my knees, cradling the small round blooms in my hands. "My roses!" I sputtered. "You broke my roses!"

Without hesitation he moved to the horse and mounted, thrusting his feet angrily into the stirrups. "You care more for those damn roses than for me."

"But you have trampled them! Your recklessness—"

"Roses are hearty things," he said gruffly. "It may yet survive."

"But not when so brutally trampled!" I lifted the snapped stems, caring little that the thorns pierced my flesh.

"And our friendship, lady. Have you not trampled upon it?"

Rising straight like a rod, I turned to him, fingers curled into tight fists. "Why did you come, Thomas? You leave as you came, it seems, with nothing. You offered nothing, you asked nothing, and you received nothing!"

"So you have said it, lady. I leave with nothing."

He wheeled the horse, gave me one last scathing glare, and rode out of the yard, the stallion's hooves casting up great clods of mud.

THOMAS GIFFARD
SUMMER, 1515
Caverswall Castle, north of Beech

II

"Live now, believe me, wait not till tomorrow:
gather the roses of life today."
−Pierre de Ronsard, 1524-1584

I was abominably angry. How could she ever completely understand my turmoil or my hurt? How could she deny me? Isabella was like a true sister, truer than my own siblings. A stone foundation to my clay monument. No. Not foundation. A statue of her own. Like a stone saint, she was perpetually in waiting until the moment of my return.

I thought of her even while I lay in the straw, nestled beside one of Father's serving wenches. Yes, Isabella was very like a saintly statue, serious, unyielding, patient, unlike the fawning creature who lay beside me.

My hand lifted to stroke a silken thigh that had escaped the straw. She purred a throaty giggle. "My lord," she murmured.

"Would you sleep during your working hours? Up, you slothful wretch!" and I playfully slapped her haunch. She yelped and sat upright, but her eyes were still hooded, hair falling indulgently across her face. She was a fetching lass, to be sure, and I could not help but smile at her. "Bessie," I said, snaring my arms about her.

"*Betty*, my lord!"

"Yes. Betty. What shall I do without you when I am far from here?"

"You're to be wed, my lord. When?"

"Too soon, my merry Betty. Too soon. Will you miss me?"

"Yes, my lord."

"Liar." I slapped her thigh again and this time it roused her to her feet. She gathered her clothing and began to dress, scattering straw as each layer covered her. I leaned back and crossed one ankle over the other and watched. "Any number of young men will fill your hours and you will not think of me."

"Any more than you will think of me, my lord."

"Ha!"

"It's that other then, you think of. Or is that your betrothed?"

"Who?"

She pushed back the hay-speckled hair from her face and insolently raised her chin at me. She smiled sleepily. "Isabella. It is a name you murmured to me."

"I? How so? You jest with me."

"Maybe so, my lord." She yawned before throwing her veil lazily over her shoulder and sashaying out the door into the sunlight.

Shaking my head, I secured my slops and pulled on my jerkin and gown. Faith! That I should be so occupied by thoughts of Isabella that I mumble her name into a kitchen wench's ear! How Mistress Launder's cheek would blush at that.

Leaving the stables, I peered into the hazy afternoon, thinking of Isabella's commonplace features and how unlike she was even to our Bessie, whose face rounded with rosy sensuality, yet they were not unlike in their stations. How incredible the difference with which I viewed them both.

I could have easily forgotten about Isabella after that very first meeting, so long ago now. Recalling it always filled me with a portion each of amusement and embarrassment. I was a young rascal then, and she a hard-featured and spindly maid. That day—so many summers past now—I rode my stallion over the roads and byways with reckless impetuosity. The concerns of Caverswall were left far behind, and Father with his nattering about my schooling could be damned! Eyes shut tight, I had absorbed the bright sun dappling its warmth upon my closed lids. There was a fleeting rich scent of primrose shimmered on the wind, along with meadow grass, sweet and moist and filled with the essence of earth. That day I *was* the earth and sky.

Too late I spied her. The horse leaned, and when I opened my eyes to observe the bend in the road, I could do little then but haul upon the reins. Even so, I saw her go down at the edge of my sight. Wheeling the horse, my heart was in my throat. *Jesu! Did I kill her?* I was hours from Caverswall and help. Panicked, I wrenched the horse to a stop.

To my immense relief, she rose from the mire of the ditch and glared at me.

"Could you not see me?" I cried. "What were you doing in the middle of the road? God's teeth!"

"That is hardly the point," she replied, shaking each foot like a hound shaking his paws. She rather resembled a hound, with her thin arms, big hands, and long, unattractive face. Even covered in mud I could tell she was probably not much older than myself. Perhaps fifteen or sixteen, for the buds of her bosom were evident from the damp of her mud-spattered chemise and bodice. Having only just reached my thirteenth year, such things as bodices began to intrigue me. "Well, then," I muttered indignantly, for indeed, what could I have said? Reaching into a pouch at my belt I tossed a coin that landed with a gentle thud at her feet.

The impudent creature stared at the disk a long moment before glaring at me. "What is this?"

"For your trouble," I said, and thought that was that. I had only tilted some urchin into a ditch and no harm was done, except to that of my good humor. That was ruined. It forced me to consider how Father would have needed to save my neck if…but no matter. The creature was alive and well and now a groat richer.

"Do you think you can buy your way out of your troubles?" she said, stepping before me again. Like some fishwife she shook a scolding finger at me. "You sir, are a poor young man indeed."

"I am no one's 'poor young man'! I am Thomas Giffard, son of Sir John Giffard." I rose in the saddle, lengthened by my own nobility. "And I will thank you to treat your betters with more respect."

"Forgive me, my lord," she said without one shred of regard, "but I expect my betters not to hurl me into the mud, nor insult me with coin as if I were a beggar. I am Isabella Launder and my father is Yeoman Rafe Launder, owner of this grange near which you ride so heedlessly. And I would thank *you* to offer the proper civility to the king's subjects who must travel this road. You may take your coin back, sir. I have no use for it."

Tightening my gloved hand on the reins, I stared astonished at the coin still sitting in the mud and then at her lank frame. I should have lashed back. She looked as if she expected it, braced for it. But the amazing circumstance of her refusal aroused in me an unexpected awe, the same often aroused in me when I witnessed my father in poised confrontation with a room full of nobles. "I…I did not mean anything…"

"I know," she offered, softening. With more grace than her loose limbs could be credited, she stooped to retrieve the coin and placed it into my outstretched hand.

"You are an unusual maid," I said frowning. But I could not sustain that frown under her onslaught. I smiled.

My confidence faltered her own short-lived courage, and abruptly she dropped those proud eyes. "So I have been told."

I expelled another relieved breath, slapped my thigh, and replaced the coin. "This is your father's farm?" I asked conversationally, putting her off guard again.

"Yes. It has been in our family for several generations." She seemed chagrined suddenly as if she did not intend to speak out of turn. Her discomfort only assured me.

"We live at Caverswall Castle," I said. She stared at the gleaming silver of my stirrup. Surely it was finer than any plate she possessed at home. That knowledge reassured me further.

"I know who you are, my lord."

As she said it, I saw all our servants and all the courtiers that have ever known me, saw them look and see the Thomas Giffard they expected, and I knew that not one of them truly did know me, know my thoughts on politics and faith, know my hopes and dreams for myself, understand how much I wanted to be my own man. "No," I answered enigmatically. "I am afraid you do not."

It was that small utterance which caused her to study my face more closely. She was only the daughter of a yeoman farmer from a long generation of farmers and landowners. She said so herself. But her long nose and incomprehensible eyes nevertheless intrigued me. How they looked at me! Perhaps through me. They never should look at me with anything but deference, and there were many occasions when my glove struck a similar expression from the face of a liveried stable boy. Yet on her, such sincerity was disarming.

"I must go," I said. I leaned forward over the saddle bow, beckoning her closer by a softer manner. "Should I come this way again, I would be bound to see you, would I not?"

An expression looking neither frightened nor encouraged crossed her eyes. She nodded, and I acknowledged it with a smile before riding away, the shadows of a distant copse swallowing me.

Later—often—I relived the encounter in my idle hours while supposedly penning Latin. Caverswall was over seven miles away from that unusual farm girl. My thoughts were not of dalliance, for there were far more attractive girls in my father's castle, and it was not long before I made the acquaintance of some of them eager to please the lord's son. Curiously, when my pleasure was spent and I fashioned their faces in my mind, it was mostly Isabella Launder I saw.

Why did she intrigue me so? My young heart was not engorged with lust for her, nor was I aroused to my usual anger at her discourteous treatment of me. Perhaps it was that very thing which intrigued the most. Her bravery. Her honesty.

Not more than a fortnight later, I found myself trotting my horse before the gate at the end of Yeoman Launder's lane. Two chatting dairymaids carrying their buckets beside her looked up and noticed me first but, after a brief acknowledging bow, they returned to their gossip.

Isabella saw me and stopped. She set down her bucket and straightened her napron. It was stained and damp with yellow, soured milk, and it briefly crossed my mind to discard the very idea. Faith! What was I doing there? Then I remembered the honesty in her eyes, and I ignored the napron while she walked alone down the long lane to test her fingers on the wet stone of the gateposts.

I smiled. "Good day, Mistress."

"My lord," she said with an awkward curtsey.

Chuckling, I glanced toward the house and the dairymaids who looked back at us, whispering to one another. "You are occupied."

"No!" She almost lunged forward, but stopped herself, hiding the action by grasping my horse's bridle and stroking the velvet nose. "That is…I have many chores, but have a moment for you, my lord."

"Mistress, I have been thinking about…well, when last we met. I cannot seem to wrest it from my mind, in fact." Her face took on a pall as if she would burst into tears and I was quick to add, "No one has ever spoken to me like you have. Well…my sisters, perhaps." This did little to alleviate her anguish. I slid from the horse and found to my distress she stood taller than I. To show sincerity, I doffed my hat. "Father says I am a bit reckless…and then to toss a coin at you…well. That showed little courtesy."

"It…it was I who…who was rude to you…"

And there it was. That same obsequious tenor I came to loath from fawning servants and lying courtiers. "Stop it! I cannot stomach it."

She drew back, long fingers covering her horrified mouth. Instinctively, I knew she would bolt, and I grabbed her before she could. With all her might she wrestled with me but I pushed her up against a tree and held her arms at her sides, her back pressed against the bark. Tears made her face even more ugly, all wet streaks and red-dappled cheeks. "Mistress, I mean you no hurt!" For I knew she feared retribution from me when all I wanted was…what? I knew not. Releasing her I stepped back and ran my fingers through my hair. I paced, my bodkin smarting my thigh. "It is most extraordinary."

"What is?" She snuffled, pushing her dirty palm over her face, making more of a mess of it.

"You. You did not seem afraid of me a fortnight ago."

"I am now!"

"I do not want your fear. Can you understand? I want…what you did before. I want your sincerity. Your candor."

"What for?" Her eyes darted this way and that. She was still trapped between the tree and myself. "Is that not what your kind want? Fear?"

I grasped the horse's reins and trudged along the road. She tentatively followed, walking on the far side of the beast, its warm flank keeping a proper distance between us. I glanced back at her over the saddle. "Perhaps you are right. But *I* do not. In fear, there is no trust, no true loyalty."

"We fear God."

I shook my head. "We fear God because He is powerful, but He loves us. When you crack the whip of fear alone without love, then…then I suppose you get back what you deserve."

"Then what is it you want from me? Love?"

The smile growing on my face turned sheepish. Here I was a full three years younger than this maid, and she no one's beauty. "You misunderstand. It is your honesty I crave. The truthfulness of your anger has been like ointment to a festering wound."

"You want my anger?" Now she smiled.

"No, Mistress. I have tasted it and need no more helpings, I assure you."

"Then my trust. Is that it?"

"Is it costly?"

She thought a moment but not with crafty intent. It was as if she were considering a contract with all its implications. "Not costly. Not to you."

I laughed heartily. After a pause I asked, "How old are you?"

"Fifteen. How old are you?"

"Thirteen. You look older. You are tall." She flushed from the offhand remark, and I blanched. "I did not mean to offend you."

She stared straight ahead, dismissing her discomfort with a deep breath. "Why did you come back?"

I shrugged and dropped the horse's reins, allowing it to trail. I batted the leather strap a moment, kicked at a stone, and then pressed my hands behind my back. "I know not. Boredom? Do you mind?"

"Appeasing your boredom?" she sniffed. "Of course not, my lord."

"By the mass! I do nothing but further insult you."

"Only by your swearing, my lord," she whispered.

I stopped, turning to her. "Are you certain you are the daughter of a yeoman?"

She engaged my eyes. "Are you certain you are the son of a knight?"

"Mistress," I acknowledged with a courtly bow that made her blush. "You are truthful. A man needs that assurance from time to time. Perhaps you will be my counselor. Or at least my personal cynic."

"A woman? You must surely have better counselors, my lord."

"Thomas. Call me that. We are alone. No one need know."

"I think it unseemly, my lord," she said in a tone one might reserve to admonish a servant.

"I rather think it unseemly that we are alone together at all, but that does not seem to distress *you*...Isabella."

An instant of panic flared in her eyes, and she cast an anxious glance back toward the house, but no one seemed to be aware of us. Tentatively, she surveyed me. An impish demeanor encroached upon her face. "Have... have you just given me leave to use your Christian name?"

"As you will. We are alone. And I hope we shall be friends."

"A Giffard, *friends* with a Launder?" A smile formed, the possibilities fluttering in her eyes. "Then..." She looked again behind for spies. "I am your friend...Thomas." She giggled, amused by the notion. "If you must have me so."

And so we were.

I smiled with the remembrance of that long ago day, but a sigh remade it to a frown. We have a history, she and I. Was it to be spoilt by a wife?

I stomped into the house, my mood soured and my thoughts running between Isabella and Father's unrelenting schemes, the latter in which I always seemed to be a pawn. The more I considered the upcoming nuptials, the more helpless I felt. The wine jug called to me, and I lunged for it before a servant could fulfill his duty. I dismissed him from the room with a wave of my hand and leaned against the great hall's hearth, relishing the painful jabbing of the stone carvings in my shoulder.

"The bridegroom!"

I turned to see Father striding under the arch. He was winded, apparently just returned from a ride. He seemed to be avoiding Caverswall of late, or trying to avoid any possible messenger from court calling him thence.

"I weary of that moniker."

"Are you? Well worry not. Soon you will be wed and called 'husband'."

"How I dread that day."

Silently he poured himself wine while a servant divested him of his mud-spattered gown. "Do not dread this wedding day, Thomas. Not only is she wealthy, but a handsome woman. Not many can say the same for their own matches."

"Wealth and beauty. Is that all there is to women, Father? Or to you?"

He eyed me a moment before joining me by the hearth. "I recognize that your tastes may run toward more rustic diversions." Reaching, he plucked a sprig of straw from my breast and raised it pointedly before tossing it into the fire. "Are you not a bit old, Thomas, to be dallying with servants in hayricks?"

"Whom I dally with is my own damn business."

"I will not have Giffards begotten all over the county. See that you comport yourself." Of a sudden, he turned back toward me. "Or is *that* the reason you put me off? Is there another to whom you have promised yourself? *Without* asking my permission? Who is it, Thomas? Tell me the woman's name!"

How often did I see that look in his eye? He was a mule over a mud hole, immovable. "There is no one." Taking my wine I walked away from the fire to stare out the window. Through the rippled glass, the distant green hills rumbled onward, and beyond that, a long road leading to Beech.

"Thomas, this is weighty business. Contracts have been arranged. Banns have been posted. Much has gone ahead. If I find you have muddled it by your own selfish interests…"

"Selfish interests," I muttered to the window. "My own happiness? That is a selfish interest?"

"Yes, when so much is in the balance. A Giffard has responsibilities."

"Why does everyone keep saying that?" A reflection suddenly shaped itself on the glass—my own scowling young face. "It is only that..." What was I to say to him? What did love or happiness to do with it? Surely he could understand friendship? Choosing my words, I said, "With these events old ties must be severed, old friends lost."

For the first time, Father seemed to consider words I never meant to say aloud. His face softened and he laid his hand condolingly upon my shoulder. "Which ties do you speak of, my son? Which friends?"

I endured it even as I raised a shoulder in a shrug. "It matters not."

There was folly in saying too much to him. I was not yet his match. But it was too late. His face mirrored his thoughts, thoughts pregnant with plots and excavation.

ISABELLA LAUNDER
MIDSUMMER, 1515
Beech

III

"Behold, the bridegroom! Come out to meet him!"
—Gospel of Matthew 25:6

It was not exactly that I missed Thomas. Memory of his dark eyes did not cause my hand to churn the butter idly, nor did the thought of his bronze cheeks or sculpted nose invoke a listless nature. No. I lived practically and deliberately. My life lent itself to its slow meander, much like the lazy crawl of a river's soupy waters. God presented me with my life, such as it was, and like a map, each thing was in its proper place.

I continued my work on the farm while the weeks passed into a month. The marriage between Sir John Giffard of Chillington Hall, Brewood, and Elizabeth Montgomery, wealthy widow, proceeded with much celebration.

Great anticipation in Caverswall followed at the announced wedding plans of Thomas Giffard to Dorothy Montgomery.

My father took it very hard indeed, for Thomas' visits were not as secret as we supposed.

They were also greatly misinterpreted.

I knew I would miss Thomas, our meetings and conversations. What was I to do with my time if I could not spend it with him? I wondered as I leaned against the rugged bark under the shade of a swaying elm. The whispering buzz of insects encircled my head. "How empty, Isabella," I sighed aloud, listening to the words, feeling my lips form the syllables. Thomas had so filled my time and my imagination! "Isabella, how bland you are without him."

"Without whom?"

I was fully startled. I never heard him approach. Indeed, I saw no sign of his horse, only Thomas, with an iron veneer I had never seen before. His brow was serious, his lips pale. He wore dark colors as if in mourning. Doublet, jerkin, slops, and stockings blended together, looking more shadow than man. "Thomas..."

He took my hand without a word and simply held it before bringing it to his lips. The bristly mustache caressed for a moment, soft lips flattening upon the roughened skin. Then he merely held it, staring at it, memorizing its contours. "Isabella. I did not want to part from you as I did, angered. I would not grieve you for all the world."

An era was slipping away, sinking fast beneath deep waters. I took my hand from his. "I have forgiven you."

"Yes, I know." He walked a circlet, kicked at a tight knob of grass, and thrust his knuckles into his hips with a sigh. Both his gloves bobbed limply from the fist of one hand like a dog's panting tongue. I stared at his back, at the fine cloth of his cloak, the jewels at his fingers, the feathers rustling at the fringe of his hat. "I met my betrothed," he said.

"That is good," I said mechanically.

He huffed an incoherent sound before turning his head to look at me. "She's a mare."

"That is unkind, Thomas."

"Why? I'm to be a stallion stud, so why should *she* not be a mare? That is why we were chosen for one another, after all, to continue this fine and noble line of Giffards." His mocking smile faded and a bruised expression replaced it. "Only another fine and noble spouse would do. It only makes me wonder, Isabella, what life is for at all. Am I not to have satisfaction in my own lifetime? Or am I merely the steward and sire for those later anonymous generations? I would travel, Isabella! I would see the places of which I have read with a true companion, a woman of intellect at my side!"

My long fingers covered my lips and I chuckled through them. "Surely you do not mean *me*! A woman of intellect?"

"What you may not have gained through study you surely have through natural gifts. And I know you could learn."

"I do not even read Latin, Thomas. You know I am a poor study."

"Only because you do not have the time. I always meant to get you a tutor—"

"Thomas! Listen to yourself. What would I do with a tutor? Recite grammar while I milked the cows? I was pleased enough to be your friend. You never needed to buy it."

The arched brows, the lightened eyes, all shadowed suddenly, remembering the present. He sagged, his heavy clothes dragging him down. All at once he reared up and cast his gloves violently to the ground. Before I could react he took hold of my arms and pulled me to his chest in a fierce embrace. "Why do you speak in past tenses? Are we not to remain the dearest of friends? What should I do without you?"

"You are betrothed and soon to wed. I have no place with you."

"I will not give you up."

"You will," I said sternly. "And you will not come again. If you care little about dishonoring yourself, at least think of me and my honor."

"What has that to do with it?" He released me and I faltered back, rubbing the arm crushed between us. "You speak as if we were lovers."

I let my coif drape over the rose in my cheek. "Do you think that others have not believed that?" He paused, looking at me… before he laughed. Thomas' laughter was always merry, often with a bawdy peal to it. Now it only annoyed, like that boyish manner he fashioned about his person. "Your laughter, Lord Giffard, is most inappropriate."

"'Lord Giffard'? Isabella, you are very grave."

"Never more so in my life. Do you think I am not just as hurt by our parting? You are moving into a new portion of your life, one fully expected of your rank. I cannot come along on that journey. Who would believe, after all, that we are only friends?" I faced him with those last words, looking at the man he had become: tall, elegant, comely. I shook my head, not only to unfurl his knotted brow, but to extract the foolish notions long ago burrowed in my own head.

He did not fully understand, and the notion of our parting did not sit well with him.

Even up until the fortnight before his own wedding he haunted the places I often walked. He would not come near enough to speak with me, but I noticed that brazen silhouette atop a nearby hill or his lonesome shadow stretching forth from a dark copse. I wandered, ignoring my shade.

I returned to my labors, swallowing my emotions in the routine of my garden, my sanctuary. I repaired my trampled roses and gave them an encouraging glance, but they lay limply against the garden wall. Still, I hoped for their recovery.

Immersed in work, I dug into the soil, loosening the clumps and at the same time loosening the scrambled thoughts from my head.

The church bell chimed, rolling its peal across the countryside. The church itself was a distant walk, but the bells' echoing pulse reached me nonetheless. The Angelus.

With a curved hand I sheltered my eyes and gazed up toward the hazy sky. Another noon. Another fleeing summer. Another day. They heaped one upon the other.

I leaned on the hoe and stared at a cabbage, eyeing the evidence of a rabbit's nibbling on its fanning outer leaves. Every one of God's creatures found its place in life, even the rabbits who so abused my garden. My brother Robert had his children, as did my sister Agnes. I was an aunt many times over. What was to become of Isabella? Be the spinster in my father's household?

The thudding hoofbeats of an approaching rider failed to rouse me. *Oh Thomas*, I thought. *Do not trouble me with your pleas. Not today.* I set to work, feeling no surprise when the rider cleared the hedge and approached.

The horse chewed the bit, large teeth grinding at the iron, while the leather squeaked and whined under the rider's seat.

"Are you deaf, woman?"

My head jerked upwards. There towered not Thomas, but his father, Sir John! Certainly the face of Thomas, only the skin was raw and fleshier, more textured with lines. He wore more jewelry than Thomas, underscoring the broad strokes of his chest and shoulders with the sweeping drape of a bejeweled chain. His collar was tied right up to the gray whiskers under his chin and he glared down at me with a scowl.

"Come, girl. Take me up to the house. I have business within."

I laid down the hoe and curtseyed. "Yes, my lord." He dismounted and tossed the reins to me, and I led the horse through the gate. We walked silently into the courtyard where I handed off the horse to one of the stable boys.

"Is this a prosperous farm? I admit I know not Rafe Launder."

"It has been," I replied. "It is managed very well."

He came up beside me and cocked his head. "You have a fondness for your employer? That is refreshing."

I sucked in my lips. He believed me to be a servant! I looked down upon dirt-lined fingers, muddy hem, and stained napron and could not help but smile. "I do at that, my lord. I toil for the good of all, and my wages are only the satisfaction at a job well done."

A deep sound rumbled in his chest. "Does he not pay you, lass?"

Chuckling, I said, "I did not mean to imply such. It is just that I am not Rafe Launder's servant, but his daughter, Isabella."

Sir John stopped. He sputtered for a moment before placing his hand upon his chest. "By the mass! Mistress Launder, forgive me!"

"Completely unnecessary, my lord. I look nothing like a daughter today. We are a small grange and we all must do our part."

"You work willingly?"

"Of course. I am a dutiful daughter. 'The Lord loveth a cheerful giver'."

"But to...to...sully yourself—"

"—with well-earned honest dirt, my lord. When I look at these hands by the end of the day, I see hands that helped to feed many mouths. Perhaps they are not graceful fingers with which to weave a tapestry or polish the armor of a knight, but they do their toil without complaint."

His frown dissolved any other expression. "Hmm. I came here to admonish you, Mistress, not to admire you."

My heart leapt to my throat. "Admonish *me*, my lord? Whatever for?"

"For bewitching my son. This pining for you must stop. He has responsibilities."

How did Sir John know of us? I froze, uttering the first thing that came to my mind. "You mistake me, Sir John. If your son has responsibilities, I am not in the way of them. He best get on with them."

"Not when he is distracted with you!" He sighed heavily and cast a glance again at the house. He smelled of horse sweat and a foreign perfume. The blended aromas aroused an uneasy feeling in my belly.

He shrugged, jangling the chain and displacing the position of cloak and jewelry. "I know you are not to blame, my dear. I recognize your character—or I know better my son's." He sighed. "I wish only to talk with your father to get you betrothed as quickly as possible. I believe that will satisfy the situation. It is best for all, lass…er, Mistress. Thomas will get on with his life and you will get on with yours."

Was it my own heart pounding in my ears? I did not know such sounds could throb throughout a body. Did Sir John hear it too? "But I have a life here, my lord." I clutched my chest. Surely if I did not, my heart would leap forth, bursting through the bone and flesh.

If Sir John took this marriage plan to Father he would have no choice but to obey it.

The church bells intruded again. They clanged inharmoniously before blending as they always did to a singular resonance of clarity. I did not immediately realize I had turned in the direction of the bells.

My vague existence consisting of family, garden…and Thomas…was suddenly given a crooked course. Nothing wore the semblance of sense any longer. "I am unsuited to married life," I muttered.

Sir John examined me with questing eyes. "What's that? A sensible girl like you? Come, come. Do not be stubborn. He is not worth your pining for him. It is unseemly."

"I do not wish to be taken as stubborn, my lord, nor am I pining, yet I say again, I am unsuited to the married state." They tumbled forth, each thought upon another. Bells, marriage with a stranger, Thomas. They closed upon me. My breath was not mine to keep. It swiftly flew from my throat, wheezing away on the wind. Sounds of insects thrummed in my head, snagging on the throaty choir of distant bells.

I realized I stood at a crossroads, lost no matter which direction I turned. Tucked into the bland folds of my life was the specter of Thomas, and there was nothing else. But Thomas was never mine, and was very soon to belong entirely to another. I knew I could do as Sir John wished and bedevil Thomas no more by marrying some young man. And this I *should* do, I knew it with the strength of my being. It was what a woman was made for, keeping a house for her husband and bearing his children. To this bondage my own mother succumbed, and her mother, and all the mothers before her. Even our Holy Mother, the Blessed Virgin, was surely an obedient wife to husband Joseph, though she lived with him chastely as brother and sister. Could I not do that with a husband? For the thought of a stranger in my bed turned my stomach.

Would any husband other than that of the foster father of our Lord ever agree to such an arrangement?

I clutched the post, pressing my nails to the wood, inhaling ancient oak. I would have to surrender to this. There was little choice for me. My father sought no suitors, but Sir John would find one right quick enough, and I might find myself wed even before Thomas. I was as trapped as he.

Raising my head to inhale the remnants of summer, the bells sounded again. Listening, I reflected on their timbre, how they called each of us to that quiet house of God's, and even how they were part of the landscape, like a tree or a fence. How natural they were to the environment, as natural as I in my garden.

Dawning slowly through the thick layers of my despair, God revealed His light. He offered a path of escape, a path I would never have ordinarily considered. The bells *were* escape, all innocence as they tolled day after day, hour by hour, speaking to my soul in whispers. I cocked my ear and heard the words more plainly. The more I listened, the more sense I reasoned from them.

My lips parted and the words seemed to speak themselves, for surely they were not of my devising. "If I have your blessing, and of course that of my father, I should choose instead to join a nunnery as a holy sister."

Astonished I spoke it aloud, I realized that it could not now be unsaid. I stared feebly at Sir John.

At least it was a choice.

"A nunnery!" He took several steps back as if struck a blow and his entire demeanor shifted from stern lord to helpless and ordinary man. "I...I never suggested..."

"Would that not equally suit your purpose?" The words rushed out of me. Incautious, Isabella! "If I am such a distraction to your son and his responsibilities, then take me out of this work-a-day world and put me in God's house." Yes. For the thought of any man but Thomas touching me caused such revulsion to rise in my gorge, I feared I would disgrace myself.

"Well...I never meant..."

"Do not fear you are bullying a maid into a dread step, my lord."

"I...I was not thinking that!"

"Of course not." I clutched my fingers to keep them from trembling. "I shall present myself with all haste. Will that suit?"

"Mistress Launder. I... Do not mistake that I love my son, but he is not worth such devotion to chastity."

"It is not for that, Sir John. It is merely the only...*sensible* thing to do."

THOMAS GIFFARD
MIDSUMMER, 1515
Caverswall Castle

IV

"Wedding is destiny, and hanging likewise."
—John Heywood, 1541

I rode the stallion hard toward my foe, feeling the weight of my armor gather and fall with each stride. I lowered my lance—so—ramming the tip into the straw manikin. It pierced so deeply the damned thing caught, and I was dragged from my mount and hurled into the sand. I lay in agony for what seemed an interminable hour, though it must have been only mere heartbeats before my attendants came to my aid.

"My Lord Thomas! Can you hear me?" My servant William shouted in my ear, and though I could hear him perfectly well, the wind was knocked out of me and I could not reply. "My lord!" He lifted me and saw that I still lived, and he raised me to my feet where I was able at last to catch my breath.

"God's toes!" I clawed at the helm's straps and William pushed my useless hands away to unfasten them. "Even the manikin is against me today." He pulled the helm free and tucked it under his arm. "I weary of this. Enough." William helped me as I staggered toward the stable, and I reached for a cup of wine offered by another servant. I dispatched the entire cup before handing it back. I knew the king favored these jousting amusements and it was good training for war. I only wished that I was already a knight and not kept from the greater tournaments of the king.

I practiced in order to take my mind from my troubles, yet it only accentuated them. William seemed to know my mind when he offered, "You are not concentrating, my lord. Doubtless, your mind is occupied with marital matters, not martial ones."

He smiled with a wink, but I did not feel like a congenial lord today. I scowled in answer, though he did not notice as we moved toward the house.

"What a grand thing to have two weddings so nigh one another," he went on. "First Sir John and then you." I grumbled my reply. "I have seen the lady, my lord. Your lady, I mean. And such a creature God has never before blessed the earth. A beauty, my lord, if a poor servant may say."

We reached my chamber and I stood in the center while William disarmed me. Servants hovered, casting aside the curtains and opening the windows. Another poured wine. Too many milling bodies, and all the while William jabbered on. It was too much.

"Out! All of you!"

The others froze for a moment before scurrying to comply. William stood aloof, wondering if I meant him as well. "Help me, William," I said as kindly as my mood allowed. He moved toward me again even as the last groom left my chamber, and I sighed my relief when he resumed untying the many laces and straps.

"Indeed, my lord," he began cautiously. "It is a heady time in a man's life. Marriage means the beginning of all."

"The beginning, William? I thought it the end."

"Oh no, my lord," he answered, good-naturedly. "Why, a wife means children, heirs, my lord. Perpetuating the Giffard name. Gold cannot accomplish that. Only the joining of man and woman under the eyes of God. Yes, the family line will continue and ages hence, your descendants will look back and thank Thomas Giffard, who will have been a knight and a mighty lord in his own right."

With the corner of my eye I studied William. Not even a squire, he was a man who had lived in my household since he was a child. He understood the place of each man, but I never considered him a confidante. It was only Isabella who wore that emblem, and I knew not why. Surely this man with his experience and loyalty was the better intimate. Yet as he spoke, I noted his speech filled with that same subordinate humor the others wore about them like livery. Yes, he was kind and caring of me, but afraid, too. He knew my wrath could destroy him as easily as elevate him, and were he not to curry to me, he would find his place diminished, and some other in his appointment.

No. He was no Isabella Launder.

Still, as sorry as I was about the entanglement of a wife, I was always of a humor to enjoy the goodly feasts of the upcoming nuptials. What young man did not seek his pleasure in these beguilements? I was not a somber man, and so I sought the company of friends to while away the time before the inevitable. They came to pay their respects, much as one does at a funeral.

Godfrey Foljambe was some twenty years older than myself, but was my longtime companion and mentor at court. Married for many years, he sired only the one child, a daughter. His wife lay in childbed again. He was in a mood to merry-make if for nothing else than to keep his mind off of stillbirths, for that was the result of the last pregnancy nearly ten months earlier.

George Throckmorton, a courtier my own age, was wed himself only three years ago, with three children to show for it, one after the other, all sons. The two of them jibbed me unmercifully for my future state, regaling me with drunken songs and stories of uxorious husbands.

"You think to be the master?" laughed Throckmorton into his cup. His cheeks were rosy from the heat of the wine.

"Saint Paul admonishes wives to be obedient to their husbands, and asks of them humility in all their ways," I replied, which made Throckmorton laugh all the more. I pictured Dorothy in my mind. When I met her, she was a quiet lady, dignified in her person, but not afraid. The Montgomerys were an old family, as old on this island as the Giffards, though grander. She was not inured to that history, yet I saw in her—though I touted the contrary to Isabella—a suitable wife befitting a Giffard. And one pleasant to look upon.

Foljambe raised his goblet in a mock salute. "A woman can find a thousand ways to naysay Saint Paul. And what did *he* know of it? He was not married."

"Yes," said Throckmorton, setting down his cup, and huffing a bloated breath. "A woman can quote all manner of scripture to support her view. A man must be an Erasmus to argue the point."

"Come now." I sat back in my favorite chair in Caverswall's hall. "It cannot be as impossible as that. A man is the lord of his household, and should a wife proclaim it differently, then it is for the man to lay down the law before her."

Foljambe guffawed. "Giffard, do you intend to keep a switch by the bed?"

"Why Foljambe," said Throckmorton, "that is a good suggestion."

Even as they abused me I knew what lay behind the words. They were only good-natured warnings of what was to come. Not one of my acquaintants married for love. These were opportune marriages, just as mine was. Men often remarried before their mourning clothes were soiled, and mostly in matches equally beneficial to their pockets or their title. Some at court did not wait for their widowerhood, but annulled spouses less desirable, to gain younger, more fertile wives with large dowries. We trafficked in spouses, building dynasties. Just as an architect erecting a castle does not pause to consider the beauty of the cornerstone, but chooses it on the basis of its strength as a foundation for the whole, its worth measured by its longevity and nobility of purpose, so, too, do we build, one stone upon another, one generation upon another, one dowry after another.

Still, I harbored romantic notions of the perfect wife with whom I could fall in love. Perhaps Dorothy was the one. Her pale skin was perfection, and the silkiness of her hair begged exploration. It was a man's duty to beget an heir, and it was obvious by the doings of Father and his behind-the-tapestry stratagems, that if the Giffards did not want the same fate as the Montgomerys with their daughters, then a male heir was paramount.

Ironically, it was the very same worry at court, for the king himself—the pride of manhood, a man for whom an heir was far more important—could not beget a living son upon his wife the queen. There were three fatal pregnancies in three years. All sons and all dead, some living only months. She was with child again and due in the beginning of the new year. Our prayers were with the good queen Catherine that she deliver up a male heir.

Throckmorton yawned as he nestled into his seat. The wine lay heavy in him and the fire was comforting. "Mark you. If Queen Catherine delivers up another dead son or even a living girl, we shall see a bastard son on the throne."

"There *is* no bastard son," said Foljambe.

Throckmorton nodded sagely with eyes closed. "There will be."

"Or a woman on the throne," added Foljambe.

"There will never be a woman on the throne." They turned to me as if I uttered a blasphemy. I smiled. "Mark *me*, gentlemen. There will never be a woman on the throne of England. How can a maid rule an army?"

"I recall something in Orleans…" said Foljambe as he, too, nestled in his chair to sleep.

"May I remind you, she was a witch and French," said I. "This is England."

"Nevertheless. Whatever Wolsey advises, the king will do. I do not like that man. He is dangerous."

"Such words for our chancellor!" I chuckled. Little good was said of the porcine Thomas Wolsey. "Worry not, Foljambe. The king is not a fool. He has many wise men about him. Thomas More, for instance. I could lay down my life for such a man as he. There is none more honest in the kingdom. Before the king listens to all Wolsey's fantasies he will talk to the likes of More."

"Giffard, when did you become such a child? The king uses his councilors, but he listens to the ones who most conform to his will. And at present that one is Wolsey."

"How tiresome." I sighed, leaning back and closing my eyes.

"He's been made a cardinal," said Foljambe. "Did you hear?"

I snorted. "The devil you say. Well, well."

Foljambe squirmed in his seat. "I know you have no love of clerics..."

"I have no love of clerics who use their robes—crimson or any other hue—to pursue wealth and status."

Foljambe laughed outright. "Hypocrite! Is that not your pursuit?"

"I do not use the cloak of the Church to do so."

Throckmorton rose to pour himself more wine, but his scowl was darker than his whiskers. "Since when have you become so self-righteous? Is there a secret hair shirt beneath that doublet, Giffard?"

Chuckling, I toyed with my empty goblet. "Do not be a fool. You know my tastes are neither in churches nor religion. I view it as a necessary evil."

Foljambe eyed the agitated Throckmorton. "Such a cynic. 'Necessary evil.' The next thing you will be telling us is that you have become a pagan."

"Churches have their uses," I drawled. "We need them for baptisms and weddings, I suppose."

Throckmorton cast his goblet to the floor. It clanged and rolled toward the hearth. I sat up and glared at him. "I do not know if I can be in the same room with you!" he growled.

"Did you not know my humor, Throckmorton? Monks, nuns. I have no use for the cloistered. The Church is an institution of tradesmen in souls and indulgences."

"Is that what you truly think, Giffard? I pity you and your wretched soul. You cannot see beyond the foul doings of a few rascals in order to witness the true hand of God in His sacraments."

"Throckmorton, sacraments are for children and women with nothing else to do, bored with their embroideries and housekeeping. A house chapel keeps an idle wife from thinking too far afield."

"What would you have religion be, Giffard?" he spat, face reddening. "A few mumbled prayers?"

"I would not have it be constant fawning and begging to a God who must surely tire of our excesses and our pleas, nor would I have my soul depend on how much gold I spoon into the alms box."

"By the Mass!" rasped Foljambe. "You best go back to your catechism, Giffard. You have forgotten more than you learned."

"He sounds to me like a heretic! A reformer!"

"I am not a reformist. I am not anything. Never fear. I do believe in the power of the Almighty, but not in the guise of these cardinals. I can do without them."

"I will hear no more of this!" cried Throckmorton. "Friend or no!"

He wrestled with his gown, and I rose to appease him. "George, I do not speak against God. Only the doings of His beadsmen. Would you base your religion on the likes of Wolsey?"

"Giffard!" Throckmorton pulled away from my placating hand, his own hand near his hilt.

"Easy, Thomas," hissed Foljambe. "Know you not George's uncle—"

I did not like Throckmorton's rabidity in my house. I squared with him. "I know of your uncle. Dr. William Throckmorton, trusted servant of the now *Cardinal* Wolsey. Are you in Wolsey's pocket, too, George?"

Drawing his sword, Throckmorton postured. "Stand and defend yourself!"

Desperately, Foljambe fell between us. "Do not be an arse, George!"

"Coward! With a coward's accusations!"

"I will let that lie, Throckmorton," I said calmly, but in truth, my blood was stirred. I itched to draw my own weapon, but even through the haze of wine, I knew to do so in anger was foolhardy. "I know you are hot to defend the right good name of Throckmorton, and none ill have I ever spoke of them before this. But it is not I alone that sports these opinions of Wolsey and all who traffic with him."

"Then you insult me, Giffard, for I, too, 'traffic' as you say, with Wolsey."

I was shocked to silence, for I knew that his uncle forged ties to our cardinal and chancellor, but I did not know of George's involvement. He could only be a reluctant pawn, for I knew George well. "Do you?" I said feebly. "I...I was not aware."

Foljambe clenched my shoulder. "For God's sake, Giffard!"

I took a breath and bowed low. "Forgive me, Lord George. I bespoke myself. Never would I willingly offend so bosom a companion as you are, and have ever been, to me."

For a moment, I did not think he would capitulate, and I dreaded that I would have to draw my own blade. But after a long, dreadful pause, he rolled back his shoulders, and sheathed the weapon.

"Well, then," said Throckmorton. "Be more cautious in your speech."

"I shall be." I suddenly looked at all of us, snarling and posturing like dogs. "Is this to be a wedding celebration, or a funeral?"

Foljambe relaxed first, clapping both Throckmorton and me on the shoulder. "What would you have it be, Giffard? For it is you who lamented this match since you got wind of it. Come now. The lady is agreeable and fair. What ails you? Is it your father?"

"Speak not of my father, I beg of you."

"A wedding is a beginning, Giffard. Soon, you, too, will have sons to add to the Giffard line."

"Already I miss my bachelorhood. Where have the days of our youth gone, Foljambe? Could it be I miss the wars in France?"

Throckmorton eased back into his chair and toyed with the hilt of his bodkin. "You think that is past?" he said slowly, coming back to himself. "The king has not yet won back his ancestral claims in France. He would best old Henry V in this and win back that which was lost. We will see the shores of France again, mark me."

I sighed. "So many treaties. They are like spider's webs; they have the look of strength, but it only takes the wave of a hand to tear the threads."

Throckmorton nodded. "Treaties are forgotten before the ink is dry."

Foljambe stretched out his long legs toward the hearth, crossing one ankle over the other. "Do you think once bridled with a wife you may not go to war, Thomas? Why do you think some wars are waged? To escape shrewish wives!"

I gnawed on a knuckle. "Will Dorothy be a shrew in time, I wonder?"

Foljambe nodded sagely. "There is no escaping it."

"I beg the exception!" piped Throckmorton. "My wife—"

"Oh, your wife!" Foljambe waved his hand in the stifling air. "By the Mass, George! Your wife must be somewhere between that of the Holy Mother and Saint Catherine."

"*What* did you say?"

"Godfrey," I hissed. "He is full of wine. We are all full of wine. Forgive our slippery tongues, George. No harm is meant."

"Well…" Throckmorton glanced sourly at his goblet lying across the room where he had tossed it. "The wine jug is empty."

"And what a poor host am I!" Leaping to my feet, I swiveled, looking for a servant. "I shall call to refill them—"

Throckmorton slowly rose and stood unsteadily. "No. Let it rest. Too much we have said already. I will to bed now."

Foljambe and I waved him away, and watched as he departed gingerly from the room. I looked at my older friend as he ticked his head at me. "You should not taunt him. He has no belly for it."

"I cannot help my feelings for Wolsey and all his kind."

"'His kind.' Does not your own father support many religious houses, Thomas? The Giffard name is stamped on half the monasteries in the region."

"He must find profit in it, else why would he? Perhaps their prayers for him are what he buys."

"Careful, Thomas." He eyed the doorway but saw no servant's shadow. "Such talk can become troublesome to you."

"It is no secret to buy yourself out of purgatory. But it will take far more than a few shillings into a handful of convents to shorten his stay, I'll warrant."

"And what of your own? Such loose talk will raise the ire of the Almighty. It has certainly bedeviled Throckmorton tonight."

"I do not over-worry about my soul. God will do with me what He sees fit. I will not purchase my way to Heaven."

"Only through the shire."

I laughed at that, for my agreeing to marry Dorothy despite my principled speeches showed I was more than willing to use a wife to gain a fortune. I lifted my goblet. "Here is to the Montgomery lands."

"To your imminent nuptials. May its issue be as profitable as its grants!"

ISABELLA LAUNDER
MIDSUMMER, 1515
Blackladies
Brewood, Staffordshire

V

Gather my faithful ones before me,
those who made a covenant with me by sacrifice.
—Psalm 50:5

The look on my brother Robert's face when he led me to the priory's august stone arch gave me pause. "Robert! Why is your look so pale?"

"I cannot believe you are doing this willingly, Isabella. It is that damned Sir John. He has coerced you."

"Is that your fear? Robert, you give me too much credit for obedience. Do you truly think Sir John could force me to this?"

"Well and why not? His son is beguiling enough."

I reddened. "There will be no talk against Thomas Giffard, Robert. I have told you before…"

"But you would not be here now except for him. Oh Isabella! Reconsider. Is this truly the life for you?"

"It is very much for me. And you are wrong about Lord Thomas. If it were not for him, I should have been here sooner."

He examined me sternly from head to foot. With fingers curled into fists, my brother—who paid me so little heed while we were children—seethed with injustice. "Just tell me true. *Are* you a virgin?"

I closed my eyes. Of course he should think it. Even Father accused me when I told him of my decision. I should be appalled at the question, but it was not without reason. "Yes," I exhaled, opening my eyes in time to witness his slackening shoulders. "You have it wrong about Lord Thomas and me. I told you."

"Then how in the name of God did you meet, Isabella? I mean…what did he see in you?"

I tried not to frown. I knew he did not mean the words to hurt, yet he always used me ill. Didn't I already know how plain I was? "I was fifteen. When I was on my way to market, he ran me into a muddy ditch with his horse. I scolded him for recklessness."

"You did what?"

"I scolded him. Told him he was a lucky fool he did not kill me. We were fast friends ever since. It seems no one dared speak to him that way before, and he desperately needed it."

He shook his head. "Only you, Isabella. Anyone else would be carted off to gaol!"

"It is honesty which makes a better world, Robert. We could all stand to be more honest with one another."

Robert grew silent until the reality of where we stood intruded. We both turned as the door opened. Light from a hearth spilt into the portico, revealing the bailiff in the doorway. "God be with you," he said, raising his eyes under a bush of brows. He wore workman's clothes and was youthful, possibly Robert's age.

"I have come to submit myself to your prioress," I said, until Robert clutched my arm.

"She will not!" He pulled me back, but the bailiff lurched forward to my rescue.

"Here!" said the bailiff. "She looks to be of age. How old are you, Mistress?"

"I am five and twenty, and have made my own mind on the matter."

The bailiff glared at Robert. "Is this your...your..."

"I am his sister." My answer smoothed the bailiff's expression and he turned again to me.

"If you come willingly, Mistress, I shall take you to the prioress. If your brother will take his leave..."

Robert turned to me, and I stared into his puzzled expression. "Isabella, at any time, I shall come to fetch you." A mix of new emotion rolled within his eyes. Was it love that propelled him, or was it the loss of the steadiness of our proper places? He dropped his face down close to mine and whispered, "Are you *certain*?"

"Robert," I sighed. "What other choice is there for me?"

"You can marry. Have children. A hearth of your own. Why must you be so stubborn?"

His tone was kind at first, but the last was uttered with his familiar exasperation at the older sister he never understood and could not control. I searched his brown eyes for compassion, eyes very like an ox's with its moist vacancy. His rounded nose and thin mouth gave him a similar appearance to Father, which wrung from me my usual impatience with him. "It is only walking out of one door and into another. It is a natural course for me. You view it as shutting away, but I see it as the place in which I have always been. I find my comfort in solitude and chores. What better place than to be with women who share this view?"

"But a husband—"

"—would get in the way of it." I laughed, only a quick, nervous burst of mirth before quieting. "Perhaps I hunger for more religion, Robert. We sowed precious little of it in our house, you must admit."

"That is why I ask you, Isabella. Such a sudden turn at piety makes me suspicious."

"Suspicious of what? My intentions? Perhaps piety is what I need. Perhaps the rest of my life was the selfish part. Perhaps I need to devote my time and thought to God. It is a worthy pursuit, Robert. As worthy as being a wife, surely."

He mulled my words, but plainly he saw I was immovable. "Very well, Isabella. If it is your will. But…let us know how you fare. Is that well with you?" he asked of the bailiff.

The bailiff shrugged and gestured to me to come in. I glanced back at Robert, forced a smile, and then moved forward. The bailiff led me to a small courtyard and an iron gate. A bell hung at the top and he pulled on the rope several times, creating a jangling carillon. We waited, and it was only then that I noticed my heart pounding.

It seemed that many minutes passed, but I knew my own nervousness slowed the crawl of the sundial's shadow. At last, careful footsteps approached, and then the dark shade of a woman opened the heavy door. She wore the black St. Benet habit, hence the unflattering but adhering designation of this house: Blackladies.

I did not choose this particular house. There were many to choose from, including another nearby in Brewood, the "Whiteladies" of the Augustinian order. But Sir John—who was a generous benefactor to this poor house in Brewood—wrote a letter of my character to give to Prioress Margaret. It was useless to refuse. Apparently, *he* chose carefully; it took me far from Caverswall where Thomas lived. I said no farewells to Thomas. God knows how he reacted to the news of my decision.

But of course, he should be married soon and forget me.

The sister approached the gate and peered at the bailiff and then me. A white wimple framed her face. She wore a heavy black veil draped overall. Her gown was also black, as was the scapular before and aft of her, tied loosely with a dark cord on which hung a rosary and a ring of keys. Her green eyes were small and rimmed with red, with pale and stubby lashes fanning outward.

"What is it?" she asked without preamble.

"I…I wish to present myself to the prioress." The nun's stare cut through me, and I lowered my eyes. Though my resolve was certain, it seemed to have scurried a few paces away.

"Why?"

I raised my head at that, clutching my mantle as a gust of wind swayed it. Why so much opposition? First my family, and now this. I tried to keep exasperation out of my voice. "To become a holy sister, of course."

Momentarily animated, the nun's thin brows arched and just as quickly lowered. "Indeed," she muttered, unlocking the gate. She swung it aside and the metal rasped. "Come," she said, waiting for me to step within before locking it again.

I looked back at the bailiff with thanks, but he had already departed. My eyes drew instead to the dark skirts before me snuffling against the ground. *It is only another door*, I told myself. Only another door.

The nun led me down a drafty hall whose floorboards creaked with each of our steps. All the windows were solidly shuttered, for I sensed from a cursory glance that none of them had glass. We climbed a staircase where scant light bloomed from one lonely candle ensconced on a wall in the middle of the gallery. It was raised higher than it used to sit, its former place on the plaster easily discerned by the holes and its soot-stenciled pattern. Squinting, my eyes darted, absorbing the strangely dim surroundings. With a cold pang in my chest, I regretted allowing my brother Robert to depart so soon.

The strong scent of beeswax and oil filled the gallery, and its shining wainscoting at least told of great care. But my fears were reawakened when we passed the nimbus of that one fat candle and entered into a secluded corner and its veil of shadows. Here the sister stopped and knocked confidently on a door I did not at first notice. Without waiting for a reply, the nun pulled the latch and pushed opened the door, slicing the gallery's gloom with a flat rectangle of light.

Prioress Margaret glanced up from the folding table, still squinting from her close work on a paper. The quill poised in her hand, and her fingertips were black with ink. *"Deo Gratias,"* she said.

"*Benedictio*," replied the nun.

"Dame Cristabell," said the prioress, though she eyed me instead of the nun. "What is it?"

"Madam," Cristabell said, inclining her head. "This young lady seeks to become a holy sister."

"Indeed." With the prioress' full attention now focused on me, I shrank. She waved the quill at Dame Cristabell, dismissing her. "It is customary that your mother or mistress accompany you for such presentation."

"My mother is dead, Madam. And I have no mistress. Indeed, I have been mistress of my father's farm for many years."

"Yet you come alone. Your name, my dear?"

"Isabella Launder."

"Launder. Launder. I know no Launders in Brewood, do I?"

"No, Madam. We hail from Beech."

"How came you here, then?"

Nervous fingers searched in my scrip and pulled forth the letter from Sir John. I then lifted the pouch of coins also from the scrip, and placed it on the folding table that served as her desk.

The prioress read the note laboriously, her lips forming the silent words until she reached the end, and with brows lifted she lowered the page. "However did you acquire the wrath of Sir John Giffard?"

"I have not angered Sir John," I said tightly. "The letter says nothing of that. It was my choice to come, and mine alone."

"Which is why you come unaccompanied? This generous stipend. Is this only Sir John's displaying his esteem for you?"

"Your lack of charity appalls, Madam." It came out a husky whisper, but audible enough for the prioress to frown and set down the letter and quill before rising.

Had I not suffered enough? I wanted desperately to turn away and march out of that room, but realized there was nowhere to go.

Prioress Margaret—shorter, composed, and small beneath her loose gown that seemed too large for her diminutive frame—approached and stopped before me. At first, her imperious manner hid the small unsightly details of her appearance; how her skirts were mended with patches slightly greyer than the deep black of the gown; how the hem was frayed, threads following her like shadows. Even the bleached wimple showed signs of age and repair.

The prioress' hands were lined and bony with a sprinkling of dark, age spots. Her face did not seem so old, though when she stood closer, I noted how that face was drawn with lines down either side of the nose, and creases crossing the line of her thin dry lips.

I was still young, even at five and twenty. How long would it be before my features took on this craggy landscape? *And what would it matter?* It might even add distinction to an average appearance.

"You think I lack charity?" asked Prioress Margaret. "I think *you* lack honesty, Mistress Launder. You are obviously willful, and so have been sent on this course to put you in a better mind and temperament. But we are neither school nor gaol. What we are is a home for women who *wish* to be here. I cannot stomach a woman who would be mistress of this manor. We are too small and too poor a house for that arrogance. And of course," she said, eyes shining, "that position is already filled." She eyed the round-bellied pouch as it nestled on the table like a hen over her eggs. "Though Sir John has been most generous to us in the past, I can easily turn aside his...his...donation...in order to allow you to return to your home."

Studying her severe yet sincere eyes, I considered. It was an honorable retreat she offered. There was little shame in changing one's mind from such a step, though left with no better choices than before, I could see no alternative.

I stiffened my narrow shoulders. "The truth of it, Lady Prioress, is that my being here *is* a convenience to Sir John. But I am here as neither a convenience nor an obedient servant to his will or any other man's. It is simply that I cannot see myself wed. It is unnatural to me. I am pleased to make this place my home in any capacity you deem proper. But my ultimate aim is to enter here, and never leave it."

A ghost of a smile flickered at the edges of the prioress' tight lips. "Your desire seems strong. It will take a strong desire to live this life. That will of yours must be surrendered for the good of the community, and your obedience to me and your fellow sisters here is expected and necessary. I trust obedience to *women* will not inconvenience you."

She smiled, but I was mortified. *Oh Isabella! When will you ever learn to govern that razor tongue!* Though small, Prioress Margaret looked to be a formidable woman. Was she cruel? Kind? There was no way to read it in her shadowed eyes.

"You have yet to mention sincere devotion to God in these protestations," she said.

There was truth in that, too, but I could not raise my eyes to acknowledge it. It was escape for me, but I did not wish to say so to the prioress. I did not think God would mind so much. I wondered then if the same could be said for the prioress.

"Do you freely give your obedience to those of this house? *Can* you?"

I bowed. "Yes, Madam."

The prioress eyed me again, scrutinizing from head to foot. "Are you a virgin?"

I cursed myself for a guilty blush. "Yes, Madam."

"There are tests. Do you wish to change your answer to me?"

Indignation drained the blush from my cheek, leaving it pale and flat. "I *am* a virgin, Lady Prioress. Perform any tests you like."

"Unless you are widowed it is not fitting to become a bride of Christ in any other state… But I believe you, Mistress." The prioress rose, took my arm, and walked me through the door. "You will need to exchange those clothes for a novice's gown. I will take you to a place whereby you may do so."

We emerged into the sunny cloister and were enveloped by the fragrance of roses lining the cloister path. It was a garden of herbs and tiny flowers, intersected by a cruciform gravel path.

"You have a garden," I sighed. "I am good with gardens. And especially with roses."

"Good. Then most assuredly, you shall work here."

I allowed myself a moment of pleasure—the briefest—almost comforted by the prioress' casual manner. But as the accustomed scent of the garden receded, and we entered the maze of rooms and halls, my bleak comfort was replaced again by fear.

Prioress Margaret guided me to a little upstairs room with two bedsteads. One had a featherbed and the other did not. She gestured to the latter. "This you will share with Dame Cristabell. The other I share with Dame Elizabeth. Store the clothes and any jewelry you are wearing now in one of these coffers. Should you choose to leave us, these things will be returned to you. If you stay, you may do with them what you like. Give them to the poor, for instance." Out of the cupboard she took a wrapped bundle and handed it to me. Without further ado, she turned and left the room, her footfalls dispersing down the creaky steps.

Bathed with quiet again I stood alone, the black woolens still clamped between my two hands. I glanced at the smudged window. Several of the rectangular panes were cracked and one was replaced entirely with a wooden shingle. The room smelled musty and slightly smoky from the cold ashes in the hearth, but it was clean.

I sat heavily on the mattress and heard the crunch of fresh straw within. *There are worse places*, I thought, taking it in. Looking down at the folded clothes, I ran my hand over the dark wool. It was rough under my equally rough palm, but it seemed to suit.

Setting it down beside me, I slowly unlaced my bodice and peeled it away. The skirt came next and I let it fall to the floor. My nearly transparent linen shift—one I altered from one of my dear mother's—was surely humble enough for Blackladies.

Shaking out the black gown, I looked it over. It, too, was patched and mended, altered many times for many different novices. Perhaps Dame Elizabeth and Dame Cristabell had each worn it at one time. Perhaps even the prioress herself.

After removing my coif I slipped the gown over my head and pulled it down into place. It was a bit short for my height but it would have to do, for there was little left of the hem to alter. Lastly I fitted the wimple over my face and the white novice's veil over that, cinching the loose gown with a cord. *There. The transformation is complete. From yeoman's daughter to bride of Christ.* I swallowed hard, ignoring the pain in my throat. My thoughts must conform. I was here now, and here I intended to stay. Away from my poor inelegant father, and the prying eyes of Sir John. Away from painful reminders of what once was, and never was. Safely away.

THOMAS GIFFARD
SUMMER'S END, 1515
Greenwich Court

VI

It is easier to resist at the beginning than at the end.
–Leonardo da Vinci, 1452-1519

The candles blazed, shining the paneled walls in a familiar glow. Did the candles burn brighter because the king was there? Perhaps the physical world itself was just as enamored of King Henry as were his subjects. We fortunate few who served at court luxuriated under this perennial radiance. It was as if we, too, ruled the world with him. We were Englishmen, proud conquerors who feared no foreign enemy. Our king, King Hal—as only his fool referred to him before his person, and as his court called him in private— came from both common and regal lineage. Welsh, English, and French blood ran in his veins. He was England incarnate. While Henry sat on his throne, he was second only to God in our esteem.

It was a merry court in contrast to that of his father, the late Henry VII. I remember attending court as a child while the other Henry reigned, and I also remembered how restrained were the offerings at table and in purses. Father grimly complained of the few favors accorded him, and of the fewer coins to be pried from the late monarch's thrifty fists.

But not this court. The wine flowed as dish after sumptuous dish paraded out from the kitchens; whole roasted animals, sliced and reconstructed on their platters; castles complete with moats devised from pastry and sugars; roast fowl dressed up in their feathers and arranged as if still in flight. No kitchen artisan lay sleeping in Henry's court, for they were put to good work for the banqueting hall.

Dancers moved, spinning colorful ribbons to the beat of the court musicians strumming on their lutes, stroking their fiddles, and drumming their tabors, all filling the hall with melodious sounds, competing with the conversation of the diners, punctuated by the king's loud bellows and guffaws. Such happy chaos!

Amid the cheer of our dinner, I glanced at Father. We sat not at the high table, but adjacent to it. We were both Gentlemen Ushers in Ordinary to the King, ready for any duty, be it amusement, or serving the meal, or even laying down our lives. Tonight, however, I doubted we should be called upon to defend the king from anything other than biliousness. Father himself ate heartily, and, between bites, exchanged warm glances with the handsome widow, now his wife. He had a right to smile. He was master of the monies and lands that she possessed. The Giffard name was now indelibly stamped upon that of Montgomery. Father plotted well.

Beside me sat Dorothy, my own bride. Stately, poised, fair. The match to any young courtier's spouse. I resigned myself to accepting this arrangement, and I took care to show a proper face at court.

The king laughed again, and the ripple of laughter shook the hall. A shock of red hair flamed the top of his head, but his face was smooth and white, with a smattering of faint freckles. Henry's childhood servant and friend Sir William Compton spoke, starting this eruption, and the king turned and made an affectionate and amused remark to Queen Catherine.

She listened demurely until her fair brows rose and she, too, laughed with gusto. Her earlier Spanish solemnity had given way to

English good humor, and she was readily accepted by her subjects. She was, in fact, held in great estimation by the court, not only for her devotion to spiritual matters, but for her motherly attention to her adopted country. The king and queen were, as Erasmus said, a mother and father to the realm. She sat at the king's right, while Compton—as well as his close friend Charles Brandon—sat at his left.

Compton and Brandon, older than the king by ten or so years, were ill-liked by the court at large, for they were common men. Brandon came to the king's household as an orphan, and began his career as companion to the late Prince Arthur. He was soon given to Henry. But instead of leaving them in their place, Henry elevated them to Privy Council positions, favors beyond their deserts. They were naturally mistrusted. Oftentimes they and the king behaved like soldiers merrymaking in foreign territory, lawless and invulnerable.

"Perhaps our dear Cardinal does not find my story as amusing as does the king," said Compton to a dour Wolsey, who also sat near the king's left, though several chairs separated him from Henry.

With greasy fingers, Wolsey tore a leg from the stuffed hen on his trencher. I thought he might gesture with it, but he only tore it again, this time the thigh from the foreleg. He flicked his eyes toward Compton as he meticulously plucked the flesh from the bone. "Why so surprised, my lord? I seldom find your stories amusing."

"Oh ho!" cried Henry, nudging Compton, whose smile faded under Wolsey's contemptuous appraisal. "Our good Cardinal does not like your humor, Compton. What say you to that?"

Compton clutched his goblet too tightly. "I say that my lord Wolsey understands not my humor, else he *would* find it amusing."

"Ribald humor on indelicate subjects," countered Wolsey. "I understand them well, my lord. I simply do not find these common tales suitable to my tastes."

"But he understands them well," chuckled Henry, eliciting a wave of tittering amongst the diners, including my father and myself.

"Indeed," said Wolsey, either ignoring the king or misunderstanding the source of the jape. "Though I am a chaste man and vowed to celibacy, I understand the matters of the bedroom, as must a cleric who counsels his fellow man. Even the basest of men surely need such counsel for the betterment of their souls."

Compton scowled and looked as if he might rise. Henry pressed the back of his hand subtly against Compton's chest, before patting his shoulder. "Base men or chaste," said Henry, eyeing Compton, whose face flushed red, "we are men, and cannot stop ourselves from contemplating 'bedroom matters,' as you call it, my lord cardinal." Henry's gaze suddenly fell on me, and a smile parted his lips. "Here is a man who, no doubt, contemplates those very matters."

The diners laughed at my surprise and subsequent blush. Dorothy lowered her eyes to her trencher and kept them there.

"Giffard. Have I heard rightly? Are you wed to this fine young lady?"

I stood and bowed to my sovereign. "Yes, your grace. To be a bachelor no more."

They laughed again. Henry leaned forward, taking up his cup in bejeweled fingers. "Indeed. Bachelorhood is much to be praised." Then he smiled and turned to his wife. "But the married state is also much to be praised. A good and obedient wife is worth kingdoms. I pray that your marriage will be as happy as my own." He raised his goblet to me while pressing the queen's hand with his.

The court saluted my nuptials, and Dorothy and I acknowledged them before we drank our draughts.

I glanced at my bride. What sort of wife was she to be to me? As I sat, I unexpectedly thought of Isabella. Not long ago, I disparaged Dorothy to her, but certainly she was a suitable wife for a Giffard. I saw how she managed those diners beside her, how her aplomb carried her through the japes and embarrassments of the king and his consorts. Yet even in that moment of satisfaction, I found myself with the strongest urge to ride madly to Beech so as to beg Isabella to come away with me and be my counselor once again. Dorothy and I did not impart the camaraderie that Isabella and I shared, though I supposed only time would grant that. Still, I was heartsick at the loss of our friendship. I wondered what Isabella was doing now on that humble grange. Perhaps sitting down herself to some pottage she made with her own hands, hands often dirty from her garden.

Looking at Dorothy and the delicate white hands that tore her meat apart with the dainty application of a knife, I decided that she had never made a meal, nor kneaded bread, nor milked a goat. In fact, the thought of my wife doing such a thing caused a smile, though it faded again upon contemplating Isabella. I knew I would miss her. No more to hear her clever words, her coarse laughter hidden behind impossibly long fingers. No more? Once I was wed and some time passed, surely I could get her to accede to my wishes again. We would still meet. She was not an unreasonable woman. And should she find herself also a bride, she and her spouse would be most welcomed in my household. Though...the thinking of it—Isabella as a servant in my employ and married to some coarse farmer—gave me an unsettling feeling, like standing on a rickety bridge that was about to fall.

I tried to turn my attention back to the colorful room and all its amusements, but the memory of a farmyard's smell intruded over that of roast fowl and hart.

Isabella wed? Selfishly, I hoped it would not be so.

ISABELLA LAUNDER
AUTUMN, 1515
Blackladies

VII

How good it is, how pleasant, where the people dwell as one!
—Psalm 133:1

Matins came far too early, though I was not the only one who delayed dragging herself from the warm covers to dress within the icy gloom of midnight. This was the first Divine Office of the day, where we, the cloistered, rise "even at night to praise Him."

We shuffled down to the little chapel of St. Mary and, snug in the worn wooden settles of the quire, chanted our first prayers by the dim of two candle flames. We tried to keep ourselves awake, mumbling vulgar Latin we learned by rote.

Raising my eyes to the chapel's roof, I hoped for the wherewithal to stay awake enough to finish our scant prayers before shuffling off to bed again, sleeping uninterrupted until six, where we were to rise again for Prime.

The chapel's ceiling almost disappeared in the smoky gloom. Its timbers rose upward like imploring hands. Between the beams was a dim scoring of planks, just enough to hold the clay tiles that secured the roof from the weather, though none too well. Soot from years of candle smoke darkened its unpainted surfaces, while cobwebs draped long into the airy space, swaying with our chant.

I liked the chant. I found it soothing, and easy to lapse into the contemplation of a prayer. And what did I pray about? I prayed to understand my new life and my new sisters. I prayed that they should like me. And—selfishly—I prayed that I should be happy, for I was coming to realize that I had only leased a portion of happiness for most of the years of my life. It was never mine to keep.

But a selfish prayer is not easily answered.

Looking to my sisters whose faces fell into dim contours and deep shadow, I wondered what went through their minds. I soon learned to be a rigid surveyor of what I gleaned from their faces alone.

Stern but fair, Prioress Margaret no doubt prayed for enough food to feed us and our servants, for not only did we support the chaplain and bailiff, but also two women workers and four men, for there was far too much for four nuns to accomplish alone. The property boasted a brewhouse, bolting house, kilhouse, cheeseloft, stables, and fields, not to mention the mill and ponds. It was quite impossible to remain self-sufficient without help.

Cristabell, on the other hand, was unreadable under any pretext. Her wide, shiny forehead was smooth except for brows that lay in a flat, though expressive, line over the rims of dark green eyes. Her skin, too, was not pale but darker than most, like sage. Her family name was Smith, and I wondered if it was from these kinsmen she received her sharp upturned nose, pixie mouth, and mistrustful nature.

Dame Elizabeth Warde's face was heart-shaped. A pale rose mouth always lay slightly ajar from the projection of rabbit-like teeth, and above that was a squat nose and gray-blue eyes, the color of gray horses in the rain. She was much older than either Cristabell or myself, and even, I suspected, the prioress.

When Elizabeth glanced in my direction I swiftly averted my eyes, angling my head toward the nard-rich aroma of our stalls.

What was at first frightening in its mystery and sanctity became comfortable by repetition. It was true: I only stepped out of one door and through another, giving up the servitude as a daughter for that of chaste "spouse." I also discovered I was here at Blackladies for a noble purpose: to enrich my friendship with the Almighty, to feed my soul, to empty Isabella of herself. I did desire this. For with it, all the pain would be gone.

I jerked awake in the quire stall. Dame Cristabell jabbed her arm into my shoulder to make me rise with the others. It was back to bed until Prime.

I found it difficult laying my head on the pillow beside that of Cristabell's night after night. Stiffly I lay abed, waiting for her to drift to sleep first before I could relax.

In the morning hours after the High Mass, when we were allowed recreation, she would eye me as I moved away from the study carrels to my own pursuit.

On the days that I scrubbed the hard cloister floor with a wide straw brush while on my knees, I could tell without looking up that Cristabell hovered in the shadows, watching me. *What is it about me*, I wondered, *that makes her so disagreeable? Was it my inexperience? My lack of education?* This latter seemed to plague all the nuns of Blackladies, for not one of them could read or understand Latin.

Sharing a bed night after night with Cristabell was no better than with my own sister Agnes, for the nun's disapproval was just as weighty.

On the occasion of my second day at the convent—a month ago now—we four women sat together in the chapter house. My head was buzzing from weariness, for we rose so very early in the morning, I was unfamiliar with the chanted prayers, and I was desperately nervous of the others who did not warm to me. They sat in their stalls in the quire that first day while I sat apart. I understood that after I petitioned for admittance formally in Chapter that I, too, would be admitted to the quire.

"Isabella," said the prioress in the chapter house, and my heart throbbed. I rose from my place and stepped before her, looking at the floor. "Kneel," she whispered and I did so. She took my hands in hers and kissed my cheek. "Now prostrate yourself."

She had told me of this earlier, and instructed me as to what I was to say, but in a panic, I suddenly forgot each of my replies!

"Dear daughter, what is it you are asking?"

And then the words formed in my head, and my white lips muttered them into the dust of the floor boards, "The mercy of God and yours."

"What is that mercy that you ask?"

"To dwell in this place, to serve God, for the punishment of my sins, for amendment of my life, and finally for the salvation of my soul."

"My daughter," she replied. The others were quiet, save for coughing and the clearing of a throat. "This thing that you ask is hard, but to those whom God inspires He gives grace, will, and power to fulfill it. Stand stable in the purpose that you began. Listen carefully, for there are three things by which you must live: to forsake your own will and live under obedience to the prioress and the elders in the order. The second is willful poverty, taking nothing from your friends, neither gold nor silver nor jewels nor any other property, for if you hold such things without the knowledge of the prioress you shall forever stand cursed. Third: you must live chastely and take God as your spouse and forsake all lust and the liking of the flesh. You must take on abstinence and fasting; you must rise to the service of God when other men sleep; give prayer and devotion for to purchase grace. Say now before all the convent, what is your will?"

"The good purpose that I have taken I shall fulfill to my life's end through the grace of God and your good wisdom." To my life's end. And why not? Though I said the words, I knew I did not have a longing for God as I should, for I still longed for earthly things. But I reckoned, perhaps naively, that I could come to long for Him, for I did indeed have till "my life's end."

The prioress blessed me, and then the other two prayed for me, and then we went to prayers in the little chapel.

But all the while, as the prioress spoke and I answered, my thoughts ran rampant like hounds on a hunt: *Will I be good for You, Lord? Will I be able to serve You as I should?* When I gazed into the prioress' weary eyes when she spoke the rote words, I wondered if God would answer me swiftly, if I would hear His rumbling thunder, or if I would be struck down even there in the chapel. For the prioress said I must renounce all lust and give up my will, and I was not certain if such things were possible.

I gazed dazedly at the puddle of soapy water I had created on the cloister path. I dismissed that month-old event, and felt Cristabell's eyes upon me with sharp annoyance. I thought I could maintain my silence and allow her whatever satisfaction she gathered by my seeming humility, but after what seemed like ages of quiet scrubbing, I could stand it no more. "Is there something you wish of me, Dame?" I said, raising my head.

My outburst did not seem to startle the shadow that lay in wait. Gradually, as if by her own thought, she emerged from the layers of dark, standing with her hands hidden under a frayed scapular. "I wish nothing of you, Mistress Launder."

"The others call me Isabella," I said. "Why will you not call me so?"

"I do not desire familiarity."

At that, I set the brush down and angled my head up at her young face. Her cheek seemed as soft as powder within the confines of its wimple. I reckoned Cristabell was my own age, but she could easily be older. Within the boundaries of the cloister, the nuns appeared ageless, as if time stopped for them, like flowers pressed in a book. "But surely familiarity is expected of so small a house."

"Yes," she admitted, flicking her eyes away momentarily before piercing my gaze with her own bright green eyes. "But I see no reason in it when you will not be staying."

"Not be staying?" Unfolding my legs I stood, standing taller than Cristabell. "Why would I not be staying? It is my sincerest desire to do so. I hope I am working toward the proper humility to be welcomed here."

Something of a smirk teased the edge of Cristabell's mouth. "You cry yourself to sleep."

I clenched my teeth. "Why should that surprise you? Is this not a strange place to be a novice?"

"Only to those who do not wish to be here."

"You enjoy your cruelty," I said plainly, startling from her a look of surprise. "I am a frank woman, Dame Cristabell, and I always speak my mind."

"Humility is what's wanted here, Mistress."

"I have seen little by way of humility here, Dame."

"You think because you bring pouches of gold that we will conform to your will? Then I am glad of our poverty…if for nothing else than to protect us from the power of greed!"

"You know nothing of me, Cristabell. And I would tell you if only it would make a difference."

"I will not be fooled by your innocent demeanor. You are no highborn lady."

"And I never professed to be. Why do you mistrust me so?"

Cristabell maneuvered away from the puddle as if its reflection could contaminate. "Clearly you do not take this seriously, Mistress."

I leaned against a chilled stone arch. I rubbed my reddened hands, chapped from wash water and morning cold. "I do take it all seriously," I said to the floor. "You must help me, Dame, for I know not how to be a nun. I have only been a daughter and a poor sister to my own siblings. And I am a naïve woman. You must help me."

Surprised wariness flickered in Cristabell's eyes. "Help you? Seek your help in God."

"But are you not my sister in Christ? May I not find help in you just as the holy apostles helped one another?"

"We are not apostles. Only women." Cristabell turned, but I caught her arm.

"Surely it was difficult for you when you first came here. How…how long ago was that? Why did *you* come to Blackladies?"

Her brow lowered over her eyes. "You are too familiar for your own good, Mistress." She pulled her arm free of me and moved down the cloister, disappearing behind a door.

I watched the bubbles form and pop along the edge of the puddle, and my mind wandered, drifting. Was it possible to seal the rift in my heart with God? I thought as much, for else why was I here?

To run from an arranged marriage by Sir John, I admitted. But what was so wrong with marriage?

My toe nudged the puddle, touching off rings running to its outer edge. I inhaled Blackladies' wet stone, its sweetly scented garden, and I felt its enclosing walls hover over me like a schoolmaster's switch.

It was Thomas who stood in my way, of course. There was no use denying it. I could not see myself loving anyone but him. No one else but God.

I cleaned the rest of the floor before going to my other tasks. Each day became a new lesson in the worth of communal life. It seemed I was nothing but a chore to Cristabell, who made it her mission to correct my faults, making mention of them constantly at our daily chapter meetings. I kept to myself, as I was used to, for I never troubled myself with Robert's acquaintances who were too rough for me, nor Agnes' silly feminine pursuits and gossip. At home, I happily tended the garden and beehives alone, and so alone I did so at Blackladies.

"Good morning, Mistress," greeted Meg Burre, our servant, as she did to me every morning. And every morning it startled me. I was used to solitude and the disregard of the nuns.

I nodded to her as I affixed my bee bonnet with its netting.

"Here, let me help you with that." She straightened it, making certain the veil pooled over my shoulders. "My milking's done. Shall I help you with the hives?"

Embarrassed for no reason I could fathom, I glanced swiftly at her in acknowledgement. With buckets and knives, we walked to the meadow near the mill pond where the woven domed skeps soon came into view mid the dying hogweed, nettles, and lavender. We smoked the tiny workers with a piece of smoldering linen wrapped around some straw inside a canister, and I lifted the woven skep while Meg pulled out the combs with a knife, and scraped the precious honey and beeswax into one of the buckets.

Meg looked up so often toward the barley fields that I could not resist turning my head to look, too. She nodded to a tall figure stepping through the browning September stalks. "That there is Tom Smith," she said, and then giggled. "He's a right comely man, but he don't give me the time o' day. He can't fool me, though." With a hoe angling up over his shoulder, he joined the other men in the field. None looked our way. "Oh!" she thought suddenly. "I shouldn't be saying aught to the likes of you, Mistress. I reckon it isn't proper. The Prioress will give me a hiding for that."

"Do not fret, Meg," I said softly. "It matters not to me. I am not made of stone. I am a woman though I wear this livery. You must feel free to speak to me unless it is to gossip."

"Now then," she said surprised. "You're a different sort than the rest, aren't you? I seen you scrub the cloister and go off to the kilhouse like all the rest, but I was thinking to myself that this here's one who knows what a day's work is. Am I right?"

Walking to the next hive, I set down my bucket and straightened the netting. "I do not believe my sisters come from a life of ease."

"That's not my meaning." She removed the next skep, waving away the flitting bees. They moved off as we dispatched the combs. "None of them are highborn, I know that. But they all come with notions."

"I had no expectations. Indeed," I said as I worked, feeling more and more at ease with her, "I did not know the least what to expect."

"Why'd you come, then, if it isn't too forward to ask?"

We finished with the last hive and I pulled the netting from my face, gazing across the flower-dotted meadow. Dandelion seeds winged around us, vying for updrafts with disgruntled bees. I was tempted to dip a finger into the bucket for a small taste of the dark honey whose fragrant perfume arose in the toasting sun. I resisted the urge, though glancing at Meg, I noted she was not plagued by such restraint. "It seemed the only place for me."

"What about a husband?"

I smiled, shaking my head. "I am unsuited to married life."

"Not I!"

For the first time at Blackladies, I laughed aloud. It encouraged a brisker pace, and Meg followed me down a rutted path beside a fence overgrown with brambles. "You have your eye on Tom Smith?" I asked.

A spark kindled in her eye. "You're a one, Mistress. Aren't you going tell me how my thoughts are sinful?"

"*Are* your thoughts sinful?"

"No. Well..." She laughed. "You're not like the others, are you?"

With a frown I pushed through the gate into the main courtyard. "I suppose not."

She skipped to keep up with me as we approached the honey house, a small appendage to the bolting house. I opened the door letting in enough light for me to open the shutter, and we set the buckets down on the table, ready to strain the honey from the wax and dead bees.

"Do you think I should try to get on with Tom?"

She reminded me of Agnes, only gentler and less deceitful. Immediately I found I liked her, and smiled. "Is Tom of a mind to 'get on' with you, or is marriage not on his mind? That is important, Meg. I would not have you thinking of sin."

"It's true. It's hard to tell with a man, isn't it? It's mostly marriage on a woman's mind, but never on his." We scraped the honey into a pot and set the buckets aside. The combs would be heated slowly to melt the wax and release the honey. Cloth-covered honey pots sat on the shelves. Most served other purposes than eating. Honey was useful for wounds, and for making a hand cream for the chapping winter ahead. The honey for eating we would take on to the buttery and sell the rest.

"But take you, Mistress," she went on. I handed her pots from the shelf and she tucked them close to her large bosom. Her white kerchief was clean. I admired this about the two women workers who served Blackladies, this care they took with their person.

We left the honey house and made our way across the courtyard again through a crowd of geese, honking in displeasure as we scattered them. I unlatched the buttery door and we entered. It smelled of sweet honey and the fresh earthen aroma of dried peas and beans, of lavender oil and pungent rosemary sprigs hanging upside down from its rafters.

"You say you are unsuited to marriage," Meg went on and I nodded to her words. "But how can a body know?"

"Mayhap you can never truly know," I said quietly.

The courtyard swallowed our steps, and the shadow of the porch's arch cut the fleeting sun with a sudden chill. We did not proceed into the house, but followed the mossy edges to another gate. Encouraged by Meg's friendship, I raised a hand in greeting to the workmen in the fields. They returned the hail by doffing their caps, including indifferent Tom Smith.

In the shed, I discarded my shoes and slipped into wooden clogs, trudging along the gravel walk until reaching the vegetable garden.

Meg watched me from the gate. I knew she had other errands to attend to, but I decided suddenly that I would miss her company. "May I ask you?" she said, leaning against the damp stone wall that always lay in shade.

"Of course," I said cheerfully.

"Why is it I do not see you with the other nuns? They don't work with you. Is it because you are a novice?"

The hoe hit the dirt. I tore free a weed and tossed it over my shoulder. "At first I thought so." I shrugged. "But now…I think it is merely that…they do not like me."

"Well that won't do! Some of them nuns have been here nigh on twenty years. It won't do to carry on so for twenty years."

I straightened and leaned on the hoe. "No. It very much will *not* do!" Meg was a plump creature, all cheeks and smiles, with hazel eyes peeking out of squinted sockets. Her sleeves were rolled up past chapped elbows, and smudges darkened the outside of one forearm. Her napron, clean only this morning, was now streaked with dirty honey. I suddenly thought of St. Martha, which was quite unusual, because I always viewed the saints as very well to-do people. It suddenly occurred to me, like an unexpected gust of wind, that the Saint Martha who was so hospitable to our Lord must not have been high and dignified like the prioress, but instead more like Meg. The thought gave me courage.

She watched me with some surprise as I dropped the hoe, exchanged my clogs for shoes again, and entered the cloister.

I found Dame Cristabell polishing the wainscoting in the hall of the main house. She looked up at me once before returning to her work.

"Mistress? Do you stand idle while others work?"

"No, indeed. But I come to ask a favor."

"A favor? That is very ill-suited to your position in this house."

"It is not that kind of favor, Dame. The favor is to ask for your civility…no. Not merely your civility, but your friendship. It seems a little enough favor to ask."

Turning back to her work she said nothing for a long time, until, "This is not the hour for talk. These are the hours for work. You have been here for two months. I would expect that you should know this by now."

And there it was again, the sensation that I was on a skiff suddenly cut from the dock to drift. I reached for the line, but no line was there, and the mist was rising.

"Cristabell." She turned to me, the same indifference smoothing her face. "I know it is not the hour for talking, but when you have done your sister a hurt, you must go at once to her and make amends." A hint of movement flickered her brow with just the merest tinge of satisfaction. I read it perfectly well. "No, I have done *you* no injustice. It is injustice to *me* of which I speak."

She leapt to her feet, the stiff rag clutched in her fist. "Mistress Launder! May Almighty God forgive you your insolence! And look at you!"

I did, and saw my muddy shoes and mud-dredged hem. The napron I tied over my scapular was also dirty from my day's work.

"You come here with your indignation," she trumpeted, "and your high ways, and your high friends. Did you expect your precious Sir John to make all things smooth for you? And what of us? Shall we serve Isabella instead of God?"

"Oh Cristabell. You have no idea how mistaken you are. I am no friend of Sir John Giffard. I am only from a farm like any other here, and my family did not want me to cloister myself, yet bowed to my decision. Surely you could have known this if only you had asked."

"Am I expected to believe you?"

"Yes, praise God! Cristabell, it is no sin to be friendly, and I have such need of it."

Her eyes darted down for a moment, and her face betrayed only a hint of something indistinguishable…and then it was gone, enmasked behind her stiff demeanor. "You come here to hide. I know your kind. You make a fine show of work, but have no virtue behind it. This is not a place to hide from your troubles. And I will be no party to your deceit."

"I have not come here to hide."

"Have you not?"

Her immovable tone infuriated, yet something resonated from her words. I took great pains to occupy myself with work and prayer and the obedience to the difficult Rule. So much so that it gave me little time to think of anything—or anyone—else.

My eyes stung suddenly with tears. Far from Caverswall and Beech, I was cut off from the news of court or of Stafford. I heard of no deaths, no weddings, nothing. No mention of people I knew or how they fared. I suddenly realized how much I longed to hear tidings of Thomas, but was saved from that cruelty by virtue of this cloister.

I knew from Father William's sermons that to sin against the Holy Ghost was the unforgivable sin, but I also learned from Cristabell another: that of lying to one's self.

"There…is much to what you say," I surrendered.

She raised a tentative brow. "And so. I am heeded at last."

"Yes. But, I hope you, too, have learned from me. If we are to be sisters to our life's end, then we must be friends. If I have offended you, then I ask your forgiveness."

Her eyes nestled under lowered lids, and her mouth set fiercely, determined to release nothing. "There is still two hours until Vespers, Mistress," she said sharply. "Make use of your time."

Nodding, I turned. Over my shoulder, I said, "We will be friends someday, Cristabell. You will see."

She said nothing, as I expected, but I was grieved by her humor. I was not by nature a likable woman, not the friendly, laughing sort like Meg, or the giggling flirt as was Agnes, but neither was I too critical nor facetious. Cristabell was a challenge, but I did not find myself entirely alone. I was fortunate eventually to find some solace in Dame Elizabeth, who warmed from my companionship. Often we sat silently in the warm light of our chamber where we did our mending, and I was surprised when one day she spoke openly to me.

Reaching forward with a bony finger, she touched some of my stitchery. "That is a fine hand, Mistress," she said, slurping her words behind her buck teeth. I looked up into warm eyes, and smiled.

"You flatter me, Dame."

"Not at all. Flattery has no place here. It is simply that you have a good, solid stitch, and I should like to learn it."

"But certainly you have more years training on me, madam."

"I was never one for stitchery. See here."

She showed me her work, and though it was efficiently done, it lacked smooth competence. "Still, it will hold a seam."

"It is artless," she said, shaking her head.

"It need not be tapestries," murmured Prioress Margaret from across the room. She did not look up from her work.

For the first time, I felt part of this little family, accepted as if I had passed a test. Part of it, surely, was that Cristabell was on her rounds checking the bars and gates, and not amongst us.

"Is it becoming clearer to you what is expected as a nun?" asked Elizabeth.

With her wimple hugging her cheeks and her toothy grin, she reminded me of the red squirrels which danced from tree to tree in the cloister garden. "Yes, Dame. It is becoming clearer. Although—"

"What is it, my dear?"

"When I first came here, I was treated as if...well...as if I were not liked." I blushed from my words, for when I uttered them aloud they seemed so foolish. "This is, in fact, the first genuine moment of affection among my sisters I have experienced here."

Elizabeth chuckled. "Yes, it can seem so. But you see, there is little reason in getting to know a novice in the first few weeks, for that is when they usually change their minds."

Her gentle tone and her explanation was a relief. "I see. Then have you now decided I shall be staying at Blackladies?"

"It is a fair guess," she said, glancing once at the prioress. "Unless there is more to occupy your mind."

"More?"

Elizabeth's voice fell to a whisper "You talk in your sleep, Mistress."

I shuddered to think what I said, and I vowed to pray that much more fervently to keep my heart upon my vocation, and not on distractions of the past. I also vowed to remember the kindness of Dame Elizabeth in my devotions, for she showed me a motherly concern that had been lacking.

Prioress Margaret lifted her head. "Has it been that trying for you?"

"Yes, Madam. Most trying."

She laughed, shaking her head. I was at first offended until she spoke in explanation. "Isabella! I know I can rely upon you to answer honestly to any question. Was it always thus with you?"

My cheeks burned, but I solemnly nodded. "Yes, Madam. Much to the disdain of my own family."

"Do you miss them?" asked Elizabeth.

Once the dike was opened it seemed the flood was upon me. "In all honesty," I said with a nod to the prioress, "no, I do not."

"Were they cruel to you?" asked Elizabeth.

"No. Not cruel. Simply that…they did not see me. I was part of the wall, or the hedge. Not that I desired to be the center of attention, never that! But the mere fact that I was seldom visible gave me pause. So you see, there was very little resistance at my decision to come here."

"It was not imposed upon you, then?"

Prioress Margaret looked up at that, measuring me with her small eyes.

"It was my decision, Dame," said I.

"Then this desire to become a nun was made by reason, much like my own," said Elizabeth.

"Tell me, Dame. I long to hear your tale."

"There is little to tell. I was the middle daughter of five siblings. Our mother was very pious and I saw in her devotions something quite dear to my heart. I was quite young—fifteen—and my mother did not wish to give me up to a convent. She tempted me with a parade of bridegrooms and promises of such household treasures I could expect as the wife of a good burgess. But I could not see myself as a wife. My conscience was aimed toward the crucifix and the passion of our Lord, how God Himself died for our sins to bring us salvation and everlasting life. That was a treasure that could not be bought with household goods. It touched me. Strange that it should touch only *me* and not my sisters nor brothers. Finally, my mother capitulated, somewhat proudly, I think. Her other daughters fulfilled her desires to see them wedded well and with grandchildren aplenty, but she seemed most pleased by her middle daughter's choice. I think it gave her comfort to know that prayers were said in constant for her family. She died a good and happy death. My one regret was that I was not with her."

"Yes," I said, comparing Dame Elizabeth's honest devotion to my empty one. "We are locked within these gates."

The prioress lowered her mending in her lap, and gazed at me fondly. "It is not that we are locked in, but that the world is locked out. Does that notion alarm you, Isabella?"

"No, Lady Prioress. It is not alarming, but comforting. I was not a woman who enjoyed dancing and country beguilements. I seldom left the confines of my father's grange. I worked in my garden. Within this cloister, I continue in this enterprise. I hope my work has proved satisfactory."

"Indeed. The garden has never looked healthier. You have a way with it."

"By the grace of God, Madam."

"Of course," she answered. "Then you are pleased to be in the company of nuns?"

"Yes, Madam," I said carefully.

"There is hesitation in your voice." Picking up her mending again, she peered at her stitches and placed the needle with care. "Could it have to do with our other dear sister?"

"I do not wish to criticize—"

"But, indeed, I can count upon you to do so."

She said it with a grin, and by that I knew she held for me no ill will. "As you say, Madam. Cristabell seems vexed by the mere mention of me, and I know not why."

"Know you not? It is simple—"

Cristabell entered at that moment and we all fell silent, picking up our stitchery where we left off. Cristabell, too, picked up her mending, and as she glanced toward me I offered her a cheerful smile.

To me she gave a cursory look of indifference and set to the task before her. We stitched quietly, each with her own thoughts, until Dame Elizabeth began to hum, and soon we all took it up.

All except for Cristabell.

THOMAS GIFFARD
AUTUMN, 1515
Chillington Hall, Brewood

VIII

"There is no more lovely, friendly and charming a relationship,
Communion or company than a good marriage."
—Martin Luther, 1569

Father suggested we come to Chillington, and I clutched at the idea, grateful for its fond familiarity. For a brief time, I could forgo the anger at my father for having arranged my marriage without informing me, for my loss of freedom, and the unwanted attention of Dorothy Montgomery, my wife. But I warmed to the situation as any courtier must. It meant a great amount of land to the Giffard coffers, making us quite the wealthiest family in the county of Stafford.

After leaving court we all rode on to Brewood, trotting through this fine little village to Chillington. I even pointed out my favorite childhood haunts to Dorothy.

"And that?" she asked, lifting a silk and velvet-clad arm as we made the juncture of Port Lane and Upper Chillington.

I looked and saw the oaken cross. "That is Giffard's Cross, madam. Shall I recount the story of its raising?" She inclined her blonde head to me, the heavy dark blue veil of her kennel headdress fluttering in the breeze. "Years ago, my father saved a woman with babe in arms from the deadly jaws of his own panther, which escaped from the menagerie at Chillington Hall. He and I pursued the beast and felled it with one arrow, and hence the family motto *Prenez haleine, tirez fort.* "'Take breath and pull strong,' words I myself whispered into Father's ear for encouragement."

She stared at the cross and followed it with her gaze as we passed it. Then she turned a wry eye to me. "Tell me husband, did this truly happen?"

I smiled and adjusted my seat on the worn saddle. My horse chuckled, mouthing his bit. "They erected a cross on the spot, did they not?"

It was more companionable between us from then on. Though it was true I was not a chaste man before marriage (*Jesu* grant me mercy for that) I made my vows to my wife in the presence of God, and I intended to keep them well. She was a comely woman, and so it was not difficult fulfilling my obligations of the nuptial bed. I even looked forward to it. It is a man's way. Does not the cockerel sire his brood over the hen? And even should he long for a hen in another barnyard, he continues his duties as is his nature. So it is my nature, indeed the nature of men, that they seek their solace from whatever their distress in the mindless abyss of the sexual act.

When I entered the chamber that evening, Dorothy sat enthroned upon the bed, a dour expression marring her blushing cheek. Immediately I sat upon the bed's corner. Petulance of this sort usually meant my imminent purchase of some bauble, and so I played my part. "Madam," I offered in my most endearing voice, "is there something amiss?"

It took a long moment for her gaze to slide toward me. Her blue eyes settled on mine. At our first strained meeting, I reckoned those eyes might offer a warm haven, as the sky is warm on a midsummer's day, but I have since learned that it was rather the blue of oceans, deep, cold, and unfathomable.

"I do not mind your having past lovers, husband. An eagle flies far afield before he settles, after all. But I do mind when they follow you."

"Surely you are mistaken, madam." I chuckled, but the thought, and the fact of her uttering it, aroused me. I took her hand and stroked the velvety skin. "I keep no cote of doves, neither here nor north in Caverswall."

"Then *I* must be mistaken," she said, enduring my touch, "for I have heard talk of you and your farm whore."

It is true what they say. The blood does drain from one's face. It pooled in my chest and burnt, while my cheeks grew cold. I withdrew from her hand. "Be careful what you say, madam."

"Very well, husband." Coyly she smoothed the coverlet over her lap. Her gold hair lay unbound down her back, her head covered by a tight white cap. "In faith, I knelt with you before God's altar, and I was declared your lawful wife. I did not foreswear myself before God, hiding behind a veil."

"Madam." I gritted my teeth. "I have not the least idea what you are talking about, but I might suggest you leave it at that."

"Leave it? Surely I would, if the very idea of this disguising were not an affront to me as a Christian woman. But I have been told that this fornicator calls herself a novice at your Blackladies priory."

"What?" Now the burning in my chest went cold. Farm whore? Surely not... "I know not of what you speak—"

"Isabella Launder. That is her name, is it not? It is free talk amongst your servants, Thomas, and even they are appalled."

Astounded, I muttered, "You are mistaken about us. You do not know how much." It was all I could reply to her. I could not trouble myself to explain to her the chasteness of that dear lady, nor of her humor, her kindness... But did Dorothy say she was now ensconced at Blackladies? As a novice?

Anger flared again within me, at that coney Dorothy and at Father. I left her in the chamber as soon as I might the next morning, and stalked down the stairs of Chillington Hall, my father's pride and joy even above that of Caverswall...that is, until the Montgomery lands caught his eye and his ambition.

I raised my eyes to the main hall's familiar arches uplifting the roof several stories high, like the ribs of a whale. Like Jonah we were, swallowed up in this monster of a house. My eyes traveled back up the oaken staircase, and I could not help but snarl at the thought that my wife was somewhere up there. I could not go to her. Not with pricking thoughts of convents fresh in my mind. I strode through the hall, the feeling of friendliness dissipating. I felt as if my chest were gouged out, like a hollow trunk of a dead tree. I sought the solitude of the parlor, but stopped at the arched doorway. Father was there, but did not see me.

Do I let him exile me from all those places I find consolation? I took a deep breath and muttered, "Take breath and pull strong," before striding forward into the room. I took a goblet from beside the jug and poured the wine myself. Then, without acknowledging him, I plopped down into my favorite chair.

I felt his glare upon me, but I continued to ignore it. Nudging my shoulder near the flickering hearth, I warmed the dark velvet of my pleated jerkin, and burrowed further into the cushions. I knew my brooding silence would wear on him, and his irritation pleased me immensely. Not once did Father ever mention Isabella Launder. It galled that he somehow knew about her nonetheless.

"I have arranged a meeting with the Brewood council today, Thomas."

"Have you not arranged enough?" I muttered. Still he heard it, and scowled.

"And what is it that so berates your brow?"

"Blackladies."

He made a sound in his throat at that, but said nothing. I turned to him. His face was red but neutral.

"Is she there? Did *you* machine that as well?"

"You are not too old for a strop, my lad. That is what is needed!"

"I have endured your arrangements and plots all my life, Father. Have I not earned the right to an honest sulk?"

"Not in my house!"

"Then I will leave your house!" Bounding to my feet, I glowered nose to nose with him. He glared at me for a long moment until a smile turned up his mustache, and he suddenly laughed and clapped me on the shoulder. Taken aback, I could do nothing to solace my anger.

"Oh, Thomas. Sit down!" He forced me back to the seat and then sat opposite, a smile still spread on his face. "Oft I speak, but rarely do you listen to me. I wish your mother had lived. It would have spared me years of your abuse."

"Do you blame me for that too? It is not my fault she died in childbed, as much as you would have me believe it were so."

He canted back, lips parted. "Do you truly think that, my son? When have I ever blamed you for that which was God's will alone?"

"All my life, sir. 'If only your mother were here, she would set you on the right path,'" I said mockingly. "'I know not what to do with you, Thomas. Your mother would have known.'"

"By the blessed Virgin. And you interpreted that as my blaming you? You *are* a spoiled child, Thomas. And I know not what your—Hmm. I know not what *I* am to do with you."

"You have done it. I am married."

"And high time. At your age I was married, sired three living children, been knighted by the king, appointed sheriff and joint bailiff of Wolverhampton, besides being a trusted member of the king's household. What have *you* accomplished?"

"Precious little, Father," I grumbled, arms firmly crossed over my chest. "But I shall."

"Of course you shall. You are a Giffard."

"Then explain this to me. Last year you made all your conniving intrigues to gain the wardship of Sir John's daughter and heir Dorothy. You obtained the license to marry her yourself. Why then did you marry her mother instead?"

He smiled, brushing up the tips of his mustache with a finger. The rings on his hand flashed in the fire glow. "The Montgomery lands are ours, Thomas, through my marriage *and* yours. The late Sir John—God rest his soul—made his daughters co-heirs. Naturally I saw an opportunity and moved on it with all haste. Dorothy was an obedient thing and would have married an old creature such as myself, as her mother no doubt ordered her to do. The Giffards are no country fools, after all. But the thing of it is...well...I became acquainted with her mother, the widow Elizabeth...and..."

I glared at my father and snatched the goblet of wine sitting beside me. I gulped a dose and licked my lips before the obvious thought finally occurred. "God's teeth, Father! Did you fall in love? Is *that* why you married her?"

Father's cheeks grew crimson spots and he shifted in his seat, adjusting the furred collar of his jerkin against the over-stuffed doublet. "Well...an alliance is an alliance."

"Father! By God's body! A man your age..."

"Keep a civil tongue. I am a man, and your mother died over twenty years ago."

I toyed nervously with the cords of my shirt collar. "And you gave up all that land for love."

"I gave up nothing. You have married it."

"Yes. I see. It must have cost you a considerable sum to gain a new license to marry a ward of the king that quickly." He did not answer, and after a while I raised my head. "Did you hear me, Father? I said it must have cost you dearly—"

"As I am a Gentleman Usher of the Chamber I was certain our gracious majesty would excuse a fleeting misjudgment based on the heart, while making certain the original license was sufficiently carried out."

"You mean to say," I said with lowered voice, "you married her without the king's permission? That was a dangerous game to play, Father, gambling on the king's good humor. He has a terrible temper when provoked."

"I *was* gambling on it. He is a good Christian and a young romantic himself. He was lenient with me, praise God."

"You…you surprise me, Father. I was certain your motives lay elsewhere."

"Can a man not look upon his life and decide on better things? Land is land, but a proper woman to run it is another thing. Elizabeth, your stepmother, is well trained, well prepared, Thomas, as is your wife, Dorothy. She, too, will be the chatelaine a Giffard man needs. A strong woman, Thomas…a *highborn* lady."

I swallowed another dose. "The integrity of the lowborn must not be underestimated," I said softly.

"Neither should the importance of being a Giffard." Rising, he straightened his jerkin and adjusted the thick gold chain arcing over his breast. "I will see that the horses are saddled. I will await you at the stables."

"*Was* it you who sent her to Blackladies?"

He stopped and swayed for a moment, but he did not turn to me. "It was her choice, Thomas."

"How can I believe that?" All the hurt was back, all father's schemes flitting through my mind, like a whirl of leaves in an autumn storm. "By the Mass! A convent! Is she a *nun*, then?"

"I do not know. She asked for my counsel, and I provided a place."

"So you sent her to a convent. Did you think she disgraced the Giffard name? Soiled it? You have a crippled mind, Father. You cannot recognize that which is pure!"

"It was her choice."

"You coerced her!"

"It was her choice to marry or choose this. Those were her *only* choices. I see now what a wise decision it was if your heart burns with such jealousy!"

"You do not know what you are talking about! She is the most chaste of women…"

"If that is true then she belongs where she bides." With that, he stomped away, and I, suddenly irritated beyond speaking, sunk deeper into the chair.

A log in the hearth spit out an ember with a loud report and it glowed and simmered on the planks. I watched as the warmth in it died, greying to ash, only a changeling of itself. *As am I, the wedded husband.* I brought the cup to my lips and drank the rest. My fingers wiped the wet from the fringe of my mustache as I clutched the goblet and scowled into the hearth. Isabella shut in a cloister, a ghastly, simpering nun! Why did she do it? Why not marry? Surely any husband would have suited better than that.

Yet even at this quite ordinary thought, an entirely extraordinary sensation welled in me. For the notion of Isabella wed, with a man touching her as I touched my wife, sent a jolt of revulsion throughout my core. Oh I knew it was selfishness, for I wanted her to myself as my apparently not-so-secret friend. But why such revulsion?

Raising the cup, I realized it was empty and set it down again. I dropped my head into my palm. A sense of dread, of something utterly lost rushed over me, and I found myself out of breath. Something swarmed to the surface and I slowly raised my face, picturing in my mind Isabella's image. How ordinary a countenance it was, but how I longed to see it, longed to see a smile spread across it at some jibe of mine, or even see her brow crease with stern words pronounced for my benefit alone. I was fond of her, yes. Deeply fond, as I would be toward a sister or a cousin. Very fond.

The more I concentrated on her image the greater the ache in my heart, and it grew, this notion, with fearful enormity. Surely it was not possible. Far more beautiful women crossed my path, delicate creatures, demure, dainty. They did not possess her Amazonian height, or her callused hands, or those heavy brows more like a boy's. They were clever with words and currying, these women, not like her blunt assessments. They smelt of perfume, not of barnyard.

In my desperation to deny it, to compare her to worthier women, my own logic faltered on something so very simple, so obvious that it never before occurred to me. My heart *was* jealous. Past the callow depths of me was a better Thomas Giffard, the one seen through Isabella's eyes. The Thomas Giffard I could be, if I had heeded her years of advice.

The Thomas Giffard who realized at last—and very much too late—that he was dreadfully in love with her!

I felt a painful hemorrhage in my chest.

So simple. I loved her. I loved her plain language and the sardonic tilt of her head. I loved how much she cared for that damned garden and those roses of hers. I loved that she was not disposed to poetry or philosophy, and had no clue how to debate the finer points of faith. She knew neither politics nor schemes, and for that I loved her, too. "Dear God in Heaven…" Worse. Did she love me, in all my ineloquence? In all the years of knowing one another? "Oh *Jesu!*"

The tingle of a shadow crossed over me and I slowly raised my head. A servant. "Sir John awaits, my lord," he said.

"He awaits," I mumbled with ill humor. "He can wait till the Devil comes!" I pushed the servant aside, sprinted down a flight of steps, and ran out to the stable's courtyard.

ISABELLA LAUNDER
AUTUMN, 1515
Blackladies

VIX

"Hark! My lover—here he comes
Springing across the mountains, leaping across the hills…"
–Song of Songs 2:8

The bells jangled in the back of my thoughts until Dame Elizabeth gently touched my shoulder. "Is it not your day to act as porter, Mistress Isabella?"

"Bless me," I sighed. "It is indeed. Little wonder the prioress has me attend the gate so often. Perhaps it is to instill remembrance of that duty for which I oft forget." I rose and left the pleasant room for the late afternoon light of the cloister. A breeze came up, and with it the aroma of autumn, of country bonfires and musty damp. It put me in a charitable mood of my present life at Blackladies. Three months had passed since I entered the gate, and I was beginning to feel at home here, and reconciled to tutoring myself to a different kind of devotion: that of God, not of Thomas. Cristabell's words still rang in my head, and I was determined to make this not a sanctuary *from* the world but my true place *in* the world. I was satisfied to call Blackladies home. As a cloistered nun, I would never leave its grounds, using my time to till the soil or work in the many places required of me. I was pleased to do so, for though Dame Cristabell still insisted on indifference toward me, I did not miss my father's grange as I thought I might, nor did I miss my father, nor Agnes, nor even Robert. Nor could I muster guilt at this confession. There was no wall or arch on Rafe Launder's farm that I longed to see again. No family member I pined for. I conformed to this place, the flavor of the Rule and its discipline. Despite Cristabell, I made good acquaintance of Meg and Dame Elizabeth, and I began to find my satisfaction within prayer and the little cloister garden.

My mind was emptied of all as I made my way through the cloister. I was even cheered as I turned the corner, anxious to give a pleasant countenance to the tradesman or farmer who rang the bell so impatiently.

When I raised my eyes, my amiable greeting caught on a gasp. The face I could not excise from my mind, the body that haunted my dreams, paced before the iron grate, sword slapping his thigh with each impatient whirl on his heel. He wore no hat and his collar was left untied, exposing dots of sweat at the base of his throat.

He heard my step and jerked his head, careering toward the grate, curling whitening fingers around the protecting grille. "Isabella! God's body! Look at you!"

"Thomas." My mind shut down. I merely stared at the toes of his boots. Such fine leather and so finely tailored to his feet. His spurs gleamed dully under splatters of mud.

He rattled the stern grating, gritting his teeth in a desperate grimace. "Open this! I must speak with you."

I took a step back and shook my head. "I cannot, Thomas. We are not allowed out."

"*We?* Oh, Isabella!" Pressing his forehead against the bars he stared at me with dark-rimmed eyes, from my feet to my veil-covered head. "Have I brought you to this? May God forgive me."

"You have not brought me to this, and it is conceit to think so."

"But this is damnable! You cannot become a ...a *nun*! How foolish and selfish! It is absurd!"

I frowned. "And what is it to you, Thomas Giffard? You are a married man. You best go back to your bride."

His lips clamped tightly, quivering the dark beard. He was a bridegroom three months. His wrinkled brow pressed against the rusty metal. "Isabella," he whispered, rolling his head along the bar. "If I only had known you would do this..."

"I did not know myself, Thomas, until the moment of decision. It was either this or marry a man of my father's choosing."

He cast himself from the grating and furiously paced. I watched him helplessly.

"Why are you here, Thomas?"

He stopped. His normally erect posture slumped with desolation. "To...to see you. I...I did not know. I only heard today."

I told myself I was stronger than this, but to see his face in all its forlorn shadows and to feel his enigmatic presence again caused my will to crumble with unwanted tears. I covered my face with my hands.

Thomas rushed to the bars and yanked them. "Curse this! Isabella, let me in!" I waved my hands in refusal, unable to speak. He reached through, trying to touch me. "Do not weep. I knew this to be a mistake! You are so pigheaded! Tell them you have made a mistake and leave here."

I rubbed my fingers across my ruined face and dropped my hands to my sides with a capitulating shrug. "It is not a mistake. We have both made our decisions and must surrender to them."

"I cannot accept that. You do not need this mummery. You can return to Beech if you desire."

"To what end? Marry?" A surge of fierce emotion welled, and still blinded by tears, I stomped to the grating and stood before it, hands curling around the iron. "What would you have me do?"

My strength seemed to sap his, and he leaned a shoulder against the bars, sliding to the ground, resting his flaccid wrists on upraised knees. I looked down upon his vulnerable head, that musky dark mane. "I do not know, Isabella. The world has fallen apart. It has lost its meaning. I am yoked with a wife I do not love, and my true beloved is now lost in a nunnery. My God. What have I done to deserve this? What great sin have I committed to lose you?"

My breath held, stifled by those incomprehensible words; words he spoke with his own lips. Did I hear them? Could they be believed? "Thomas...do you call *me*...beloved?"

Gently shaking his head, he turned to look at me. It was the same face, the same Thomas, but the look was different. Oh, he had smiled indulgently at me many times before, or chuckled at some ineptitude of mine—always at my expense, but never with cruelty. This time it was a potent expression of something that I longed for only hours ago in restless slumber.

He rose, and, laying his hands on the grating, his gentle eyes gazed into mine. "I have been a fool, Isabella," he said softly. "I did not see what was always before my eyes. I did not see that my dearest friend was also my own heart. And I have only just discovered this, too, today. Dare I say it aloud? Isabella...I love you! Not as a sister. Not as a cousin. But as a man loves a woman."

"No!" I clamped my hands over my ears. "Why? Why now, Thomas? Why too late?"

"Never too late, Isabella. I am here now. Open the gate."

"No." Even as I said it, I could not move. I offered no resistance when Thomas snatched the keys from between the iron grate, unlocked the door, and flung it aside. Even watching him approach, I could do nothing. He stood above me, and then my stiff muscles released when he embraced me. I shied like any untried colt, and sought to move away from the strangeness of his arms, of his chest pressed against mine. I felt that chest swell as he panted. Was it I who caused such distress? Plain Isabella? The thought amazed, barely completely formed, when he leaned toward me. I stared at his chin, counting the hairs of his beard, so close was I—yet this helped not at all, for it put me in view of those lips drawing slowly, parting in a smile.

"Isabella, you cannot possibly be afraid of *me?*"

I held my breath. His smile softened and drew closer. His lips lowered until they rested upon mine, growing soft and warm.

No man had ever before kissed me. I closed my eyes, absorbing the unbelievable sensations of Thomas' mouth caressing my lips. The fit was perfect, like two hands clasping.

I became aware not only of the velvet of his lips, but of his heart hammering, of the bristly feel of his beard on my skin, of the pungent scent of him, the strength of his fingers clinging to me. Losing myself, I returned the affectionate embrace with clumsy passion, feeling the tendrils of his hair between my fingers.

How tenderly he kissed, a match to my own virtuous efforts. How many years did I dream of this? Lips, moist and warm, a part of my own. Breath sweet upon my cheek. His strong arms about me, gently embracing, fingers kneading my flesh beneath its tattered gown.

But gradually, his encircling arms tightened, his mouth insisted, opening with maturing intensity. Following at first, I became frightened by his need...and that of my own.

The dream faded. Reality, like a splash of frigid water, awoke the sleeper. I tore my lips from his, pushing the edge of a hand against his chest to dislodge myself.

Thomas, gasping with passion, merely stared at me, our kiss still moistening his mouth. No longer were his arms a welcomed place, but a foreign one on whose shores I no longer belonged and dared not tread.

Dreadful, this sudden change in something so longed for!

"No, Thomas!" I whispered.

"You deny me?" he rasped.

"With my very being. It is wrong. For both of us. You chose to marry as I chose this place. We made vows. Would you be unfaithful to them?"

"I do not love her!"

"Then you must try! With nobility comes responsibilities…and consequences." I brushed a tear from my cheek with the back of my hand. "It is your heritage at fault, Thomas, which cannot truly be blamed."

"Then to hell with my heritage!"

"Easily said by a rich man."

He glared at me. "What is meant by that?"

"'It is easier to pass a camel through the eye of a needle than a rich man to enter into the kingdom of Heaven.'"

"Why are you so cruel to me? Do you not see how I suffer?"

The knot in my belly tightened. "And what of my suffering?"

"I am not a fool, Isabella. I know you suffer. But for a woman—"

"You think it easier for a woman? Well…perhaps. We are practical creatures. We know our limitations. We…accept."

"But we are so well-matched, you and I, like pieces on a chessboard."

"Opposing colors, Thomas." I well understood the lay of a chessboard. Certain pieces may move across its landscape with impunity while others are confined by virtue of their purpose.

His eyes were moist as they gazed at me. His affliction was real. For the first time in his life, he was being denied. He was truly helpless, as helpless as I was. It must have been a blow to his pride, and a Giffard's pride was a grand thing, indeed. There was also a boyish vulnerability to that face of three and twenty years, trying to bear its nobility with dignity.

Partly in empathy, partly with sadness, we peered silently at one another.

"I know it is my fault," he whispered. "I never knew before. I never knew how you felt. And then I did not know until today that I felt the same. I should have stayed away." He closed his eyes. Did he think by his will alone that circumstances would change? Slowly he opened his eyes and gazed tenderly. "But a *nun*, Isabella! You know my mind in these matters."

"It is my mind that is of consequence, Thomas, is it not?"

"You are so stubborn." His pout dropped years from his face. "Will…will you be well?"

I sighed. "I am well, Thomas. I am adjusting."

"But shall I?"

His warm fingers pressed over mine, and for a moment I thought to snatch mine away, but the touch was so familiar—God forgive me—I could not bear to move. It was Thomas who moved first, leaving me shamed and repentant. He walked back through the gate and slowly pulled it closed.

"Perhaps I am meant for a better purpose, Thomas," I said. "One cannot know why conditions turn as they do. Only God knows."

Grimacing, he shook his head. "To be a poor nun in this sty of a priory? I cannot see that this is to a better purpose."

"We cannot know what our Lord plans for us. That is what I meant."

"I know what you meant. But this place…could you not have chosen something better?"

I bit my lip. To suggest that this was also Sir John's choice was to annihilate any relationship he had with his father.

I held my tongue and stared at him, at a face on which I longed to cultivate a smile, on whose lips I would plant another kiss had I courage enough to defy God. "You must return to your bride, while I tend to my own duties here. I, too, am to wed in a year's time." I fingered my rosary.

"Is there nothing I can say?"

I already turned, unable to withstand the forlorn plea in his eyes. "That time is past." The words constricted my throat, but I instantly knew them to be true. It was time to put away childish things, to face the life now offered. To greet the Bridegroom. Stiffly I walked away, but I knew Thomas did not move, watching my every step.

THOMAS GIFFARD
LATE AUTUMN, 1515
Chillington Hall

X

"If you pressed me to say why I loved him,
I can say no more than it was because he was he and I was I."
–Michel Eyquem de Montaigne, 1580

Weeks passed since last I saw Isabella veiled and swathed in a novice's livery. But still I brooded. Dorothy's bed held no comfort for me, and so alone I spent my nights. My days were equally spent in solitude, walking the grounds of Chillington.

October fled like a robber from a house, leaving in its wake the cold breath of coming winter. The green leaves began to crisp, boldly glittering their gold in a mostly white sky. I tried to breathe in its earthy damp or the sweet esters of a field mown to stubble, but my spirit was as empty as last year's rabbit warrens.

Isabella. My Isabella. Not mine at all. Not sister. Not cousin. Not lover. Too late did I know my own mind, something my own father—curse him—could recognize that I did not. If I had only known before, I could have had the happiness I sought, become the man only half-imagined.

I could have been married to her.

I kicked at a shriveled apple that had fallen dried and hardened from its tree. It rolled down an incline into a trickling ditch.

But *would* I have married her? That damnable question did not cease coursing through my mind even in sleep. Would I have had the courage to defy Father and marry whom I wished? Isabella would gain the Giffard legacy nothing. The dower was too small to consider with any sobriety. She was not even the heir to her father's grange. Marrying Isabella would have been the folly of the county, and yet it would have been my fondest desire. I told myself I would have been brave enough to do it, but I doubted the sincerity of that even as it brushed my mind. I would have lost all: lands, monies, respect, and viability at court. It was not a proper match for a Giffard.

I brooded over it even as I glanced toward the house. It was not uncommon at court for men to put aside their wives in a decree of nullity for a better match, though profit was usually the reason, not love. But I could not put Dorothy reasonably aside without great scandal and loss of her dower rights. That would put me in no better stead than I was before.

"What is the matter with you, Thomas?" I scolded myself. "Is money all that matters?"

"It is a damn sight better than poverty."

I lurched back. George Throckmorton emerged from the hatching of shadows.

"George! God in Heaven!" My racing heart slowed, and I looked his muddy clothes up and down. "What brings you here? Let us back to the house so you can clean yourself."

"Not just yet. I was passing through, and thought to stop in on the newly wedded lord. Instead, I find you fumbling about in a dead grove, alone, and without your wife. Do you tire of her so quickly?"

A sigh heaved my shoulders and I shook my head. "Ah, George. What have I done?"

"What *have* you done?" When I said no more, he stopped and took my arm. Throckmorton's reddish-brown beard lay long upon his chest, for he wished to fashion himself an older more mature man at court. "Thomas, something deep vexes you. Can you not say?"

For a moment I thought I might, the words rolling over themselves in my mind. But gazing into his eyes, I suddenly thought better of it. Feebly I offered, "Marriage is not what I expected."

He smiled heartily. "Is it ever? Our expectations are greater than our realities. We are like diners at a sumptuous feast, only our eyes are bigger than our bellies. Worry not. The sooner you grow *her* belly, the better you will feel."

"George..." He coaxed me forward, and we walked shoulder to shoulder. The chill breeze billowed his fur-trimmed cape. "Tell me true, George. Did you love Catherine soon after marriage? Or even before?"

"I fancied her before we wed," he said, squinting into the falling sunlight. "And once wed...well, there is a fortnight or so of becoming used to a wife; the same woman before you at every meal and the same in bed at night. It is, after all, the difference between strangers and kin. Once no longer strangers, the nights are a comfort, and the days away a longing to be back."

"Do you love her now?"

"Yes. I do."

"I envy you."

"Have patience, Thomas. Three months wedded is not long enough to seal this kind of life-long alliance."

"Dear God! Life-long!"

"Did you believe otherwise?"

"No. It is only that... If you love, George, but...not your wife..."

He stopped, measuring the lengths of our shadows. "Thomas, I know you are not an avid man of prayer..."

I scowled, thinking of nuns' habits. "Church, with her damned cloisters."

"—but you are a man honorable to his vows. I know this from knowing you. Church or no, you have made a vow before God that you would forsake all others."

"And I meant it...at the time."

"The march of time does not change what was vowed. Surely you fear the wrath of God."

"God knows me better than I know myself. He excuses my faults."

"So you say. But adultery—"

"Who said aught of adultery?" I tugged my cape across my chest. It was cold from the weather but also his words. I could not imagine Isabella succumbing to such, she who was still a virgin.

"Ah!" he said knowingly. "It is the manner these days to love and long without fulfillment. But I thought you above that, Giffard."

"I did not seek this," I muttered angrily. "I do not give a damn for manners!"

"I can little help you then, except to offer this advice: Forget this other woman. It will only bring you grief. Put your stock in your wedded wife. Do not fashion a shrew of her so early in your marriage, or you will regret it."

I nodded. It was all true. I best not scorn Dorothy's affections so readily. And Isabella was so far away in body and in truth. How safe she was in her cloister, far from other matters, far from the experiences of court and the politics that plagued us all. Looking at Throckmorton and the sincerity on his face, I put it aside.

"Let us change the subject, then."

He was pleased to do it. Yet the only other subject that came readily to mind was that of court matters. The queen was still big-bellied, and the doctors said the pregnancy moved on apace. Soon I would be expected back to court for the birth celebrations. We all hoped that the expected male child would be delivered.

As I walked with George and listened to the court news, my own thoughts rumbled. I did not tell him that Dorothy's belly *did* grow with my seed. Soon the Giffards would have cause to celebrate alongside the king. Pray God they would both be boys, and the two of us would see our duties fulfilled. At least it would give me an excuse to leave her here while I traveled away to court.

The queen's pregnancy unsettled me, even as hopeful as the news was. I sensed this child would be a girl. Even so. If the queen should deliver a girl, all was not lost. A royal daughter was a bargaining tool to be bartered to the crowned heads of Europe. The king's sisters well-used that route, but were no longer saplings. Their day was done.

The political wheels would still turn, and court life would go on as before, with or without my help. The bells of St. Mary's Church in Brewood parish would still toll the hour, and the bells at Blackladies nunnery would still call their nuns and novices to Vespers.

ISABELLA LAUNDER
LATE AUTUMN, 1515
Blackladies

XI

He who conceals his sins prospers not,
but he who confesses and forsakes them obtains mercy.
—Proverbs 28:13

I think it most difficult to live in common with those neither of
your blood nor of your humor. It is the challenge, therefore, to live
as Christ asked of us, neither taking more than is necessary, and
offering more when needed.

My sisters were the mirrors in which I sought to see myself. It
was a distorted image at best, as I tried to conform to their ways,
even as one of them could not seem to conform to me. It was a
dreadful month. Not only did I still struggle with the chant and my
duties, but Thomas haunted my dreams more than before, and the
taste of him now cursed my lips. Surely it was the Devil, whose
timing in this was most acute, to rob a poor novice of her time at
prayers.

Thomas in love with me! It could scarce be believed, yet now it
hung in my mind, churning ceaselessly, when awake or asleep. How
I prayed for his face to leave my sight, his words to leave my ears.

And yet, I garnered a portion of satisfaction that the great lord Thomas Giffard was now in love with the plain and poor Isabella Launder. And so I further sinned with this pride.

I did not yet go to the prioress or our confessor Father William. Only God knew why. True, I was embarrassed to fall into such a trap of lust, and I was guilty. But it was not for fear of punishment that I kept my own counsel. Nor was it a wish to encourage daydreams already much too frequent. No. I did not feel worthy of absolution. There still clung to me this damaging desire for the outside, for Thomas, and I knew that I must thrust it from me if I was ever to find my peace.

The day after Thomas' terrible visit, I took my thoughts with me to the milking. The goats were being particularly uncooperative and constantly kicked the bucket. I succeeded only by clutching the bucket between my ankles, and holding the goat's lead in the one hand, and milking with my other. "I should call you Cristabell," I told the stubborn creature, "for you are just as vexing." The thought cheered me, and it seemed in this I could put thoughts of Thomas aside. I was close to gathering the courage to face the prioress and my confessor, to leave this sin behind me.

With the milking done I took the buckets to the cheeseloft, pouring the milk into the bins to work it into cheese. There was time left after this to go to the garden, and I hurried, anxious to find my peace in the familiar. The roses' blooms were almost spent, and I wanted to examine the stalks to make certain of their strength for the coming winter.

I walked across the courtyard and ducked into the shadow of the arch, reaching the cloister and the solitude and comfort of that little square sanctuary. Dame Elizabeth walked along the little path, murmuring as she held her rosary.

She suddenly faltered to one knee, and I cried out in genuine distress and hurried to catch her arm. "Lean on me," I told her.

"Bless you, child," she huffed, until I led her to a seat. "It is a slippery spot there," she said, chuckling.

"Madam, are you well?"

"In a few moments I shall be. Let me catch my breath."

"Shall I bring you water...or ale?"

"No, no. It is all well. Come now. Sit beside me."

Gingerly I sat, measuring her calm while my own heart hammered. "Are you certain I should not call for the prioress?"

"And have her worry as much as you? No, mistress. One worrier is enough."

"Dame, I saw you fall. It is not needless worry."

"Yes, I know. Well. Such is old age, my dear. The foot is not as secure as it once was, you see."

We sat in silence, each listening to her own soul. At last she turned to me. "Take me back to our chamber. The garden gives me a chill." I braced her arm and we walked carefully back toward the little warm room overlooking the garden. "You keep your own council, Mistress Isabella," she said as we entered and sat in our places. (It is not that we were assigned our chairs, but so often were we accustomed to being in particular places that it naturally fell to this arrangement: the prioress used the one chair that sat closest to the window, while Elizabeth sat on a bench 'neath the other window along with Cristabell. I sat upon another bench against the far wall nearest the heavy cupboard.)

"You have been here three months," Elizabeth went on, her toothy smile endearing itself to me as if a rabbit were sniffing out who I was, "and all I know of you is that you do not miss your family, you chose to be here, and you have a good hand with a needle, as well as with the garden."

"There is nothing more to tell."

"Indeed? Certainly there must be more."

I frowned without meaning to. "There is no more to me, Madam."

"Not so harsh, mistress. I did not mean 'more' as such. You take too much to heart in simple words."

"Even simple words can hurt."

"Have you been hurt by words? Do you think I mean to hurt you?"

Embarrassed, I sat beside her with lowered head. My mind fell unexpectedly on Thomas again. "No, of course not," I said. "The fault is mine. I take offense easily. Forgive me."

"Nothing to forgive," she said, patting my leg. "But truly. Why so reticent? You seem more so today. Since yesterday, in fact."

"It is not reticence, Dame, but prudence. I would not weary you with the trivialities of a farmer's daughter."

Coyly, she said, "Is Thomas Giffard a triviality?"

It took my breath. How did she know? I could not speak, my lip trembled so. She rested her hand gently upon my arm.

"You were seen yesterday, Isabella."

"I have sinned," I muttered. "I shall never be allowed to profess my vows."

"And do you still wish to?"

"Oh yes. But now—"

"You put a sour face to it, Mistress. An indiscretion while you are a novice…Tut! It is lamentable, but not unsalvageable. You must, of course, confess it to the prioress and the chaplain."

My uncertain future hovered just before me. Was it within reach, or did it drift too far away? "Yes…then… Do you think there is still a chance?"

"Sir John's son is an important man, or at least has that potential. Is it your will to deny him?"

"With my very breath! If God's grace did not fill me, I would not be here beside you now."

"And what of the next time?"

"The…next time?"

"I have lived a good many years in the cloister, Isabella, but also a goodly number in the world. Think you I know nothing of men? He will persist."

I shook my head. "He is married."

"And you are a sister, or soon to be. Did that stop him?"

I stared at that wrinkled face bolstered by its starched white linen. "But…a holy sister?"

"If you were ever tempting before as a farmer's daughter, surely you are more so now."

"Before, I did *not* tempt him." Did I say it sadly? "We have been friends only. For many years."

"And now, more?"

"For so many years I wanted it to be so, but now… Oh, Elizabeth!" Dropping my face into my hands, I wept. Was it for Isabella or for Thomas?

"There now. Finish weeping and then awaken to your new cause. If you truly wish to be a sister then you must forgive like one."

"Forgive?" I raised my face, feeling the cool wet of my cheek as a breeze cast up from the open casement.

"Dame Cristabell, of course. She is the one who saw you yesterday and reported it."

"I should have known." There was no anger for Cristabell. How could I blame her for merely witnessing my own weakness? "I will never endear myself to her now. What makes her so cross with me?"

"Ah. It is interesting that you think you have so little in common, for I see more now than ever before."

There was no time to ponder this, for the bells suddenly chimed. It was not the thrumming tower bell. Slowly, I came to know the sounds and rhythm of the cloister. When tradesmen came, the little bell was rung to let the sisters know to meet the bailiff at the iron grating or at the dwelling gate. And when the bell tower rang out, it was a call to the chapel for prayers. The latter rang often, and I tried to become used to abandoning whatever task I was given to go silently and obediently to prayers, the Divine Office.

"I must see to the gate," I told Elizabeth and she nodded to me.

I scurried down the halls to the cloister, finding myself near the buttery. Not only was I becoming accustomed to the sounds, but also the sights of the convent in each stage of the day; how the shadows lengthened, brushing aside the autumn sunlight as if with the careless wave of a hand; how—on a cloudy day—the light lay lifeless upon a wall, barely changing its color from musty buff to a dull gray. Shadows, too, possessed their own personality and were seldom cause for fright in the dim evening or in the slanted light of late afternoon.

I thought nothing of the buttery door that was as old if not older than the heavy timbers that made up Blackladies herself. We were not a rich house with foodstuffs to spare, but there was often a goodly supply of cheese and peas, barley and rye. We kept the door closed and secure, hoping to keep it free of vermin.

So it was with some curiosity that I observed the buttery door resting ajar.

I stopped. An unnatural caution propelled me, and there in its indistinct layers of shadows, I saw a figure lingering just in the doorway. Its movements were strangely vigorous, and I was suddenly afraid. What apparition was this? A demon? I longed to cry out, to frighten it away, but my own throat was swollen with fear, and I could do nothing.

At that moment, the figure made only a small step into a stripe of illumination, but it was enough to see fingers dipping into something wet and sticky. I could see the shiny, translucent strings of it lengthening as the fingers drew away and were brought to its open lips, which wrapped about the two fingers and sucked upon them.

Sickened with horror, I took a step back into the protecting shadows. Terrified, I watched until I realized—belatedly—that my own imagination made of a simple honey pot a macabre scenario. Still, my greatest surprise was the perpetrator.

"Holy Mother," I whispered, not knowing whether I called upon her help or her witness. What was I to do with such information? Was I to denounce the thief upon the spot, or go to another authority with these tidings? I touched my lips with my fingers and leaned my head back against the wall. Such a little thing this was. Was it not something I could keep in my heart and not pass my lips? For what good was the telling of it to me or to the thief? A little bit of honey, a taste of sweetness in a bitter life. How could I begrudge that?

The bell chimed again, and without hesitation, I left to attend to it.

I wondered as the next day passed why I heard nothing from the prioress, for surely Cristabell had rushed to her with news of my disgrace. But nothing came of it. Cristabell did plague me with a secret smile, but it was not until late afternoon in our chamber that she dared broach the subject.

Her expression was dark with taunting satisfaction as she sat opposite me, picking up her yarn and weaving it about her hand into a ball, never looking at the yarn but at me. "Soon the prioress will ask to speak with you. It is regrettable, but I am certain your family will welcome you back."

"Welcome me back? Cristabell, you speak of journeys I will not be taking. Why?"

"Come, Mistress. It is over. All know of your liaisons."

Prepared as I was, the blush still tinted my cheek. "You must be referring to the visit of Thomas Giffard two days ago."

"Aha! So you admit it."

"I admit what is true. He came to see me to confess his love. And I must admit, I have longed to hear it. But. I am a practical woman, Cristabell. I am only a yeoman's daughter and he a great lord. Never was there to be anything but friendship between us, and never was there."

"I saw more than that," she hissed.

"I know. It was regrettable, but not unforgivable. I turned him away."

"You did not—"

"I did. He is a married man, and I intend to profess my vows. Surely you must know that."

"I saw only the carnal nature of you, Mistress, which I suspected from the start. The prioress will never stomach such behavior. You will be out."

"If only you would listen to me, Cristabell."

"Lies. The high and mighty Isabella Launder. Caught in her own deceit at last! I knew this day would come. I shall pray for you." Red-faced with satisfaction, she cast the yarn aside, jolted from her chair, and left the chamber.

Sitting alone, hearing her voice in my head, I wondered what the prioress *would* say to me.

She called me to her parlor that very hour. I bowed as I entered and stood, awaiting her instruction. She did not bid me sit as she studied me, tapping one curled nail upon her table. I wanted to blurt out, "Denounce me!", but I kept it in check, telling myself to await her pleasure in this.

At last her dry lips parted and she took a breath. "Isabella, I have asked to speak with you on a certain topic. A topic I hoped you would broach first."

"Yes, Madam. Do you mean Thomas Giffard?"

"Yes. That it is." She nodded her head. "It is said he was allowed into the cloister...and more."

"He kissed me, Dame. And in all honesty...I kissed him back."

"Honesty is one thing, Mistress, and humility quite another—"

"There was nothing humble about it, Lady Prioress, and so my intention is to be honest."

"Your intention, in this instance, should also be to silence." I heeded the warning, stilling my wayward tongue. Her brow furrowed, regarding me with a somber expression. "Is it insolence, Isabella? Answer only yes or nay."

"No, Dame."

She seemed mildly satisfied with that, and sat back. "Truly, Isabella. I am surprised by this. You seem by all accounts to be a sensible woman, a good worker. No trouble at all. It now brings into question your continued virginity."

I closed my eyes before steadying my gaze on hers again. "There is nothing to question. I am a virgin, Lady Prioress."

"Do you intend to encourage him?"

"No. I wish to become a nun."

"Still?"

I should not have been rankled by her surprise, yet it was so. I lowered my eyes again in an attempt to regain composure. "Yes, Madam. It is my whole desire."

"Why did you never come to me?"

"I…could not."

"But it is incumbent upon each of us to look into ourselves, to find our faults, and purge them for the betterment of our souls. Can you not do this?"

"It is difficult, Madam."

"It is more difficult living this life with true honesty."

"Yes. I see that. Forgive me, Madam."

"What will you do should Lord Giffard return?"

"I will have no words for him."

"Then we shall put this to the test. For he is here."

The sound I uttered was strangled, for I thought the jest cruel, more the doings of Cristabell. But the prioress persisted, until I realized that it was no jest. "Oh, Madam! What shall we do?"

"We? It is for you, Isabella, to decide what to do. Will you see him?"

"No, Madam! You should forbid it!"

"And if I do not?" Her face was smooth, but the set of her brows proclaimed her misgivings.

"You wish for me to see him, then?"

"I do. Only then—facing your demons, Isabella—can you come to your vows with any hope of truth. We are not building straw manikins in habits. We are fashioning God's handmaids. Not of impenetrable marble, but of human flesh, with human flaws and sins. You cannot hide here, for the world intrudes regardless. I will not have this place be a haven from the world. Rather, it is a place to come to when the world's hold has loosened from you."

I squeezed my hands, wringing them red. "I am not strong enough," I whispered.

"I think you are. There is a woman of character behind those somber eyes. Your blunt way with honesty attests to that. Go to him. But know that my solemn prayers are with you, guiding you."

I stood unsteadily. I was to be sent to the lion's den. I could not help but feel Prioress Margaret's confidence in me was overstated.

Turning gravely on my heel, I walked from her parlor down the stairs and through the long gallery to the cloister door.

Thomas paced in the cloister garden, just as he was wont to do at my father's farm. All merriment was gone from his person, a figure that lived for merriment. He did not yet see me, and so I gazed upon him in all his rich velvet grandeur. Riches beyond my humble understanding adorned him. We could have clothed all the nuns on the sale from one of his rings alone. What was such a man doing tempted by the likes of me? What did I do to encourage this? The fault must be mine.

I whispered his name. Immediately he turned to me, and like any courtier, he fell upon his knee, grasped my hand, and pressed his precious lips to it. How my skin burned from his touch! I pulled it free, rubbing the pain away. "Why are you here, Lord Thomas?"

Slowly he rose, his head still dejectedly bent. "I tried to stay away. I knew that the only consequence of our being together meant that I should lead you into sin. I could tempt you to it. I know that." He raised saddened eyes. There was a ghost of a smile at the edge of his mouth, framed by that dark beard.

Oh yes. He could, indeed. He had only to take me in his arms again.

"Yet each time I considered it," he continued, his gloved hand raised to his chest as if pressing on the pain of his heart, "I knew also how bitter you would come to be, and how much you would someday despise me for it. You see, I know you better than you think." Then he smiled, but there was bitterness and anguish there. And maturity. Thomas had become a man before my eyes, but it was a rueful confirmation. "Because I love you, I will see to it that you…and your sisters here…fare well. It means also that I may visit you from time to time."

"In the cloister, Thomas? How is it allowed?"

"Your prioress. She is a very pragmatic woman."

"You paid your way." I turned my back on him, but it was a mistake, for he took the opportunity to grasp my shoulders. The fingers curled, pressing into my flesh.

"How often have you chastised me for not knowing my place?" he rasped, close to my cheek. "Well I know it now, Isabella. There are privileges with rank, and I will take them." He moved closer, his lips just touching the veil at my ear. "Do not mistake me. If there were a way to take you from here without sin, I would do it. Perhaps someday there will be. I can wait." His fingers tightened for only a moment before releasing me, and he stepped back. He brushed his gown to straighten it, and tautly pulled his gloves. "Will…will I be welcomed should I return?"

"Thomas… I do not know how to reply to you…"

"I *will* come again. Unless you say me nay. But for the love of the living God, Isabella. Do not say 'no'."

"To what purpose, Thomas? I tell you it is not good for you, or for me."

"To see you. To know how you fare. And if for nothing else, then it can be our own personal purgatory."

It was my first smile upon seeing him. It felt very much like the old days on my father's grange. But then that, too, was fleeting. I sighed and shrugged, couching my hands within one another. "Was there ever a counselor as abused as I? Never did you take my advice."

"Never?" He turned to me, distant but reaching for the kind of camaraderie that was once our stamp. "Oh, surely I must have taken it once or twice."

"Perhaps."

A spray of rosemary stood between us, no more than the length of a man's arm. Thomas gazed at me for a long span before dropping his eyes to the herb. He stooped and snapped a stem, touching the fragrant sprig to his nose. "Rosemary is for remembrance," he said, and then he glanced to the roses that ringed the little garden courtyard. "And those are you," he said gesturing toward the roses with the rosemary. He turned to me one last time and bowed. He tucked the rosemary into the slash of his doublet and walked sedately from the garden.

I did not weep as he left, for he promised to come again, and in that lay comfort, for we were good friends. I was also pleased I did not succumb to him, nor did he force me to. I was very pleased with Thomas for that grace.

With a sigh I pushed my skirts aside to go, spying the prioress in the shadows of the cloister. I inclined my head to her, and she to me in answer. Such a wise woman was Prioress Margaret. I only hoped I could achieve her wisdom in the time allotted to me on this earth.

THOMAS GIFFARD
FEBRUARY, 1521
Greenwich Court

XII

"What family of citizens offers so clear an example
of strict harmonious wedlock?"
—Erasmus on the English Court's Royal couple, 1520

My father made his mark at court, and I, too, served as a Gentleman Ushers in Ordinary to the king's household. His majesty favored us with offices of respect. It was not forgotten how my father held the king's standard in the wars in France, nor how he was one of the many knights deputed to meet the French king on the Field of the Cloth of Gold only last year.

The king fancied clever men who knew how to make an honest fortune, and with my having married the king's ward—a Montgomery—I was wealthy without ill favoring myself. I was satisfied with the knowledge of that wealth, giving a nod to Father and all his plotting. I would have been an unhappy man as a pauper and wed to the farmer's daughter. But never far from my thoughts was Dame Isabella, as she was now called, sweeping down the drafty halls of Blackladies in her black nun's weeds. My feelings for her, despite my reconciling to my place, did not cool as I had hoped they might. But I took George Throckmorton's advice, and attended to my wife, and there I cobbled a marriage of it, the equal of any courtier I knew.

Dorothy was with the ladies in another gallery—praise God. All the chattering and giggling preyed on one's nerves, and there was work to do. Court was a pleasure of course, but its purpose was more for what could be gained than reacquainting oneself with old friends. True, old alliances were remembered, old ties rebound. And there were amusements in between these toils. It was a place bright with gold, pomp, music, and disguisings.

King Henry was a man who devoured amusements, be they feasts, or wardrobe, or masques, or women. He enjoyed the company of many a charming lady. My sisters Cassandra and Dorothy stuck close to their husbands while at court, though they did not often attend. It was a place for Father and me to make ourselves available should any important appointments be offered.

My daughter Elizabeth was holding her own court back home at Caverswall. A dainty creature at five years, she was nevertheless robust, and tried the patience of her nurses. At present, she was my only progeny. I cooled to my wife's attentions after discovering where Isabella resided...and of my feelings for her.

Dorothy had been with child one time more, but the babe was cast out of the womb far too early, and died. It was a boy. Such was also the fate of our king, for the good queen delivered at last a living babe, but it was a girl, the Princess Mary. She was nearly the same age now as my Elizabeth, and such a cheerful child. The king often referred to her as his "pearl of the world." The last time the queen was pregnant was three years ago, and no more were likely. It seemed our "pearl of the world" would be reigning queen after Henry. He said as much to the Emperor's envoy. The last reigning queen in England was the Empress Matilda nearly four hundred years ago, and that sad queen's history did not readily appeal to our courtiers. After all, when that first King Henry named her his heir, there was civil war, and it was her cousin Stephen who seized the throne.

The nobles were unhappy with this turn of affairs, for history was leaden in us all. The robust king could not seem to produce a legal heir, though he did sire a bastard, Henry Fitzroy, on his mistress Bessie Blount not long after the Princess Mary was born.

"But what is a king to do?" said Philip Draycot in my ear. A courtier some ten years my junior, he became my fast friend through his merry wit and sharp ear for news. I glanced sidelong at him and at that pride of wheat-golden hair that reached in a curled edge to just below his ears. It seemed he could read my thoughts aloud, though it was a subject pressing on everyone's mind.

"He can beget more bastards and name them to the throne," I answered, "but I doubt he will keep the bloodline to the throne from his lawful heir, his daughter."

"A woman on the throne? Have you not always said, Thomas, that there would never be a woman on England's throne?"

"Well…" I brushed my mustache with a fingertip. "Perhaps I was wrong."

Draycot laughed into his hand as we both perused the room of gallants and bedecked females. Wolsey was also there, fervently instructing a crony who wore a dark plain gown—a commoner named Thomas Cromwell—while the king watched a musician pluck "As I walked the Wood so Wild" on a lute.

"This is a day worth celebrating," Draycot said close by me, as others turned to look at us. "A Giffard admit he is wrong!"

"Stranger things have happened, Draycot. When a cardinal can be chancellor, then maids can be queens."

"Careful when you speak ill of the Church lest you be taken for a Lutherist."

"I am not a Lutherist. What do I care about the rantings of a German ex-monk? And I speak no ill of the Church, Draycot. Only its envoy."

"Wolsey sticks in everyone's teeth like last night's mutton, but do not let George Throckmorton hear you. You know he often transacts business with Wolsey. Land grants or some such."

No sooner did I turn my head to look for Throckmorton, than I saw him making his way through the throng toward us.

"Lord Giffard," he said with a perfunctory bow.

"Lord Throckmorton," I returned in kind.

"Both your brows are so heavy, you must be speaking of the succession."

Draycot made an expression of mock chagrin. "Do you mean we are the only ones?"

Throckmorton shook his head with disdain and turned his back on young Draycot. "It is said that the Princess Mary may soon be betrothed to the Emperor."

"Is she not already betrothed to the Dauphin?" asked Draycot, not in the least offended by Throckmorton's contumelious treatment of him.

"Betrothals are like games of cards," offered Throckmorton, instructing. His eyes glanced here and there about the room, cautious of heads cocked our way. "One jack after another is discarded for a higher hand."

"The Princess Mary is the hope of the realm," I said. "If not as heir, then as *mother* to the heir."

Throckmorton nodded. "Yes, that may be the way. Better the king's grandson as heir than…others."

Edward Stafford, Duke of Buckingham strolled across the hall with his attendants, his attention strictly on the king at his gaming table.

"And there goes the 'other'," whispered Draycot between us.

"He has made certain of his royal claims," said Throckmorton. "He now has York blood with his son married to Ursula Pole. I think he makes crowned heads uneasy."

"He is too ambitious for his own good," I agreed, smiling only a swath of teeth at an acquaintance nodding at me from across the room.

"He does not forget slights easily," said Throckmorton. "Thomas and I were young at the time," he said to Draycot, "but no doubt you have still heard of the occasion when the king had his…indiscretions…with Buckingham's married sisters."

"Yes. I recall talk of it."

I pivoted to watch the king's dice game. "Buckingham defended the honor of his none-too-chaste siblings and never forgave William Compton for acting as pimp to the king's pleasure," I said.

Draycot nodded and swept his gown hem aside to place a fist at his hip. "Buckingham has no liking for commoners, even when they are the king's bosom friends like Compton. Or Wolsey."

Throckmorton sniffed. "Nevertheless. He never forgot how unwelcome he was at court after the incident. Though it was ten years ago."

"Memory runs long at court," said I.

"I would keep clear of Buckingham," said Draycot soberly. "I fear he thinks too much of himself in these uncertain days. He listens too dear to his friends who would set him in high places."

"Too high," I agreed.

Draycot talked on, but I listened very little. A great fire roared in the hearth and the torches burned equally bright. I cocked an ear toward several courtiers my own age standing in a loose circle, discussing their lands and their hopes, while other young hawks talked of war with France, and fretted at the hilts of their bodkins. I listened to all distractedly even as the musician played on, and the king gathered his fellows over the dice table: his brother-in-law Charles Brandon, duke of Suffolk, and Edward Neville, among them.

I, too, was thinking about what I should do with my life; about when I would be knighted; about the estates. I was fit for all of it, of that I did not doubt. It was the timetable that troubled me, for I should like to make something of myself. At thirty, I was getting old, and my career already fell behind that of my father's. It irked me. Having married well, I knew these things would soon accelerate. A male heir was the first step, after all, to a dynasty. Yet even so.

I looked, and also saw the queen at the other side of the hall, surrounded by her own pleasures and ladies. How weary she looked. How old. Yet she was barely older than myself. Never a robust lady, the years and her many unsuccessful pregnancies must have taken their toll.

It suddenly occurred to me that there was one more option for the king's heir: his widowerhood. When Catherine died, he could marry again and yet father a legal male heir.

Was it a good thing to contemplate the death of a queen...or of a wife?

I turned to the ladies' gallery to spy Dorothy laughing and chatting with her many contemporaries. Was I to leave my estates in no better claim than the doomed Montgomery's, awaiting the Giffard buzzards to swoop in and pick their bones clean? Leaving my estates to a woman, where any jack could come along...

Frustrated, I rasped a sigh. The idea of Dorothy in my bed while Isabella dwelled nearby in that convent was a cold winter to my desired summer.

The king won at his game and roared his approval, echoed by the surrounding courtiers. The king's fiery red beard set off the roundness of his face, giving it a merry mien when he laughed, and an equally fierce countenance when he angered. He grew the beard in an obstinate avowal. He would not shave, he said, until he met the king of France on the Field of the Cloth of Gold, but he kept it ever after, pleased with its added maturity. It was said the queen did not favor it, but Henry was a man of his own convictions.

His courtiers laughed again at one of the king's jests, and it occurred to me to become part of the fawning milieu, until I reckoned the many faces already occupied with such. I could not bring myself to become part of that. I would prefer to accompany the king on a battlefield and earn my knighthood rightly by toils rather than by obsequious expressions of false flattery.

Buckingham maneuvered his way beside him, and rolled his dice upon the gaming table but was foolhardy enough to win, and this did not please the king, who growled and reluctantly handed over his gold pieces. I looked quickly at Draycot and Throckmorton and wondered if Buckingham possessed a wit of common sense to lose. Again, he cast his dice with care, and won another two gold pieces from the king. Praise God Neville stepped in and nudged Buckingham none too graciously aside, letting Henry win again, but not too obviously.

"That is how to keep your head," hissed Throckmorton in my ear.

"I do not think the king would behead a man simply for besting him at dice," I answered. "But see how sour Buckingham is. Do you think he will make a fool of himself?" Buckingham was one who believed his ambitions would lead him to a throne. He did not know that much of what he plotted was well known and would someday cast him down. Court was a hazardous place if one did not watch one's step—or one's friends.

The king rose from the gaming table at last, knuckling Neville in the chest. Neville could be the king's twin, so alike did they look, and used it for more than one jest. His majesty lumbered toward the gallery, no doubt in search of the banqueting hall. To my surprise, he headed straight for me. An unexpected flutter tickled my heart as he approached.

"Giffard!"

"Your grace." I made a graceful bow. Throckmorton and Draycot, too, made their obeisance, withdrawing subtly into the crowd.

"Thomas. You have not been at court of late. No doubt you languish in the country, eh? You are wed to someone Montgomery."

"Dorothy Montgomery, your grace."

"And so. A former ward, eh Thomas? How long now married?"

"Six years, your grace."

"Six years! Is it six years already? How the years cascade one upon the other." Chuckling, he put a hand on my shoulder. "You have a daughter, Thomas."

"Yes, your grace. She is the same age as the Princess Mary."

"You do not say so. Perhaps she should wait upon the princess. Would you like that, Thomas?"

It was, of course, a great honor he offered me, but with Elizabeth so young, the notion tore at my heart. "Your grace, she is my only child and precious to me. I fear I dote upon her too much to let her go very far at so young an age. Forgive a man for his weaknesses."

"Yes, Thomas," he said, putting his arm about my shoulders. "We fathers do indeed dote upon our little girls. What jewels they are, eh?" He squeezed my shoulder uncomfortably before releasing me. "I like that country in Staffordshire. It's bold land, rich with fields and woods." The king took in the men around him and, obviously in a convivial mood, swallowed them up in his presence. "Is it good hunting?"

"Yes, your grace. We would be honored to have your majesty guest at Caverswall."

"It might be so, Thomas. I do not often venture to my estates in Stafford."

My mind whirled with incomprehensible thoughts. I had the king's ear. Now what, by the Rood, was I to do with it?

"Ever been to tournament, Thomas?" he asked me. His eyes scanned my lanky frame. My figure was deceptive, for though tall and lean, I was strong and a worthy fighter.

"I have, your grace."

"Your father. He's a good rider. A good man. But you look as fit as he. I should not think it will be long before you win many competitions yourself."

"As a knight, your grace?"

An expression of varying hues tinted his face. It began as surprise, turning to amusement, and finally to warning. He smiled. "There is no hurry," he said, before barreling into a throng of other courtiers, leaving me depleted in his wake. The earlier familiarity was gone. *Damn, my own impudence*, I rebuked in my head. Others followed after him like puppies, but I remained as I was, dismissed. Until I felt a shadow at my elbow.

"A bold lunge," said the voice I did not recognize.

I turned, running my gaze perfunctorily over the plump person beside me. He wore velvets in a style somewhat excess for English tastes, almost to bad taste. "Do I know you, sir?"

"No, Lord Giffard. There is no reason you should. I am Thomas Legh. Only a secretary."

"Truly." I lost interest while looking for Draycot and Throckmorton. "It is a wonder you are here." It was meant to dismiss the man, but clearly his intentions were otherwise. He meant to fraternize where he did not belong, and I wondered briefly whose secretary he was, though did not deign to ask. I moved away, but the creature followed.

"The king's interests are many. He populates his court with many rising morning stars. But beware, Lord Giffard. A morning star still sets."

I stopped and glared at him. "And what are you, sirrah? A shooting star? They streak quickly across the sky in a flash of light, and are soon extinguished, seen no more. Any morning star may set, but it rises again."

"'Tis true, my lord, but—"

"You are too familiar with me, and I know you not. Stand aside." I swept past him, noting how he glowered at me as if memorizing my features. In his insolence, he must have believed he was of some importance at court, yet like so many others, his ill-chosen words to the wrong man would depose him. I glanced back again, and saw Cromwell approach him and rest his hand upon his shoulder. So. It made more sense to me, then, these two in Wolsey's employ. Like jackals. I did not know whose bones they waited for, but I was determined they would not be mine.

ISABELLA LAUNDER
MARCH, 1521
Blackladies

XIII

Lord, my heart is not proud; nor are my eyes haughty.
I do not busy myself with great matters; with things too sublime for me.
Rather, I have stilled my soul, hushed it like a weaned child...

—Psalm 131:1-2

It was two months since, but still I wept for Margaret Cawardyn, late and faithful prioress of Blackladies nunnery. Mother, aunt, sister, friend, she was my mentor in all, and still more than I realized, for it was only last month that Bishop Blythe, after reviewing the carefully penned letters and reports by Prioress Margaret, appointed the new prioress among us: myself.

Entirely unexpected, I received the news along with the others. Father William read the letter to us in our workroom. The bishop wrote in Latin and none of us were proficient enough to engage such a letter with any understanding. Dame Elizabeth looked particularly pleased, and my niece Dame Alice Beche—who came to join us as a holy sister two years ago—nodded her solemn approval (she did not seem to share my sister Agnes' mistrust of my abilities).

But Cristabell received these tidings with an unwholesome measure of disbelief, even to the point of accusing Father William of fabricating the letter. I tried to assure her as well as the others that there must, indeed, be some mistake, but Father William pointed out—with some amount of satisfaction—the many references to me, of Beech, and the Launder estate. It was all decided without my knowledge or my encouragement. Dame Elizabeth was excluded from such a promotion, being very old and not in good health, and of course Dame Alice was too young, not even twenty. Certainly Cristabell felt she was slighted, assured because of her longer tenure at the priory that the position would naturally fall to her. The years did not gentle her mood toward me, and now that I was her superior, I worried over her faithfulness. Prudently, I let it lie, preferring to allow circumstance to tutor me.

In the meantime, I spent long hours over the records kept in the prioress' office, deciphering her small, careful script with difficulty, for I was not a good reader. The accounts were muddled and uncertain, and I grieved over how I should accomplish these new requirements.

The small letters wearied my eyes, so I rose and walked to the window. There was so much to do, and I did not know where to begin.

From that view looking north, I could see the cloister yard as well as the muddy lane and plains beyond. Ladies Brook, once it passed the mill stream, was little more than a vague glitter meandering toward The Hawkshutts in the distant green mist. Spring was late, and the iciness of morning still frosted the edges of the diamond window panes in feathery lace. Dew darkened the spindled trees as they heaved their bare limbs into a raw gray sky.

The men tempered the brown fields with their hoes, putting me in a mind to think about the garden below. Many days had passed since I worked among the returning herbs and roses. *Perhaps a little time there*, I told myself. I could clear my mind far better by scraping about in the garden than nosing in dusty books.

My steps hurried as I neared it. I retrieved a napron and exchanged my slippers for clogs. I first went to the roses which marched across the southern side of the cloister and up where the gravel walkway led to the dwelling. They were still little more than dead twigs, like clawed hands curled upward, branches pruned to stumps. Thorns guarded them, still formidable even in slumber. No mole dared eat its tender roots. There appeared the tiniest bit of greening and an occasional black, tightly wound leaf bud. I was pleased to see this, for often we ornamented our table and our chapel with these small blooms, and seasoned our salads with the flavorful buds. Even when the bloom was spent the rose hips made a soothing broth. It was a most useful flower.

The rosemary was as strongly scented as always, but the chervil had yet to rise and the sage looked poorly. Perhaps rabbits. The pennywort thrived as did the mullein and borrage. I snipped sprigs of each and tucked them into the pocket of my napron to later purge the staleness of our bedchamber.

The gate bell chimed. Glancing to my girdle I noticed that I did not yet give the gate key to Dame Elizabeth. "Where is my mind?" I set the snips aside, and grooming myself as best I could, I went to the gate.

Robert, our bailiff, stood beside two young girls, the older no more than nine or ten years, while the younger appeared to be five. They were shivering in their very thin shawls.

"Here, Lady Prioress," he said, though hearing that particular title was still strange to my ears. "You must take these two girls. Their mother left them at the gate and would not come back."

"What is it you say, Robert? Not abandoned?"

"Yes. That's it. She told me when I come out 'take me babes to the nuns, for I cannot feed them anymore.' I called out to her to return, but as soon as I could get the key, she was gone into the woods."

As Robert spoke, the children began to weep, and my heart nearly burst with it. Their clothes were gray from age and filth, and their faces were streaked with dirt and tears. Their hair was in terrible disarray, and they were mortally thin. "Did you know the mother?" I asked him, touching the closed gate. Robert shook his head and glanced helplessly toward the weeping girls. Without further consideration I unlocked the gate and stepped forward. They did not look up at me even as I rested my hands on their quivering shoulders. "Come now. You must tell me your names."

The older of the two finally raised her head, opening wide eyes of startling blue. "My name is Jane, my lady. And this is Mary."

I knelt so to be at eye level with them. Such sorrowful faces, and little could I blame them. "Well, Jane, you are the eldest. And it is you who must take care of your little sister, eh?" She nodded. "We must pray that your mother will be back soon. But until then, would the two of you like some bread with honey? And maybe a little milk?" As afraid as she was, Jane's eyes lit with the promise of food, and she needed little prodding from me to enter into the cloister. "Robert," I said over my shoulder, "please tell Father William to come as soon as he might." I took them through the shadowed garden and along the stone walk to the undercrofts where the kitchen lay. I seated them by the fire on a bench, surprising the servants Meg and Kat Alate.

"Lady Prioress!" cried Meg. "Beggars only come to the almsdoor. Not inside."

"This is a special case, Meg. Do we have any extra clothes for them?"

Kat curtseyed, staring with curiosity at the girls. "I'll go look, Madam."

As she went in search, I retreated to the buttery to get a loaf and a pot of honey. I set the bread upon the table and took up a knife. "Meg, have we any more milk?"

"It's on the sill."

"Could you be so good as to get a cup for them to share?"

I cut two fat slices of bread and drizzled them with honey. They all but snatched them from my hands and dug in like ravenous wolves. Meg returned with the jug and poured the milk into a clay cup and set it before them. Jane picked it up and drank the whole lot, and so Meg stooped to fill it again for Mary.

They appeared happier after they ate, but still they worried about their mother. I, too, worried over this. We were not a house for foundlings. We were barely capable of seeing to the needs of the many mouths we had to feed as it was. Which put me in a mind of those records again and how I should go about the task of running such a place. Thankfully, Father William's entrance foiled those anxious thoughts.

He looked over the two as Meg fed them another slice of bread. He pulled me aside. "What have we here, Lady Prioress?"

"Just what you see, Father. Foundlings."

"What do you intend to do with them?"

"Well, I should think I would take the advice of St. Benet and house them…unless you think otherwise."

"Where, Madam, would you put them?"

"Oh, dear. There is very little room…" I glanced toward Meg, who bristled at my suggestive gaze.

"I share a very small bed with Kat, Madam," said Meg sternly. "There is no room for two more."

"Indeed." Tracing the bow of my lips with my finger, I pondered. "Then I suppose I shall make room in mine." Dame Elizabeth shared her bed with Prioress Margaret, but upon the Prioress' death relinquished it to me. She and Cristabell now shared the other bed in the little chamber and I shared with Alice. One girl to each bed should provide enough room. That settled, I needed only to inform the sisters of our new charges.

It was later at Chapter when I did just that.

"They cannot sleep in our room!" cried Cristabell. Her eyes rounded and her dusky skin blushed a deep color. "It is not allowed, Lady Prioress."

"I consulted first with Father William, Cristabell. If it were not allowed I should think he would have told me."

Elizabeth sighed. As was her habit, she sucked on her protruding teeth. "We have much to do already. Are we to raise children as well as crops?"

"I understand your reluctance, but Meg and Kat can see to them for most of the day. They will be put to tasks. But they are in great need. Their own mother abandoned them and we have no way of knowing if she can be found. It could be they are already orphans."

Cristabell intended no surrender. "We are not equipped! There is barely enough food as there is."

"But we are one less here, sisters," I said, glumly reminding us all of our loss. "Surely the late prioress' food can feed two small girls."

"—who will grow to young women," said Cristabell with grim finality. "It does not seem the sensible thing to do."

"Then what *is* the sensible thing to do, sisters? Send them on their way? To where? Are we not God's servants? Are we not to practice charity? 'Suffer the little children unto me,' our Lord said. 'Whomsoever wishes to enter the kingdom of Heaven must be like one of these.' Perhaps they were sent here to be examples to us in our failings."

"Are we to raise them, then? All their lives?"

"Cristabell, I think that has yet to be determined." I reached for the comfort of my rosary, but found the ring of keys instead. "We only speak of sheltering them now in their hour of need. The mother might yet return."

But even after many days, she did not. And the children were often vexing in their disobedience and thievery. I cautioned patience to my sisters, for what else could these innocents have been taught in their subsistence but to steal? Yet it was a trial. I wondered if I would have had the courage to leave them to a better life as their mother had done. Or was it sin that led her to this decision? We could not garner their circumstances from the children. They only confessed that the mother's name was Maud

Sharp. The vicar of Brewood could find no such name in his registry.

More than once the children's presence made me consider how different my life might have been had I allowed Sir John to force me into marriage. I would have children of my own by now, possibly the same age as little Mary. Looking to my niece Alice, I noted how she bore a slight resemblance to me, and in her I saw what might have been. In these two foundlings, too, I saw a glimpse of another history. Two little girls.

I had heard that Thomas had a little girl. He never told me this when he made his visits. I heard it instead from those in the village.

Thomas continued to call upon us even as I tried to discourage it. His father was ever generous to this house—or so he said it was from his father. I could make little complaint, though Cristabell's green eyes were spikes in my back.

Thomas' daughter. The miserable thought intruded with regularity that this child might have been mine had everything been different. She was called Elizabeth after his wife's mother. Oft I wondered what Thomas' offspring looked like. Was she dark like Thomas, or fair like her mother?

One little girl. Why were there no more?

My hands, unbidden, smoothed out my gown over a womb that would now never swell with a babe. I was two and thirty, a professed nun, and now prioress of a community of holy sisters. It was long past the time when I would be a mother. '*Yes, blessed is she who, childless and undefiled, knew not transgression of the marriage bed; she shall bear fruit at the visitation of souls.*' Thus through such solemn words of scripture I was made to understand that I was a mother of many, just as our Lady was mother to all. I was mother to poor Cristabell who sorely needed one; to my own kinswoman Alice, whose mother nearly disowned her when she spoke of following her Aunt Isabella to a nunnery; to even Dame Elizabeth who was my senior by many years, and who imparted her wisdom to me. And now to two more little ones. Such a family! Even our extended family of servants looked toward me, as a brood of quail looked to their mother, for I was a mother also to Meg and Kat, to Thomas Bolde, William Morre, Tom Smith—who had not yet succumbed to Meg's charms, to Phillipe Duffelde and our bailiff Robert Baker, and even to Father William who asked my advice on matters from time to time, deferring to me in most affairs. Blackladies was a humble place, a place of purpose, sheltering and feeding, offering work, wages, and prayer, all precariously balanced on the head of a pin made of passions and anxieties.

In short, it was like any other family in any village anywhere in the world.

Little girls had difficulty being quiet mice in a place that thrived on its silence. The old walls of Blackladies at last rang with children's laughter, but its timbers shook uneasily. I found an unexpected joy in Jane and Mary. They loved hiding and running in the garden. It was a fairy playland to them, with its hiding hedges and aromatic blooms.

"Lady Prioress! Lady Prioress!" Mary ran toward me at full bore, crashing into my skirts. My arms were encumbered by firewood, and I could not stoop to pick her up as she gestured for me to do.

"Mary! What is all this ado?"

Jane careered around the corner of the arcade, clearly after her sister in a playful game. Mary squealed as Jane caught up to her, and they chased one another, with me as their maypole. "Now stop. The two of you are making me dizzy."

"I caught you, Mary! Did I not, Lady Prioress?"

"You certainly did. And yet, it seems that Mary has caught you as well."

The both of them held tightly to each other's skirts, tugging and laughing. At last, they lost their balance and fell hard against me, and with my own laughter rising to the treetops, I, too, fell over, my sticks of firewood scattering.

Footsteps approached at a run, and I looked up from the bundle of sticks and children to spy the disgruntled countenance of Cristabell.

"Madam! In the cloister!"

"Cristabell, you *could* be more helpful by assisting me to my feet."

Belatedly, she held out her hand for me to grasp and I pulled myself up.

"This is unseemly!"

The girls' chortles quieted under Cristabell's harsh trumpeting and I, too, sobered. I patted them on their heads. "Run along. There must be chores for you to do. Go find Kat or Meg." They groaned and shuffled their feet as they moved off. "'The Lord loveth a cheerful giver'," I called after them. Once they disappeared under the main arch, I turned to Cristabell. "Very well, Cristabell. Tell me. What vexes you now?"

"I see," she said tightly. "My worries for this cloister are only vexations to you. I shall keep silent on it then, for my words of advice are ruinous to your goodly humor."

"Dame, let us speak plainly. You disapprove of the girls in this convent. This I know. But they are here now, and their lives are the better for it. Can you begrudge me for enjoying them?"

"They do not belong in the cloister."

"But they enjoy the garden so."

"The cloister is for the nuns alone."

"I have given my permission in this. Do you go against my judgment?"

Lips tight, Cristabell lowered her eyes. "I cannot. You are the prioress."

"Yes. That is so. I ask your respect in this, then. Try to accept it in charitable obedience."

"Yes, Madam," she said with a bow. But when she left me, she turned back a countenance that possessed no hint of obedience to it.

THOMAS GIFFARD
APRIL, 1521
Blackladies

XIV

"Do you not know, my son, with what little
understanding the world is ruled?"

–Pope Julius III, 1491-1557

Apprehension was my shadow whenever I rode to Blackladies. Part of it was my excitement at seeing Isabella. The other was how she would receive me. Always she was cordial, yet a barrier lay between us. And rightly so. Visiting Chillington was only my excuse to come to Blackladies, and Dorothy knew it. But I am lord of my household, and no glacial stare from Lady Giffard could sway my intent.

I finally made my way up Kiddemore Green. Villagers doffed their caps and bowed. It was a familiar sight to see Thomas Giffard ride toward Blackladies. What could be made of that, they must have wondered?

The affairs of court kept me away from Brewood. Intrigues and trials characterized the wearying months there. Buckingham was executed for conspiring to murder His Majesty and take his throne. It was treason at its worst, yet there was much displeasure among the people at this action. Though Buckingham was a hothead, and a line could be easily drawn at court as to who liked him and who liked him not, there was unease among the nobles that a shift of power crept in under their noses—and it wore the crimson of a cardinal. Not that I thought often of Wolsey as a beadsman, for there was never a more greedy and scurrilous cleric than his bilious person. But he was mad with power, and the frustration of it was, the king listened to him.

What disturbed us more than Buckingham's intrigues was the manner of his seizure, for he only paraded himself as *possible* heir. He was guilty perhaps of arrogance and ill humor, but it appeared that he was deemed guilty mostly by improper thoughts! Were a man's own thoughts now to be suspect and treasonous? Was he not allowed a conscience? This was not the England we knew. I could only blame Wolsey for such ideas whispered into the king's ear.

The grumblings at court did not silence with Buckingham. Much was still made of the king's lack of a male heir. True, I disparaged the rule of a woman, but I was not alone. A queen was still a woman, and a woman by God's law need defer to her husband. If the Princess Mary ruled, would her husband and consort not then be king? Would *he* not rule England? And who was to choose this consort? Wolsey? Such thoughts sent shivers down our spines. We were a divided court. Henry Fitzroy thrived, but would England put a bastard on the throne?

By God's body, it was a vexation!

I looked down at my hand. The reins were wound so tightly about my wrist it was like to cut off the blood! Easing the strap from my hand, I settled back in the saddle. This was not the time for such ruminations. I came to Brewood, after all, to forget court for a time! It was the hour to quiet myself and enjoy the country in which I was raised, this little village which was a second home to me. A quiet refuge of cottages, charming church, greenswards, and woodlands.

And…I was to see Isabella.

I reached Old Coach Road and saw ahead the forecourt of Blackladies. It was a simple stone building with a prominent three-story façade, serving as the dwelling for servants and nuns alike. The nunnery itself was too small for its own church and was served by a small country chapel all of wood, which lay toward the rear near the mill stream. In the forecourt of Blackladies, the bailiff's dwelling sat to the east, and at the west end of the court were the stew ponds, which one of the servants was tending with a long-handled net. He only disturbed himself enough to glance my way, but by then the bailiff heard my mount and was already unlocking the gate. It was long past the time I was announced and kept waiting. He bowed, swinging the gate aside with a "good day, Lord Giffard." He took my mount and allowed me to go up to the house unattended, whereupon I rang the bell to the cloister.

Waiting, I listened to the calming strains of the mill wheel beyond the sheltering trees at the north corner of the main house, and the mill race as it burbled on its way to Ladies Brook.

A dark figure all in black swept around the corner. Her head was angled modestly, but she raised green eyes to me for only a moment before tightening her lips and opening the gate without a word. She was called Cristabell, I think, and her disapproval could hardly be missed as she led me to the great hall of the house. "I shall await in the garden," I told her. "Will the prioress see me there?" Prioress Margaret often dispelled with these niceties, but I thought it politic to greet her first.

Dame Cristabell gazed at me oddly, bowing her head. "As you will."

I stepped through the portal and deeply inhaled. When Isabella first came to the priory, the garden was merely a pleasant diversion, but upon her years of attendance, it blossomed into a sanctuary of sweet-scented roses, herbs, and hedges. Delights were found round each carefully cultivated turn; imaginative designs of boxwood terminating to a pot of stately lilies; a modest wooden statue of a saint garlanded with morning glory vines; a fragrant stand of herbs huddled together in extravagant display. It was her hand in it, I was certain. Her graceful hand. How I longed to kiss that hand and those lips that tortured me in my dreams and in the odd hour of a simple supper at my own table in Caverswall. To think of all those wasted years when I could have loved her, could have possessed her…

I pressed my head to the cool stone of the cloister arch. Would that this were an earlier day! A day in our youth. No, the years had not tempered my passion for her, my longing. Day and night, adulterous in my thoughts, I repined for Isabella. My Isabella.

And then she stepped into the sunlight from the shadows. Tall, stately, her gown and veil blended to one velvety vision of chaste womanhood. The white wimple cupped her cheeks as I longed to do with my own hands, framing her oblong face with virtuous modesty. She was more beautiful thus than she ever was in her yeoman's napron. Was it the black veil that gave her such loveliness? Or was it now these new eyes with which I beheld her?

With light steps, she approached me and bowed her head. "Lord Thomas."

"Dame Isabella." We played this game. It seemed to satisfy her proprieties. "But I thought I might first greet the prioress."

Her small mouth curved, and something of the old mischievous Isabella crept through. She paused only a moment more before she said, "You *are* greeting the prioress."

It took a heartbeat for me to discern her words. She looked no different except for a wooden cross hanging from her neck and a ring upon her finger. All at once, the notion of her new status seemed to further distance her from me with unexpected finality. I hid my discomposure with a light laugh. "*Prioress?* Prioress Isabella? Unbelievable…but inevitable. You are a stone, Isabella. A foundation stone."

"I am only a worker bee. One of many in the hive."

"Surely the sweetest honey." At that, I could not resist taking her hand and glancing a kiss upon it. She gently pulled it free.

"How long shall you be at Chillington House, Thomas?"

"We have only arrived today. I will be wanted at court before too long. I enjoy coming to Brewood, as you know. But you will not put me off." I took her hands and held them out. "Look at you. *Prioress.* When did all this occur?"

"Two months ago. Three months ago our dear prioress…"

"Ah. Of course. How stupid of me. God rest her soul."

We becrossed ourselves and solemnly contemplated that dear lady, while birds winged and chirruped above our heads, and white blossoms fluttered down from their breezy flights.

"It was unexpected," she said at last. "Her death and my appointment, I mean."

"I will wager your Cristabell thought *she* should be appointed."

"Hush, Thomas." She blushed, searching the shadows. "You must not speak so of one of my charges."

"What makes her so sour, anyway? You are not cruel, are you?" She saw my smile, but did not add hers to my merriment.

"I do not know, Thomas. But it is not to be discussed in such a manner."

"Forgive me, Lady Prioress," I said with a bow. I walked a little way along the path and she followed, her footsteps lightly crunching the gravel. "So you are mistress of your own household at last. I expected that you would be more pleased. Instead I find you solemn. It is not as I am used to with us."

"Much is changed."

"And there is much that has not."

She raised her head to look at me but quickly dropped that gaze away. "What is the news at court? We receive no word from anyone but you."

"The news…" I stepped over the gravel to stare at surely the largest rose bloom I ever encountered. How proud it was! How stately! Only Isabella's hand could have coaxed such a thing from nature. I bent to sniff it, enraptured by its fragrance. "The news is not as sweet as this bloom, I am afraid. But you need not worry about court. The doings of men are of no concern to you."

"Why is it the doings of women are always effected by the 'doings of men'?"

Chuckling, I turned from the roses. "Isabella, I *have* missed you. Well, then. If you must know, the news is not good, for the most part. Have you heard that Buckingham was beheaded?"

Her look of horror and belated becrossing aroused in me a visceral sensation. Was I jealous of even poor dead Buckingham?

"How is the queen?"

"The queen does not well, and it is doubted that more pregnancies are possible."

"Then the Princess Mary will be queen?"

"It may be so, but more hopes are pinned on her son as heir."

"She is just a child. It will be another seven years before she may wed. In seven years, anything may happen."

"Well, Buckingham will not be king, that is a certainty."

"Did he aspire so? Is that why he is dead?"

"Some say he did. It is known he desired it. But the nobles think more that he was arrested and convicted for having disagreeable opinions. And as you know, most of us at court have disagreeable opinions."

"But you are close to the king, are you not? Surely he does not think such things about you."

"I try to keep such opinions to myself when in His Majesty's company." Her brow was troubled, and it made me smile. "Do you worry about me?"

Her features turned to a rapid blush. "Court is a dangerous place. And you are sometimes too impetuous."

"I know when to keep a civil tongue. And who my friends are. If the king would not have taken Wolsey into the chancellor's seat—"

"He is a man of God. Surely his advice—"

"A man of God? It is a wonder he can wear a crucifix without it burning his skin!"

"Thomas!" Her voice echoed in the cloister, and she glanced furtively at its reverberations. More quietly she said, "He is a cardinal and you must not speak so. He is my superior. And yours, when it comes to it."

"Wolsey is my superior in name only."

"And that is all that matters at court. Learn from Buckingham."

The color was back in her cheeks and I cheered from her stern words to me. This was the old Isabella I knew, and I was glad to see it peeking out from behind that veil. Yet almost as quickly as its familiarity appeared, it receded again.

"Perhaps we should not talk of court," she said. "It only causes strife between us. It causes me also to forget myself and my manners, for I must offer our thanks for your many gifts of late. Would you like to see what good use we put to your generosity?"

She led me through the house and to the forecourt of the dwelling. She raised her hand to show me, but distracted, I could only look at *her*.

"We built dovecotes," she said. "Already wood pigeons come. We will have eggs and fresh meat all year. The more self-sufficient we can be the better."

"How enterprising," I said, studying the large, inexpert structure. Grey breasted squabs perched and cooed from its rooftop as if to thank me as well. "Have you raised doves before?"

"On my father's farm, Thomas."

"I forget. It seems so long ago now."

A burly fellow busied himself with a shovel, digging a series of holes along a hump of trees, and beside him were little packages of holly bushes, their roots neatly bundled in cloth. He must have been at this business a long time, for I noted more little bushes newly planted about the grounds.

"There seems to be great industry in planting holly here. Since when have you been overly fond of the stuff?"

"To feed the livestock in winter. It is all practical, Thomas."

She led me back into the dwelling and through to the garden once again. "Not all practical, Lady Prioress. This garden, for instance. Surely it is a vanity to your pride to toil on something so frivolous."

She blushed and I warmed to see it. "It is neither vanity nor frivolity. You would have us live in a perpetual state of gloom. That is not the purpose of holy orders. It is to celebrate God's gifts, His beauty. These flowers are gifts from God. And it is as fitting a place to pray or meditate as a chapel or a church. It is only through hard work that such things are accomplished. This, too, is the Opus Dei. You see, I do not while away the time until your return. This is not my father's grange. I have a life now."

"So I see. Am I now superfluous to it?"

She smiled. "I do not think that will ever be the case. After all, you and your father are our patrons. We rely on you."

"Not as I would hope."

She caught the petulance in my voice and manner before I could hide them, and sternly fastened her eyes upon me. "You must not hope in that vein, Thomas. Hope instead in the grace of your future life in Heaven. I will pray for that."

Leaning against the stone arch, I kicked at the walk with my spur, fanning bits of gravel with each stroke. She chastened right good, yet behind her solemn expression was one of fondness, and my body responded, crying out to embrace her. "Your prayers, Isabella," I said softly, pushing away from the wall, "are far more worthy than mine. Do pray for me." I stood beside her, close enough to touch, though I dared not. "I am assured Heaven from such lips."

Wisely she did not raise her eyes to mine. "Thomas, if you cannot control your words to me, then you best not come again. I value our friendship, but you take too many liberties."

"Madam, you expect a great deal from me. My feelings for you have never altered."

She whirled on me, her black habit giving more the appearance of a raven than a virgin. "And when did you realize this great love for me? When, Thomas? When you discovered I was a novice here? Untouchable? Safe?"

I frowned. "I know what you are implying. That is insulting and quite beneath you. Who understands the workings of the heart, or the moment of those workings?" I paced, feeling the solid stone of the cloister arcade beneath my boots, the intensity of those steps echoing back to me. "And you, Lady *Prioress*," I accused, turning on her. "When did you acknowledge this passion for *me*? Hmm? This passion you say you deny? Once *you* were just as safe? A happy spinsterhood, this. You, too, can enjoy your romantic longing, as is the fashion. Guinevere to my Lancelot."

She looked as if she would strike me. I would have welcomed the relief. Instead, she stepped slightly away and bit her lip, causing a crimson line to momentarily brighten her mouth to pink. Still as tall as I, she could not hide her face, and I saw how I won my vengeance in the hurt of her eyes. She breathed a sigh, and with it her plain words: "I was sixteen when I loved you first. A hopeless love."

All my thunder was suddenly spent, and all the blame with it. My mouth fell open in an unexpected moan of repentance. "*That* long?" I had no idea, never a clue. Was I so very ignorant and blind? Did she love me through all the times I spoke of women, lamenting with a young man's heart my love for one noble creature after another, my conquests with wenches? Was I that heartless a knave to have never noticed the sad shadows in her eyes because I did not deem her face beautiful? Oh, but how beautiful she was to me now! And how I would make amends if only I could.

I turned from her to hide my horror.

"We have been friends, Thomas," she went on. "Why should it change so? We can pretend that these moments never occurred. We can be Thomas and Isabella as we always were when we were young."

Yes. When we were young. Harboring your love of me and my never knowing it. Fie on my own faithless heart! "That is not enough," I heard myself say aloud.

"It is all there is."

"All or nothing? I am not given to submitting to ultimatums, Madam."

"A self-imposed ultimatum, then. Truly," she said, puffing an exaggerated sigh. "I have not the time nor stamina to argue with you. I have a priory to run." Strong as an oak, I believed Isabella capable of anything, yet all at once her will seemed to crumble, and she suddenly burst into tears.

I knelt to her. "Do not weep, Isabella! I will do anything you say!"

"No, no. It is not for that." She cast the backs of her hands over her face, wiping the tears away with blunt artlessness. "I am not worthy to run this house! Why did the bishop select me?"

It was natural to enfold her in my arms. I allowed her to weep into my shoulder, filling my nose with the sweet, warm scent of her. The woolen veil and the precious head beneath pressed against my cheek. I closed my eyes and remained the courtier.

"The books," she muttered, pulling herself slowly away. "I know nothing of books, Thomas. I cannot make heads or tails of them, but I must, for I am bound to send an accounting regularly to the bishop."

"The books? Is that all that disturbs you?" I took her shoulders and held her at arm's length. I wiped a tear from her face with my finger. "Why, I can decipher a set of books standing on my head."

At length, that image must have clarified in her mind, for she suddenly smiled and even laughed. "Your head need not be so inconvenienced, Lord Thomas, if you would but put your mind to the reading of them. I should be very grateful, Thomas, if you would."

"I am your servant, Madam," and I bowed.

There followed many a pleasant afternoon in her parlor correcting her accountings, while she occupied herself with some bit of mending by the window.

It was as close to domesticity as we could come.

ISABELLA LAUNDER
AUGUST, 1521
Blackladies

XV

I, then, a prisoner for the Lord, urge you to live in a manner worthy of the call you have received, with all humility and gentleness, with patience, bearing with one another through love, striving to preserve the unity of the spirit through the bond of peace...

—Ephesians 4:1-3

On my knees before the crucifix and sheltered within the cloister of my veil, I found peace such as I have never known. In my younger years, I imagined I sowed such peace in my garden, or in those few heart-thumping moments when Thomas Giffard deigned to visit my father's farm. I thought that religion came through common work, the sacrifice of the day to labor. But I was wrong. True, in these things we prove our love of God and man, but I found—quite late in my career as nun and prioress—that prayer is the food that feeds the inner self. It would seem obvious to an outsider, but I myself felt like such an outsider for so long that I never took a moment to understand the true good of prayer. It cracks the hard shell of pride, and picks through to the meat of our souls, our true selves.

My solitary time in the chapel in the late afternoon was my favorite moment of the day. We strove for that sense of community when we are in prayer during the Divine Office, yet our Lord often went alone to His prayers to teach us the wisdom of this most private vocation.

And so I knelt.

In the chapel, the day washed the crucifix with clean country light, as amber as honey, as golden as the throne of God. There was no sound but for the finches in the trees outside, their song muffled by the roof, and the terribly still air of August.

When I noticed myself again, it was to look down upon my hands. My flesh was impressed with the wooden beads of the rosary. Had I finished the last decade of prayers? Had I slumbered? Somewhere between prayers and peace is something akin to sleep, but not sleep. A meditation so deep it might be construed as sleep.

I have, indeed, grown into my habit.

Even though the occasional girlish thought of Thomas flit through my mind, it was stamped down through the grace of God, and I reformed my mind to more constructive contemplation. It was not to say I was free of worries. For the letter from the bishop stating his intention to visit bored a hole in the scrip I wore on my belt. (He took to writing in English—bless him—for we informed him there was not a nun among us who could read Latin.)

I gazed up at the humble statue of the Virgin, nestled in the shadow of the crucifix. "Ask your Son to watch over us. There is still so much discord, and I would not grieve the bishop with our contentiousness."

As if on cue, Cristabell entered, bowing to the crucifix.

"*Deo Gratias*." I acknowledged her with a gentle nod.

"The bishop arrives tomorrow," she said, omitting the formal greeting to me.

"Yes. I hope all is ready."

"Indeed. There is great anticipation. There will be much to report to his Excellency."

Stiffly, I turned my head to look upon her expression of triumph. It brought me to my feet. "What mischief do you speak, Cristabell? Out with it! I have endured your taunting for too many years. You respect me not, even as I stand before you as your prioress."

"Respect *you*? In all your sin? I do not think you will be prioress much longer."

"Oh? Do you think I will step down? Is it that you desire so much to be this convent's prioress? If that were the case I should step aside now."

"I do not desire to be prioress."

"Just as long as *I* am not? I will not step down, Cristabell. Not from pride, nor from vengeance, but because I was chosen. I will serve this community as I have professed so to do."

"We will see. After I speak to the bishop, the choice will be out of your hands."

"And what of thievery?"

"Thievery?" Her head in its veil cocked to one side, rather like a magpie deciding what part of the worm to devour first.

"Thievery, Dame," I answered, quieting. "I keep myself busy in this convent, performing my duties in the garden and its environs. Including the beehives. As you must know, Meg and I extract the honey and attend the honey pots in the larder. I am often in and around them. I see much, but am observed little." Her face, so animated in its regard of me and my disgrace, flattened to paleness. "There is little that escapes my scrutiny in the larder, Dame. I see those who toil and those who despoil."

"And?"

"And you, Cristabell."

She bristled. "Me? What lies are these?"

"Not lies. I did see you. On more than one occasion. You were eating the honey right from the pots. Oh not such a noticeable amount...yet there you were."

"So! Biding your time you would denounce me in revenge! Honey pots! Such a crime!"

"More than honey pots. The alms box as well. I found the coins in your bed." She glared at me wild-eyed. "Why, Cristabell? Why secret these meager coins? To what end?"

She did not change her posture. Chin still raised, her eyes glittered their challenge, until an eyelash flickered. Of a sudden she cried out so loudly that I pitched back in surprise. "To what *end*?" she proclaimed. "To *leave* this place!"

"Leave?"

"Do you think I can remain here and watch you and your lover?"

"Cristabell!"

"Do you think I can serve you in all your wantonness? I was saving that money to leave here—this place, this village—and find a new life."

"Leave the cloister? But Cristabell..." I clutched the statue's foot for support, never taking my eyes from her scowling, tear-streaked face. Pain twisted her lips, gnarling them to hateful contortions. "How can you leave your home? Your vows?"

"When the bishop can appoint the likes of you as prioress, then there is no choice but to leave or be a hypocrite."

"Hear me, Cristabell." I grasped her hands before she could quit the chapel. She wrestled with me but I, the stronger, held her firm. "Thomas is only an old friend. A dear friend. And yes. There was a time when his advances would have cheered my heart. But that day is long gone. I am a devoted sister of this house. I love this life and this Church. I would never leave it for any man. Never!"

A horrible silence followed. Cristabell's eyes glossed. Their green irises fluctuated from sage to loden until they drew wide with great, shimmering orbs of tears. "*I* would!" she cried, a wrenching, soulful wail. Her hands yanked free of mine, and she fell to her knees, weeping into her hands with terrible rasping breaths. "Had my Edward come for me, I would have gone. If he came tomorrow I would still go!"

For a long moment I stood looking down at her as she bobbed over her hands, keening inconsolably. Slowly, I crouched before her and drew her against my chest. "Tell me how you came here."

Remarkably, she leaned into me, her veiled head just under my chin. Her voice was even again, though her tears still flowed upon my gown. "I was sixteen. He was seventeen. My mother found us together. We were to wed. We promised ourselves to each other. What did it matter if I were a maid no longer?"

She sat up and dragged her arm over the tears of her face. "My mother brought me here, told me it was for to save my soul because it was in danger from my sins. Edward vowed to rescue me. But...he never came. I thought, someday I could find him—"

"But that was sixteen years ago. Surely he himself is wed and committed. It was long enough ago for him to have—"

"No! He would not have forgotten me! He would not have forsaken me! Something must have prevented him."

"But your vows..."

"And what of yours?" She pushed away from me. "You forsook your vows with that man. Why should you be the only one to indulge in her lusts? Why should I wither away like Prioress Margaret, when I can have what you have?"

"Cristabell! What I have? What I have is you, and Dame Elizabeth, and Dame Alice, and Jane and Mary. Thomas wants me, yes. But I am not his to have. I am the Lord's. I am promised to Him alone. Can you not see that? Why will you not believe me?"

"I can believe my own eyes!"

"You see wrong, Cristabell."

"I see you have harbored this information about me only to bide your time, waiting for the best opportunity to denounce me. Well, now you have more against me. I suppose the bishop will instruct you to chain me in the dormitory."

I rose, my bones aching from the stone floor and from Cristabell's dreadful expression of vindictiveness. "I will not tell him. In fact, I have told no one of your thievery. Not even my confessor."

"What? You lie! Another brazen deceit!"

"Are you so blinded by jealousy that you cannot see the truth when held up to your eyes? Cristabell, know me! And know that I have no intention of allowing you to leave. But not with chains. By your own will."

"Why would I stay? So you can lord these secrets over me, using them at your will?"

Exasperated, I turned away. "You can tell the bishop what you like. If it suits you to renounce me falsely, then do it. And when the bishop himself asks me what has gone between Thomas Giffard and myself I will tell him the truth: That I am a faithful servant to this house. That I am a maid. That I know Thomas loves me…"

Thomas' face flashed before my eyes, his insolent smile, his glittering dark eyes, his graceful body. How composed I thought I was! But unexpectedly, desperate emotions welled within me, grasping my heart, squeezing with the pain of longing. I gasped aloud all my desires, all my soul, "—and…and I love him, too! Oh God!" Never before did I speak those words aloud. Even after all my years under the guidance of God and His house, after all my prayers and devotions, even then, only under a thin crust, my heart burned for Thomas, for his forbidden touch.

I had only fooled myself, thinking prayer could keep me safe. Was I to become like Cristabell, in mourning and waiting forever?

I wiped the tears from my cheeks, and slowly turned toward her. Her cheek shined with a triumphant glow. "We can help each other," I said quietly. "We can be true sisters, if only you would let me. We are more alike than you might wish to admit."

"No. I am not like you."

"We can help each other."

"We will let the bishop decide. You with your tale, and me with mine."

"I will tell him nothing about you."

"Only as long as I say nothing."

"No! Whether you speak or not, I will say nothing."

Stiff as a pillar, she stood and eyed me, marshaling all the forces of her mistrustful aspect.

Just then, Alice thrust her head into the chapel and, breathless, hissed at me. "Lady Prioress! The bishop is *here!*"

"A full day early," I muttered, catching my breath. I wiped my tears with the back of a hand. Turning to Cristabell, I sighed. "A day less for you to decide what to do."

"I need no time to decide."

"Very well." I hitched up my hem. "You must do what your conscience tells you. May God have mercy." Hem high, I ran after Alice as she hurried to the gate. Cristabell scurried to help Dame Elizabeth, and they both turned the corner when the Bishop appeared with his retainers and Father William. I unlocked the gate, whereupon we took our turns kneeling and kissing his ring. He celebrated the Divine Office with us, and through his presence I was able to capture some peace of mind where Cristabell was concerned. I tried not to worry over it, but my heart was heavy at what she would tell him. I was innocent of her lies, but it would destroy me nonetheless. How certain were Elizabeth and Alice that Thomas and I did not indulge in improprieties? How could they support me in so insupportable a claim? Why *did* I allow him access where he surely should not be? I should be censured. There was no doubt, but still I wanted it kept as it was, like a flower pressed into a book of memories. I should be ashamed. I should have confessed it all. A thousand times, I knew I should have.

I took Bishop Blythe on a tour of the grounds, taking care to show him our many improvements. Though I could tell he was askance at our poverty, he was clearly surprised and pleased at the meal we offered him of squab and pottage as well as our cheese, damsons, and white bread. We had no wine to give, but beer and mead were plentiful.

"You set a fine table, Lady Prioress," he said to me. We ate with Elizabeth and Cristabell in the hall, but we were unaccustomed to speaking during mealtimes. There were so few visitors and Thomas never stayed long enough to dine.

Often, I glanced at Cristabell. Very soon, I knew, this might be the last time anyone addressed me as "Lady Prioress." Perhaps it was for the best.

"We do our best with what we can devise, Your Excellency."

"Yes. But the rest of the priory is—how shall I say—in wont of care, Lady Prioress."

"If you mean by such words that the buildings are in decline, then I can only agree with you. We have only so many workers and so little in funds to be able to repair, it is hardly a wonder."

"Your reports to me are ever optimistic, Lady Prioress. I do not understand this turn."

"Bishop Blythe," I began kindly, "I wrote in honesty of our progress here. But never did I consider buildings a main source of what we were to accomplish. You see us as we are: humble servants." I glanced at my fellow nuns for concurrence, but they all had the look of deer caught by poachers.

Drawing silent, I glanced at my own plate of broken meats and crusts. I was glad of only the one retainer dining with us, for as it was, Alice had to stand by waiting her turn to eat, even after having borrowed the extra bowls and spoons from our servants, bless them.

We finished our repast and adjourned to Chapter where the bishop took my seat and questioned us, his retainer acting as scribe and writing all down. "Your letters, Prioress Isabella, tell of mundane matters, but do not allude to property. Have you an inventory of the household goods and property?"

"Why, no, Your Excellency."

"And why is that?"

Dame Elizabeth saw my distress and bowed to the bishop before addressing him. "We have no inventory of the house, Your Excellency, because we are such a small and poor house. What little we have is adequately shared by all, as St. Benet said, and I know not what our Lady Prioress has but to guess that it is as little as the rest of us."

The bishop scoured the little chapter room with heavy lids. "I see the truth of it, Dame." She bowed again and sat, and I blessed and thanked her with my grateful glance, for I did not know how to answer the bishop in this. I was not instructed as to all that I should do as mistress of this house.

The bishop then asked each sister to tell the earnest truth about Blackladies, and all held their breath when he came at last to Cristabell.

"Dame Cristabell. Can you tell me whether the Lady Prioress runs a goodly house in fair measure?"

Tight-lipped as ever, she spoke in soft tones. "Our Lady Prioress is fair, Your Excellency, in *most* of her dealings, but I do have cause for concern."

"Oh?" He glanced at me, but I lowered my flaming cheeks, unable to look him in the eye.

She glared at me, despite my years of being a mother and a servant to her. "Our Lady Prioress allows that which is not to be, Your Excellency. I have kept my council, but now, in your presence, I am forced to say." Her complexion darkened. "Our Lady Prioress…" She switched her gaze from one nun to the next. They glanced at her with dispassion, knowing well, it seemed, what she intended. "The Lady Prioress is indiscreet, Your Excellency."

"Indiscreet? How so, Dame?"

"She…she…" But here, the smallest tremor quivered her lips. Was she afraid of me, that I would denounce her thievery even though I told her I would not? Did she trust me so little? "She…our Lady Prioress…" Pressing her lips firmly, she licked them and started anew. "The Lady Prioress allows young girls to share our dormitory with us." Shocked, I stared at her, unable to lower my eyes from her stern countenance. "It is not right that they sleep with us. It disturbs our slumber. We have too much work to do."

The bishop raised a brow at me. "Is this true?"

Numbed, I nodded. "Yes, Your Excellency. We have nowhere else to put them. They have no home, no family."

"You must find them another situation, and right quick. This house cannot support this charity. Your heart is good, Lady Prioress, but misplaced. You are allowed four nuns here and your servants, and that is all. There is no room for more. Is that clear?"

"Yes, Your Excellency. But they have come to know us well, and feel this is their home."

"Lady Prioress. Should you comfort every wayfarer and foundling, there would be no food enough for those you shelter already. Should I remove some of your household to make room for foundlings? Would you be only two nuns here?"

"No, Bishop. I bow to obedience."

"Well then," he said, eyeing Cristabell. "Is there anything more?"

I waited again for her to speak, a sense of dread gnawing at my belly. She glared at me, and I saw all her intentions in those verdant eyes.

I was angered at myself. It was I who put myself at her mercy. I never should have allowed Thomas such access. It was not allowed by the Rule, yet I flouted it. She was the better nun, then, to denounce me. I welcomed it. How could there be secrets within a cloister? How live honest lives if we hid our true selves from one another?

Cristabell faced the bishop, jaw clenched, before lowering her head and shaking it slowly from side to side.

It was unexpected. Should I take this opportunity to denounce myself? I swallowed my breath, unable to decide what to do.

But it was such a little thing, Thomas' visits. And he was such a good friend to this priory. If Cristabell thought it mete to keep quiet, then surely I must do the same.

I blushed with shame. How was it that in the span of a breath, I could change my resolve so easily? My heart was relieved, but what of my soul?

The bishop's visit wore on us all. More so than I thought it would. I was so vexed by what might befall us that I found little sleep in the days preceding. The day after he left, I held our

Chapter. The room which was normally cool even in summer, seemed unusually hot to me, and more than once I blotted the sweat from my chin with the back of a hand. "Sisters, we did well with the Bishop's visit. He saw our accomplishments and our needs, and I think he shall be more attentive when next we ask for a necessity… But." I drew a breath, which seemed to take an eternity. "Cristabell. Why did you tell him of Jane and Mary? You know their lot is wretched. What are two little girls to us? So we eat a little less in order to feed them…"

"I could have told him more, Lady Prioress," she said, her head down.

"I know. But we are so few here. We four against the world. We must stand together, sharing what is in our hearts here in Chapter where it belongs. If you still harbored discontent with the girls, here is where you should have said."

"Forgive me, Lady Prioress." Raising her head she stared at me. "I did tell you. I did not cease in telling you. You call it charity, but I see it as disobedience. I have been a nun a long time, Madam. Longer than you, in fact, and I was taught that obedience is utmost of our vows. Who will clothe them when they grow? We can feed them from our food now, and that we have done, and I have not complained. But shall we go about naked to clothe them? You would answer 'yes', but I say we have done what is required. We succored them when it was needed, but now it is up to the community of Brewood to find them shelter. The village belongs to Christ, too." Her mouth set into a thin line.

I paused and considered her sincere words. Did I wrongly convict Cristabell in the court of my mind, condemning without trial? For the issues she now raised were entirely reasonable, and I felt ashamed that I took no note of them earlier as a prioress should have done.

"Cristabell, my sister. I have wronged you." Alice and Elizabeth snapped up their heads in surprise. "Your concerns for this house and for the Rule have oft been ignored because I falsely misconstrued their intent. I ask your forgiveness in this. And further, I concur with your assessment. The girls should find new homes with the families of Brewood unless they wish to enter a convent themselves. But it shall not be this one. For the bishop made it clear we are a house of four nuns only. Four is a good number, Cristabell. I should not want that to change."

Her face was full of misgiving and confusion. Certainly she did not expect to be received with sincerity. It only made my heart cry out the more to her.

A flush of heat reddened my face, and I wiped a drop of sweat from under my chin. There was so much more I wanted to say to her, to make her understand, and yet a swelling headache made it difficult to concentrate. When I raised my eyes to her, it was as if I were looking at her through a rippling pond. I grasped my rosary. "So much I wish to tell you," I said, before a tunnel of darkness consumed me.

THOMAS GIFFARD
AUGUST, 1521
Blackladies

XVI

*"Covetousness is like fire: the more wood that is fed to it,
the more fervent and greedy it is."*
–Sir Thomas More

In mere moments I was there. The word came so quickly, and then I rode, yet I remember not the riding. At my insistence, I was brought to her room, a place in the convent I never before laid eyes upon. It was small and cramped, and the air close, hazy with dust. She lay very still, yet a sheen of sweat sheathed what skin of her face I could see for the wimple. "Has the physician come?" I asked, kneeling beside the bed.

"Physician?" asked Dame Alice. "We have called no physician, Lord Giffard."

"I have done," I answered. I longed to hold Isabella's hand, but it lay under a light blanket. "Pray God it is not the sweating sickness."

Alice gasped. No one wanted that malady anywhere nigh. The king himself oft left court this time of year to escape it, as well as the plague. The king reeked of vinegar, a tonic thought to keep such disease at bay. Everyone drank it or doused themselves with it. The nuns' room was the only place that did not stink from it.

Beside Isabella's bed, I prayed it was neither the sleeping sickness nor the plague. I prayed she would open her eyes and look at me.

"Isabella," I whispered, hoping to coax her to consciousness. "It is I, Thomas. You must not frighten your sisters so by fainting in Chapter as you did. That was incautious to say the least."

"Incautious..." My heart leapt, for her cracked lips opened and spoke the words. Tilting forward, I took the wet cloth from her head and softened her lips with it. "Incautious is a married man within a nun's cloister," she rasped. "For shame, Thomas."

"I have come to bring you a doctor. Oh, where is that cursed man?"

"Another man in our chamber? No, no. I will not allow it."

"You will allow what I tell you to allow, Lady Prioress."

"No." She shook her head against the pillow. It was an effort. "You must take me downstairs. Please, Thomas. We must observe some level of decorum."

"You should not be moved."

"I insist." Grunting, she made as if to rise, but Alice gently pushed her back.

"Lord Giffard," said Dame Alice, imploring me. "What shall we do?"

"I will carry her," I said, and rose.

Isabella said nothing as I scooped her from her bed, bed linens and all, and carried her like a babe down the stairs. She was surprisingly light, and I feared for this, imagining it was her weakness that made her so. I vowed when she recovered I would send a cartload of barley and rye flour, and droves of fowl.

Alice greeted a surprised Dame Elizabeth, and the older nun instructed me to take her to the chapter house, it being the coolest room. I kicked open the door with my foot and trod through, looking for the best place.

"The chair," Isabella croaked. "If I am to die, I would have it done in the prioress' chair."

"You are not going to die, you stubborn woman," I hissed into her ear before setting her down into the hard chair. I knelt and rested her feet upon the footstool.

"Now go, Thomas. You should not be here."

"The pope himself could not bestir me now."

She gave in with a sigh and melted into the bedclothes.

We waited interminably for that damned physician, and when he arrived at last I nearly fell upon him.

"This is highly unusual," he kept saying.

Clearly he had not my experience with convents, but his slow considerations were vexing me. "Well? Can you do something?"

"Lord Giffard, be assured. Despite this unusual setting, I shall do all I can for the prioress."

He summoned the nuns to prepare hot water and to bring linens, and then he instructed me to leave.

"I shall not!"

"Lord Giffard. These are delicate matters. Do the lady a kindness and cease your hovering."

"Let me take you to the chapel, Lord Giffard." Dame Elizabeth took my arm with surprising strength, and pulled me away. Looking back at Isabella, I could see the wisdom in this at last, and I allowed myself to be led.

I stood alone in the humble chapel, staring at the rustic crucifix. I reached for the altar rail and knelt, bowing my head. "Precious *Jesu*, let nothing harm her. Have mercy on her. Heal her." I further asked for blessings for Dame Alice who had the wits to call me. No ill should befall Isabella. Never in my life have I known her to fall ill. "Is it my own sin, Lord, that causes this? For I would never wish to taint her with my faults."

After a long while on my knees I stood again, stamping back the feeling in my calves before pacing the room. What was taking so long? This damnable cloister with its gates and secrets! A person could die for lack of care in such a place. Though it might be incautious in a chapel, I nevertheless cursed Blackladies and all the houses like it. Monks! Nuns! What a foolish occupation! At least the rest of us made no pretense at piety and chastity. Too many of these houses were filled with greedy lascivious creatures, or so it was rumored. Rome took its coin and appointed its clerics—like our fair Wolsey, and what did it ever offer in return? Pregnant nuns and hypocritical priests!

Raising my head I glared at the chapel's walls, daring it to naysay me. I swiveled my head toward the altar where I expected to see the riches of the Church in all its piracy, but saw only a mended linen cloth draped over the stone. The tabernacle was small and fashioned with dented plate, and I recalled its one silver goblet as well as its paten, not even made of precious metal. Could I truly imagine Isabella comporting with the Devil, or any of her nuns? Ashamed and looking about me at the coarse structure, I recognized that not all of England's monasteries could be as corrupted as was said. Ill rumor, I suppose, had a way of begetting itself.

Moving toward the meager quire, I lowered to the bench, wondering vaguely if Isabella sat where I settled. A touch of spicy incense permeated the old wood and it drew out of me an unwilling glut of nostalgia for masses I had attended, for celebrations of the Lord I gloried in. I shook my head and asked of the murky gloom, "Why am I such a cynic, Lord?" Was it because I was older, more experienced? Did I know better now, like a weaned child, mature as I played my games of court? I knew how the Church trifled with lives, and souls, and coin purses. To have Isabella join their ranks...

I leaned back against the wood and glared at the dusky ceiling. Why did I torture myself this way? If she were married with a score of brats at her dugs, would I have bothered?

Gazing at the solemn statue of the Virgin, I was forced to admit with a despicable sense of myself, that I would not have. It was this very sanctity that compelled me, that if she could not be mine, then she would be no one's. I stared at the statue of the Holy Mother, content.

It seemed I contemplated that statue a long time until I was surprised to be awakened by Dame Alice. She carried a candle, which glowed her cheek with golden light.

"Lord Giffard? Are you awake?"

"Dame." I rose, embarrassed, having no care for the ache in my bones from sleeping on so hard a surface.

"I am afraid we forgot about you. And as you see, night has fallen. Will you sup with us?"

"How is Isabella? I mean your prioress?"

"She is well. The doctor said it was only a fever, but the strain of the bishop's visit caused her to collapse. He recommended rest for the next few days, but I do not know if she will abide by it."

"By God, she will!" I cried, and strode purposely to the door. Dame Alice rushed to catch up to me.

"Lord Giffard, the hall is this way."

"What?"

Isabella's niece gestured to me in the other direction. She was nothing like Isabella in stature or in appearance. But she was fond of her kinswoman and prioress, and in this she pleased me. I allowed her to lead me to the small hall.

It was dim inside the room with only two small oil lamps on the table. Four mean wooden spoons and wooden plates sat at the ready, with fat slabs of bread, leeks, and poached fish sitting atop the platters, while a thick barley soup steamed from the four porridgers. The other nuns joined me at table, staring at the unusual company. Dame Alice placed one set of the platters on a tray and lifted it. "I will take this to the prioress."

It took all my strength not to rise to my feet and offer to take it myself, but I stared at the meager portions of food instead as Dame Alice made her way into the gloom of Blackladies. "Where is Dame Alice's place?" I asked, my voice shrill in the solemn silence, noting now only three remaining settings.

Dame Elizabeth raised her head from her dish. "There are only four settings, Lord Giffard. She must wait her turn until all are fed, and then she will eat."

"This is absurd. I do not need to eat your food, Dame."

"But you would not insult your hosts, would you Lord Giffard? You are so generous to us, we would be pleased to offer our hospitality."

"Generous, indeed. Yes, Dame. I recall supplying this house with decent pewter plates. All I see left of that are a few porridgers."

She took up her spoon and delicately scooped the barley broth. "We sold them."

"You did what?"

"Dame Isabella's wish was to provide for the local poor. We did not need more place settings than nuns, and so we sold them for money for the poor. But she kept some of the porridgers as they are very sensible." With a smile, she scooped more soup and slurped it from the spoon.

I said no more and ate slowly so as not to finish like a glutton, but I offered to relinquish my plate to Dame Alice upon her return.

"Did the prioress eat?" I asked leaving the bench so that she could sit.

"Yes. She ate well. She said to thank you for your kindness, Lord Giffard, in calling in the doctor."

Dame Alice commenced spooning food onto my discarded plate while I stood by in the dark, wondering what next to do. I wanted desperately to see Isabella, but knew if I asked, I would be refused. I decided, then, not to ask. "I bid you all farewell," I said to them. "I thank you for your generous hospitality."

Dame Elizabeth rose. "I will unlock the gate for you, Lord Giffard."

The damn gate! I forgot. I hoped I appeared polite as I nodded to acknowledge her.

Dame Elizabeth took me down the cloister and into the gallery of the dwelling. "The gate lies that way," she said pointing toward an arch glowing from fading sunlight. "And the dormitory is up the stairs to your right."

She turned to leave me, and it was then I suddenly called out to her. "Dame Elizabeth?"

"Lord Giffard, if you would see to the prioress I suggest you make it quick. We will have Vespers soon and retire ourselves."

My gratitude must have glowed in my eyes, for she smiled once before slowly returning to the hall. I took the stairs two at a time, and found Isabella propped up in her bed gazing out the window, a rosary glittering in her hand. When she turned, she did not seem surprised.

"What conspiracy is this?" I asked.

"No conspiracy," she said with a sigh. "It is simply that your nature has been discerned."

"I do not know if I like that implication," I pouted, standing at the foot of her bed. "How are you?"

"Tired. But I am well, Thomas. Thanks to you and your good care of me."

"My good care of you, indeed. You sold my plate. The plate I bought for you."

"For the house, surely not for me. And I thanked you for it. We got a goodly sum, and paid it out to the poor. Would you begrudge the poor their due, Thomas?"

"Isabella," I sighed, shaking my head. "What am I to do with you? You are too stubborn to even be properly sick."

"I have too much work to do to be sick. The good Lord knows that."

"The Lord knows you also need to rest. I will have Dame Alice report to me if you do not take the doctor's advice. I will come back and lock you in this room myself if I must."

"You need not do that. But you could do me a kindness by granting a favor."

"Anything."

"We have two waifs among us. Little girls. You might have seen them."

I recalled two gangly children romping in the fields outside the cloister and within its walls. "I always supposed they were the children of your servants."

"No. They are orphans. We have been told we may no longer care for them."

Such pain in her eyes as she said it. I did not realize the sacrifice Isabella made upon coming to this convent. Yes, she was a perpetual virgin in my heart and vowed to that end because of her own heart. But these children would be the only babes inhabiting her chaste life. How long had they been here? How attached was she?

"What would you have me do, Isabella?"

"Find a place for them. You have many estates and many servants. Surely there are those who will, in charity, take them in. Please, Thomas. They have found a home here, and now they must leave it. Imagine the sorrows they have known, and so young."

I nodded. There was nothing I could deny her, especially when her eyes looked as they did. "Yes. I will send someone for them in the morning, if that will suit."

Slowly, she inhaled and expelled a great sigh. "Thank you, Thomas. Bless you. And now," she said, gazing at me fondly, "you must quit this room before the others return. You should not even be here. But you already know that."

"Yes, I do." Still tightly wimpled, still draped in her dark veil, she seemed to blend into the shadows encroaching from the darkness. She watched me like a raven curiously watches the doings over the next wall. "Be well, Isabella. I will pray for you."

"And I for you, Thomas." But as she said the last, she dropped her face, seeming embarrassed by the saying of it.

ISABELLA LAUNDER
EARLY SUMMER, 1526
Blackladies

XVII

He who pleased God was loved...
—Wisdom 14:10

I swung the hoe hard into the dusty soil and shuffled the weeds away from the green stalks. Dame Alice worked beside me. The workmen tilled farther away. It was hard work, but I enjoyed it, for from this harvest many were fed. The work satisfied.

"You have the strength of Moses," huffed Alice, resting an arm on her hoe. She watched me work for another moment before I, too, stopped to rest.

"'To pray is to work and to work is to pray'," I told her. "I am most fond of these words of St. Benet's."

"Yes, I agree." She glanced to the trees lining the boundaries of Blackladies' fields, and how they waved and glittered in shades of yellow green. "I received a letter from my mother yesterday."

I stole a glance at Alice's pinched expression. "Oh? What news has she?"

"My grandsire is dead. She took as much caring in the telling of it as when she told of your father, Lady Prioress."

I becrossed myself. "God have mercy. Yes, I remember."

"She says she and Father have moved to the farm at Swynnerton. She says she also hopes the Church is boxing some sense into me. She never did like my choosing it."

"Why did you?"

She took her time. So long, in fact, that I wondered at her reticence at something that happened years ago, and I turned an inquiring brow toward her.

"May I be frank, Madam?"

"Of course, Alice. Always you may be so with me."

"When my mother was trying to talk me out of coming here, she would tell me things. About you."

"Oh?" I picked up the hoe and brushed the blade carelessly across the ground. "What sort of things?"

Alice's sigh was tinged with a note of embarrassment. "She said you were always insolent and that you lorded your company of Lord Giffard over her while she lived at Grandsire Launder's grange."

I spun on her. "*Lorded* it over her? By the mass! What must she be thinking?"

"So she used to say, Madam. That you expected to be the wife of...of Thomas Giffard, and your disappointment brought you here."

"Agnes!" I rasped, thinking of my sister and all her envious affronts. "Alice, I tell you true, I *never* expected to be the wife of Thomas Giffard. The notion is ludicrous."

"I told her as much, but she persisted. She said...well, she said all manner of ill things against you."

"None of it—whatever it is—is true, Alice. You must know me well enough by now to reason that."

"Yes, Madam. I did not believe it. Still..." She nosed the hoe into the soil. "Lord Giffard *does* spend time here within the cloister, and I always wondered at it."

"Agnes never understood me," I went on. "In her jealousy of my long friendship with Lord Giffard, your mother no doubt misinterpreted my need for solitude. After all, she went to the feasts and celebrations in the village when I did not. She took it for haughtiness when it was only...only my reserve at being with others who did not want my company. Look at me, Alice. I am not a beauteous woman. I never had a suitor."

"Was Thomas Giffard a suitor?" Her eyes were wide with anticipation.

"No, child. We were friends." I felt a twinge at this half-truth.

"It does not surprise me that she should have said what she said about you. I knew there was more to her words. I sensed she was envious of something about you. I thought it was your sanctity and love of God that she could not understand."

"And now?"

"That was partially true. But now I see she was also jealous that Lord Giffard paid you any attendance...and her none at all."

Nodding, I cut at the weeds.

"So...why *does* he attend to you, Lady Prioress?"

Squinting at the sky, I gazed deeply into its endless blue, swept at the horizon by curls of white clouds, awaiting their afternoon drizzle. "It was a friendship borne of my candor. He likes my honesty."

Alice laughed. "*That* is something my mother never would have liked!"

I desperately hammered at the soil, groping for any change in the subject. "Does she say how your Uncle Robert fairs?"

"No. But I am certain she would put such information into the letter in her blunt way if anything tragic occurred to them."

I smiled, turning it from Alice. It was not good to agree so heartily on another's faults, especially when they were one's own kin, though Alice seemed to understand her mother well. "Do you ever regret your coming here?" I asked, curious at her reply.

"No. But sometimes I wonder what sort of mother I would have been. What children I would have borne."

"I saw you with Jane and Mary," I offered, thinking of Thomas' letter regarding their care. "And also with the sick of this parish, Alice. You *are* a mother, you see. A kind one. When you minister to them and they look at you, it is the Blessed Mother they see. That is who we are: reminders of what is to come."

"I never thought of it in that way. Thank you, Lady Prioress. Bless you for that." Cheered, she raised her hoe, but froze, catching sight of something behind me. I turned, and saw it, too, and rested my hoe in the soil.

Cristabell ran toward us. Dame Elizabeth had taken to her bed, and each day we expected that she should go to the Lord. My heart thumped against my chest as Cristabell neared, a look of strange discomfort on her face. Winded, she came to me at last, and I clutched the hoe, awaiting her expected words.

"There is someone at the gate, Madam...*Lady* Giffard."

Lady Giffard? I becrossed myself and dropped the hoe. *What could she want of me?* Everything passed through my mind, from the smallest detail to the greatest scandal. Rolling down my sleeves, I tried to summon a prayer as I made my way from the radiant fields into the cool of the cloister.

When at last I reached the gate, I spied her standing patiently and sedately, striped by the shadows of the bars. She was a small woman in velvet and furs. Her attendant—arrayed almost as fine as she—stood behind her mistress, keeping an ear tuned to any sound that might affect her charge.

The sunlight seemed to shimmer off of the bright folds of her skirts and headdress, while I moved through shadow, dark in my nun's habit.

I reached the gate and stood with iron bars between us. "Peace be with you," I said with a bow. Raising my head, I looked into sky blue eyes, fair lashes, and even fairer hair parted down the middle and framing her forehead under its headdress.

She stared at me, her brow wrinkling. "Are *you* the prioress Isabella Launder?"

I inclined my head. "Yes. I am Isabella Launder, Prioress of Blackladies."

"You?" She looked once at her attendant and shook her head. "There must be some mistake."

"No mistake, Lady Giffard. What may I do for you?"

Another long moment passed while she studied me most insolently from head to foot. "*This* is Isabella Launder?"

I frowned. "I have already told you that, madam. What more may I do?"

"I would speak with you. Is there a place without these bars?"

With unsteady hands I unlocked the gate and pulled it open. "This way, Lady Giffard. May I offer you and your lady some refreshment? The day is hot."

"No, thank you. This will not take long."

With leaden feet, I preceded through the cloister and to the garden where I offered Lady Giffard a seat on a bench. She whispered to her attendant who then wandered to the other side of a hedge, allowing us privacy.

"A most pleasing garden," she said, almost more to herself than to me. "So tranquil. So lush. One would scarce believe such a place was in a convent. So merry and diverting. It is more akin to the gardens of court. Have you ever been to court, Lady Prioress?"

"No, my lady. I have never ventured from Staffordshire."

"No? A pity. You would like the gardens of Greenwich." My throat was dry as Lady Giffard adjusted her voluminous skirts before finally looking up. Her head gently tilted toward me. Her white skin never changed from its alabaster hue to a blush, even as her eyes squared on mine, like a hawk stooping. "So you are the one who so captures my husband's heart."

My own heart jolted, and I clutched my fingers to keep them from shaking. "Did he say so?"

"No. Not in so many words. But a wife can tell." She smiled. "And your own blush tells me more than his sparse words on the matter."

"M-madam," I began, "I am guilty of nothing! We have been friends for half our lives. There is no more than that."

"But a man allowed into a convent? Surely this is unusual."

"Lord Giffard has always been an unusual man and used to his own way."

"Indeed. He is patron of this house."

"As is Sir John."

"Yes. True." She cocked her head at me, her expression similar to Cristabell's many bold appraisals. "You are not what I expected. Quite frankly, I thought you would be young and beautiful."

My cheeks and ears burned. "As you can see, madam, I am neither."

"It is most perplexing. How many nuns reside here, Dame?"

"Four, including myself. It is a small and humble house. Rustic, some would say. And far from private."

"Implying?"

"Implying that nothing could happen as you suspect it might have done. What did you hope to gain from such an interview?"

"Let me be frank, Lady Prioress. I want my husband to know that he is no longer welcomed here. I want him to be told that he has no further congress with you. In short, Dame, I want my husband back."

"You have him, lady."

"No. I never possessed him since the day he discovered you were here. It is because of the capering he does here with you—"

"*Madam!*" I raised my hands to my veil, trying to cover my ears from such condemning words. "We are not lovers, Lady Giffard. Never were we."

"You expect me to believe this? Year after year he comes to this convent to merely *talk* with you? Does your bishop know of this? Does the king?"

I whirled on her, my blood running cold from my face. "The king? Do what you will to me, madam, but do not put him at the mercy of the king!"

"So." She rose, glaring at me with narrowed eyes. "'Do what I will with you?' Yes, Dame. My will is to see that you are punished for your whoring."

I did not will it. I did not expect it. Unwittingly my hand struck out at her, slapping her face. Immediately, I put that guilty hand to my mouth in horror.

Her attendant jerked toward us, but stayed as she was with one subtle gesture from Lady Giffard. Smoothly, Lady Giffard touched her own cheek marked red from my hand, all the while gazing at me with a triumphal smile. "The prioress awakens."

"You…you wrong me, madam, by such a name. I am innocent. I am a maid."

"Nevertheless, the king should hear about his own courtier and how he uses his convents for treachery, abusing his own wife."

I did not hear the gate bell chime, or the heavy bootfalls tromping through the cloister, but we both turned at once upon hearing the masculine voice roar, "*Madam!*"

"Thomas!" we cried as one, but it was to Lady Giffard he marched, taking her roughly by the arm.

"What mischief is this? What evil are you doing here?"

"I came to inspect the object of such wanton desire. I was weary of being left to myself, not treated as a wife."

"Then act like a wife!" Thomas' face reddened with unsavory anger. Never have I seen him such like before. He turned to me, and I shrunk from him. "Did she threaten you? What did she say?" Silent, I shook my head, but he only chuffed a sneering laugh. "Do not protect her! She is not worth it."

"She is your wife, Thomas. She deserves your respect."

"Do you hear that, madam?" He shook Lady Giffard's arm. "Even as abused as she surely was by your razor tongue, she defends you. This is the woman you would destroy."

"She says she is a maid. Is she?"

He choked on his rage, but swallowed it, finally casting her arm aside as if it burned him. "Yes. As chaste a woman as was ever born."

"Is it because you could not summon your flesh with her *either*, husband?"

The tart moue of her mouth might have been charming in another context, with other words. Such words! I feared Thomas would strike her, and I moved to place myself between them.

"Get you home, Dorothy," he said darkly. "Get you home now."

"Yes." She moved away from us, ticking her finger to her attendant. "I will go home. To Caverswall. I leave you to your... *friend.*"

"You will speak to no one of this. Do you hear me? No one. No bishops. No courtiers. And not to the king. For as I live, madam, I will see that you never benefit from such treachery. Is it you want me in prison? Yes, I can see that much vindictiveness in your eyes. But there is much a man can do from gaol with his friends on the outside. You think your life a misery now? See how my wrath changes all. Get you home, madam!"

Icily, Lady Giffard swept us with those chilled eyes, and strutted down the cloister, followed by her frightened attendant, until they both disappeared past the wall.

The moment she was gone I crumpled to my knees. I could not catch my breath, and it was made worse by Thomas' clutching me. I pushed him roughly away, and crawled a distance, until I could gasp enough air to rise. Nauseated, I pressed my arm to my belly. "Do you see what sin is there in your relentlessness?" I whispered. "Do you see at last?"

"I see a vindictive woman who wants nothing more than to hurt—"

"Only as much as she has been hurt! Why are you so blind?"

"If I am blind it is only because of my love for you, Isabella. I care not what the consequences may be."

"Even if she tells the king some half-truths, any of your enemies would be happy to hear about a nun and about you. Your love is strange, Thomas. And most unwelcome. I forbid you to come here again."

"Isabella!"

163

"No! I forbid it! If you come you will be turned away. I will no longer allow it. May God forgive me for delaying so long that which I should have done from the first."

"Isabella. You cannot."

"I can and I will. Now go, Thomas. God…God be with you."

"Isabella. You would tear what is left of my heart from me?"

The heat rose in my throat and my eyes blurred with tears. "Just go, Thomas! For the love of God!"

Unable to look upon his distress, I whirled from him and found myself face to face with Cristabell. She stood stiffly. God knows how long she was standing there.

"God forgive me, Madam," she said, becrossing herself. Her own expression was void of all, except for a deep wound in her eyes. "But it is Dame Elizabeth. She has only just now passed from this world to the next. God have mercy."

THOMAS GIFFARD
GRASS SEASON, 1527
Hunting Lodge in the country

XVIII

"This day is the end of our slavery, the fount of our liberty,
the end of sadness, the beginning of joy."
–Sir Thomas More on the wedding of Henry VIII and
Catherine of Aragon

Snarling and tearing the bracken, the boar darted from the
hedges and lunged toward the dogs, but His Majesty reared up in
the saddle and thrust with his javelin, hitting the boar at the
juncture between head and neck. Down it went, and the hound
masters quickly pulled the dogs from our victim. The others moved
in to jab their own javelins into the king's boar until the beast was
finished. King Henry threw back his head and chortled a war cry
into the drizzling gray sky, his blood no doubt running hot from
the chase and victory. It was good to see him so invigorated, for
there seemed much of late to put him in a melancholy mood.

We returned to the pavilion tents where the boar and other
goodly meats were prepared for the feast to follow. From my place
at the banqueting table, I saluted George Throckmorton from
across the room, and he winked at me. Today, I was seated near
His Majesty, or at least beside the dais whereupon his table lay. As

usual, the revelry went on long into the night, King Henry dancing merrily with the music. Ladies danced with gentlemen, yet their eyes seemed to rove about the room to other secret partners. The queen was not in attendance, having fallen ill, but there were many pretty maids to take the king's mind from his wife's difficulties. There was one with whom he seemed to dance most often, a dark-eyed creature. She was not the prettiest, but she possessed a presence about her not unlike Isabella.

I groaned into my cup and drank more than I should have. All my thoughts cavorted about the person of the Lady Prioress. I languished for her, like some fresh-faced youth. The more it went on, the more foolish I felt, and yet I could not let the possibility go that I might woo her. Though I often wondered if I won her whether I would fall tired of the game. Where would that leave her? Such labyrinthine thoughts! They chased one after the other; a mad hoodman's blind caper catching nothing but air. At six and thirty, I should have possessed enough maturity to relinquish such sport. Instead, I wrote her letters. She, in her wisdom, did not reply. Although a year had passed, she still would not allow me access to Blackladies. Perhaps she thought this would exorcise my passion once and for all, but it only served to rake the coals to flames.

How could she treat me so?

Drunk, the king at last was ready to retire. I rose unsteadily to attend him. Several other courtiers rose as well, including Wolsey's secretary Thomas Cromwell—who was growing more in prominence at court. The king waved them off when he saw me, and leaned his full weight upon my shoulder. "I will take this Thomas with me," he said, scanning his courtiers and all the Thomases who gathered.

He chuckled as we made our way to his pavilion. Once entered, he let himself fall back upon the bed with an exhausted huff.

"Shall I get the grooms, your grace?"

"No, Giffard. You can assist me. First pour some wine."

His face was already red and bloated from too much indulgence, but I nevertheless obeyed and poured the red liquor into a goblet from an ornate flagon. He took the cup and drank. His lips were slick when he set the cup aside. "Do you know why I picked you over all those other Thomases, Giffard?"

I shook my head, feeling the effects of my own overindulgence. "No, your grace."

"Thomas Wolsey, Thomas Cromwell, Thomas More, Thomas Giffard...So many Thomases. Why so popular a name, hmm? Should not all have been named Henry?"

"I know not, your grace. Surely you must ask our sires."

"I tire of the other Thomases. I am berated with their opinions and demands."

"Demands, your grace?" He sat up, and I was able to remove his heavy fur-trimmed gown. I began to unbutton his jerkin.

"Yes, Thomas. Know you not that there are great demands made of a king? As great as I am, even as the Lord Himself anointed me, I am not my own man. Does that surprise you?"

"Indeed, your grace. I know that Parliament speaks for the people—"

"*I* speak for the people!" he shouted, pushing me aside. The king's wrath came easily, and just as easily blew off like a billow of steam from a kettle. Still, I stepped back lest he strike out as he was wont to do, until his face softened and he smiled again, gesturing me to continue to undress him. Cautiously I approached, pulling the bejeweled jerkin away and laying it gently to the side. He scratched his chest as he loosened the slops himself. "I am *Fidei Defensor*, Defender of the Faith, after all," he said more gently. "The pope would not have named me so if he thought I could do less for my people."

He drew silent for a while, and I was able to finish disrobing him and get him into his nightclothes. He drew a gown on over his shift. "Stay awhile, Thomas. I seem to see little of you these days."

"My estates occupy me, your grace."

"Yes. To be king means to be occupied with many things at once. Sometimes I think I would have liked the pleasure of being only the lord of an estate deep in the country. Few cares there, eh Thomas?"

"There are still cares, your grace, though not on the scale which occupies your majesty." He rumbled his reply. I was weary, and hoped he would soon wish to retire so that I could go to my pavilion. Heartsick and exhausted, I feared to injure his humor if I stayed longer. "If you need me no further…"

"Wait, Thomas. You have a blackness about you. What vexes you?"

"Nothing, your grace."

"Nothing? With that sour a countenance? Come." He rose, and spoke in confidential tones, even putting his arm about my shoulders. In his gown and nightshift, he was still a formidable man. He hugged me close. His breath reeked of stale wine. "Thomas. Do not think of me as your sovereign. Think of me as your cousin. Or better yet, your uncle, eh? Surely you can tell your Nuncle Hal your woes."

Oh God… There was no fleeing from this. In truth, I wanted so to talk to someone of my troubles, though I did not imagine it would be the king. These matters were delicate, and I knew it could very well be misinterpreted. Dorothy saw the sense in keeping what she knew to herself, but this night I already spoke incautiously to him. Were he sober, he would not take offense—and certainly never insisted on this confidence. Alas, I needed to unburden myself almost as much as he believed—in his insobriety—that he wanted to help me.

"Sire…it is…a woman."

"Aaah!" He nodded sagely, pumping his head upon his neck. "Thomas, Thomas. Of this sorrow I know well. Women. The glory and the curse of our lives… I take it we are not speaking of your wife?"

"No, your grace."

His features grew serious, and he contemplated the problem with all earnestness. "Does she spurn you? Is that why your shoulders hang so heavily?"

I was not aware that my soul was visible through my very posture, and I sobered immediately. "It is true, your grace. She will not receive me. My only wish is to be in her presence, to talk with her."

"This is a generous love. A gracious love. A love from afar?"

Careful, Thomas! "She...she is a maid, your grace."

"Aaah! I admire you, Thomas. Then we speak not of adultery. Good, good. Such chaste affairs are noble, but most difficult. Most difficult. May I tell you something?"

"Anything, Sire."

"Would it surprise you to hear that your own king, your Nuncle Hal, has such a love?"

I tightened my jaw. Surely this was dangerous for me to hear! Were he not in his cups, he would not say. "Sire, I am unworthy of such confidence—" I tried gallantly to leave the tent, but he would not allow me to go.

"Nonsense! You are a member of our household, Thomas. There was never cause to think ill of you or your kinsmen. You are like a right arm. Should my right arm be unaware of what the rest of the body is doing?"

"I know not, your grace," I said desperately. "Sometimes it is best."

He laughed. "You fear Wolsey? You are in the king's grace. Have no fear of cardinals."

"Your Majesty." I bowed low to show my relief, but my heart knew no such thing!

"Love. If only love were all there was to it. There is more than that. Much more." He eyed me steadily, licking the wine from his lips. Slowly, his mind, like a millwheel in a slow stream, seemed to work as he measured me. He smiled and touched his mouth with a finger. "Perhaps you are right. There are some things to which you may not be privy. You are wise, Thomas. You are cautious, but not deviously so. I have always admired that quality in your father. Now I see the son is as discreet. Very well. No doubt you are anxious to get to your own bed. Hurry you, now."

"Thank you, your grace. God give you rest."

Slipping past the heavy tent curtains, I brushed my hand along my brow to wipe away the sweat, and breathed a sigh of thankfulness. "Almighty God! I thank You for this relief." It was a wise man who stayed close to the shining flame of power, but not too close as to be burned by it.

So the king possessed a love. And so. He had many, and some proved to be fruitful, but I sensed more to this than was healthy to know. The scowls on Wolsey's and Cromwell's faces all week attested to that. Often they met in unholy circles, with that other Thomas, Thomas Cranmer, hovering nearby. It was a strange coven of Thomases, indeed.

With that thought, I moved straightway to my own tent, but slowed when I heard fervent voices low and determined. Four shadows stood near a brazier, four I recognized by form or by their voices. I looked behind and saw back the way I came to the king's chamber. Ahead were the four in conversation. There was nowhere to go.

"The king's convictions lie with Leviticus," said the deep-jowled voice of Wolsey. "Therefore, it is in Leviticus we will trust the king's virtue."

Cromwell spoke next, quoting the scripture to his fellow secretaries Stephen Gardiner and Edward Fox. "'And if a man shall take his brother's wife, it is an unclean thing: he hath uncovered his brother's nakedness; they shall be without sons.'"

"You missay, Cromwell," said Wolsey. "Not *filiis*. *Liberis*. 'Childless', not 'sonless'."

"Your Eminence," he said with a cursory bow. "I have it on the king's authority that he believes the present scripture to be a false translation and that *liberis* should instead read *filiis*. I take the king's word in all accounts."

Wolsey snorted, glancing from one man to the other. He said nothing, but grasped the wide sash about his waist, rocking on his heels.

"Yet I have oft heard that in such cases Deuteronomy supersedes the other," said Gardiner, coughing into his hand as he softly spoke, "coming later in the texts as it does. As the queen was so married to the king's late brother the Prince Arthur, so King Henry, too, married his brother's wife, the former being an unconsummated union. 'If one of them die, and have no child, the wife of the dead shall not marry without unto a stranger: her husband's brother shall go in unto her and take her to him to wife.'"

Wolsey laughed humorlessly. "This, I am told, only applies to Jews."

"Your Eminence!"

Cromwell put out his hand to calm Fox, who said nothing more. "The situation is clear, gentlemen. The king wants his great matter resolved, and quickly. He is impatient for Mistress Boleyn, and he tires of his—that is, his soul grieves that he continues to live in sin with the Princess Dowager of Aragon."

I held my breath. What the king in his discretion could not tell me, I was now hearing in all its treasonous grandeur. At that moment I feared for my life, for should I be discovered, even the king's witness could not now save me. I prayed to be as quiet as a mouse while the cats plotted mere inches away.

"Your Eminence," said Fox in a husky whisper, "do you mean to say that the king desires a divorce?"

"Of course not, Master Fox. The Church would never allow such a thing and shame upon you for uttering such heresy."

"Forgive me, Cardinal..."

"The king would have the question of the invalidity of his marriage resolved to clear his conscience, much as the king's own sister Queen Margaret of Scotland did only two months ago. No, gentlemen. He has entrusted us to make certain. To that end we shall convene a solemn court."

"I do not understand," said Gardiner. "This is Rome's jurisdiction. Bulls need to be prepared."

"We will try it in England. I am the papal legate. His majesty expects his bishops to agree to the invalidity of the marriage. Presently we will call for an *inquisitio ex officio*."

"In secret?" cried Fox.

Wolsey turned to him, and though I could only see his broad silhouette, he seemed to measure the man a long time. Wolsey's perusals had an effect rather like the Gorgon of turning the offender into stone. "It cannot remain so if it is shouted to the rooftops," he cautioned.

"Forgive me, Your Eminence, but the pope will never agree to this subterfuge. An official examination in secret, without—I presume—the queen's knowledge..."

"The king's conscience will not allow him to continue in this sham of a marriage. He believes—as do I—that this is why God does not give him sons. He needs a son. England needs a son. I shall serve my king," said Wolsey.

"As you serve us," added Cromwell to Fox.

They all fell silent, until Wolsey rubbed his hands toward the brazier. Its shadows resembled hellish, flying creatures winging up the tent walls. "At any rate, the pope has troubles now of his own. It is said the Emperor's troops are in the foothills, breathing down Rome's neck. Since he is otherwise occupied, I think he would expect his legate to do the preliminary work."

"I need not tell you, gentlemen," said Cromwell to the assembled, "that secrecy and discretion need be utmost."

Fox and Gardiner agreed with murmurs, nods, and bows to their superiors. Sensing their meeting at an end, I stepped back into the shadows, pressing myself as close as I might to the tent poles. They passed through to the outer tents, and none saw me, praise God.

I breathed again. I could empathize with the king, for I, too, lacked a son as heir, and all the court agreed the king needed a son.

But a sovereign, anointed by God, putting aside his own lawful wife to do so…

It chilled my bones. Cromwell and Wolsey seemed to put forth that the queen was not the king's lawful wife, that some error took place. But she had avowed that her previous marriage to Prince Arthur was never consummated, and the king himself said as much once he wed Queen Catherine, swearing she was a virgin. Was he now to call himself false? Did he think we forgot this bit of news? All knew that the pope at the time of the marriage offered a dispensation to marry to alleviate any controversy, because she had been the wife of his brother.

All the implications spun in whirlpools in my head. If he declared his marriage to her invalid, then Princess Mary would most certainly have to be declared a bastard, for she would be a threat to any future heirs to come from a new marriage, which was to be with that Boleyn woman, the Queen's own lady.

The consequence of my pining for my beloved seemed now to pale against this new intrigue at court. As soon as I could, I would set off for Caverswall. It was imperative I discuss these tidings with Father and plan accordingly. Suddenly, I was glad I was a Giffard.

ISABELLA LAUNDER
SUMMER, 1531
Blackladies

XIX

Lo, the hand of the Lord is not too short to save,
nor his ear too dull to hear.

–Isaiah 59:1

We spent much time of late in the Divine Office, praying for the soul of England. So much had happened at court in the last few years, that we worried over all the tidings. We begged news from the bishop when he came, but his anxious scowl only vexed us more.

It was never spoken aloud, but I could tell it in the eyes of my sisters that they wished for Thomas Giffard to come again and tell us honestly what was transpiring, for we were like a boat adrift at sea with no view of land and no oars to propel us.

It was three years since I cast eyes upon Thomas Giffard, and I knew I was the better for it. Each month he sent me letters. I should not have opened any of them, but each time they arrived, I laid them upon my desk, looking at their waxen seal, until finding the courage to tear them open. I devoured his careful script, his discreetly chosen words. I longed to keep them, but knew the foolishness of such a thing, and cast them into the fire instead.

Many months had now passed since I received a missive from him. Perhaps he had given up at last.

Despite the terrible talk of divorce at court, we in our little world of Blackladies persisted on our course. Dame Alice became a very industrious nun and my right arm, while Cristabell remained indifferent to my ministering, though I was gratified that she continued to stay with us. Many times I feared I would awaken and she would be gone, but always there she was.

I still grieved at the passing—three years ago now—of that wise and eloquent nun Dame Elizabeth. A year passed before we acquired her replacement from Farewell Priory, a suppressed convent whose scattered flock found themselves all over England. Dame Felicia Bagshawe came to us with a strong will and ideas she'd grown accustomed to in a larger house. At first she was appalled at our poverty, at sharing a bed with another, at our diet, but to this, too, she became—after a fashion—accustomed.

"Lackaday, Lady Prioress!" trumpeted Dame Felicia, as she was wont to do with her strident and powerful voice. It seemed inappropriate to the small size of the chapel, but she was nevertheless compelled by her nature to be at all times at the top of her voice. "We suffocate under our ignorance! We should write to the bishop to discover the truth of what is transpiring at court, so that our prayers may better suit the circumstances." She screwed her tiny and nearly transparent brows into her gray eyes, wrinkling her long, straight nose.

"Is it necessary to know all when we only ask that God's will be done?" offered Dame Alice.

"I have found," Dame Felicia said, "that often we must encourage the Almighty in the direction of His most powerful will, else His will might put us in worse stead."

"Then that, too, is His will," said Alice.

"Sisters," I reminded softly. "We are in chapel. This is not Parliament where we quibble about this law or that. We are supposed to be in prayer for our good queen. We should pray for her continued strength to endure, to persevere against all the odds.

Whatever is to become of her should Cranmer and Cromwell prevail against her?"

"'Nan Bullen the mischievous whore,'" quoth Felicia, though I was shocked by her blunt speech in such a place. "That is what they are saying in the village. They are also saying she will be queen."

Alice shook her head, her veil shuddering. "How can this be? The queen *is* the king's lawful wife. How can he say otherwise when he knows right well? Does he not fear the wrath of God?"

Felicia drew herself up. "He deposes those who stand in his way, even if they represent the Church. Look at Wolsey. Deposed, imprisoned, under sentence of death for treason, and now dead before he could meet the headsman. And what was he accused of: *praemunire*. Simply by exercising his authority given to him by the pope, he stood under the king's judgment. Though now he will get his just judgment, to be sure."

"By that logic," said Alice, "any papal envoy may be charged with questioning the king's authority."

"Sisters!" I rose, leveling my glare at all of them, even the silent Cristabell. "We are in *chapel!* I pray you, work on the Divine Office, for in this we do for the world. These matters at court do not affect us. We will continue our work here and do what we have always done. Now, sisters, let us to it."

They silenced at last, and we completed our prayers in proper order, but when off to our business about the convent, I heard them pick up their conversation where it left off. Only Cristabell was unnaturally silent as she walked with me to the fields.

"You say nothing," I said to her.

She merely blinked and looked back once over her shoulder to the other two busily talking. "These matters do not concern us."

"Even so. We must pray for their speedy and just resolution."

"Do you think our prayers will do any good?"

"Well, if no good than no harm." I chuckled, until I realized her earnestness. "Why, Cristabell, of course our prayers do good. If they did not, then what is the point of our being here at all?"

"But how do you know?"

"I know by my faith. How do we know God exists?" I pursed my lips into a small smile at her scandalized reaction. "We know it by our faith. Did not our Lord give the very same to the apostles before He ascended into Heaven? He could have stayed with us in the flesh, but He chose instead to be with us in our faith. How does a child know that his mother will not drop him? He has learned to have faith."

"Many of us were 'dropped', as you say, by our parents, Dame. The faith of which you speak is harder come by for some of us."

"Surely you have faith in God, Cristabell."

She shook her head and whispered, "I know not."

"But I see it in you, in your work, in your sincerity."

She eyed me sidelong. "How can you be so certain of what is in my mind when I am not?"

"We know the tree by its fruit, Cristabell. Though it is true that occasionally we have received sour apples from you, most of them have proved quite sweet."

I felt her stare at me a long time before she unexpectedly raised a hand to her mouth to hide a smile. She took an extra moment to compose herself. "Your faith is greater than mine. Perhaps it always has been."

"Yet you stay when I thought you might not."

She turned a surprised expression on me. "Did you think I would leave?"

"You told me as much many years ago."

She shook her head with a rueful smile. "Why, Lady Prioress. It appears, after all has been said, *you* have little faith in your own good works. For you yourself convinced me to stay."

"How did I do that?"

Cristabell stopped and she threw her head back with a laugh. "Your honesty, Dame. Your brutal honesty. If you could stay at Blackladies in all its poverty and distemper, even when the eminent Lord Giffard offered you much more than this, then so could I."

She measured me. "I also know," she said quietly, "that you would sooner die than denounce me for all that I did... For all that I might have done. I know you have never told a soul. What I do not understand, is why."

I gazed at her like a mother hen. "I knew the good in you, Cristabell. You have learned to love this life despite your feelings. Despite anything I could have told you."

"That is true. I do not know how you knew this, but I am grateful for it." She bowed to me with a solemnity she generally reserved for the crucifix or the bishop, and then she walked away to her duties.

I stood looking after Cristabell and thought of our bold Felicia and tame Alice. Such a colony of unlike temperaments! It put me in a mood, and I could think of no better course but to return to the chapel to pray.

Raising my eyes to the rood in its golden light, I knelt and becrossed myself. "You have been generous to us, Lord. We have suffered little, have wanted for little. Even those who have crossed our path seem to have been the better for it. Even our Cristabell." I nodded, eyes closed in acknowledgment of something greater than I, before resting my eyes again upon the familiar wooden *corpus*. "But I do worry over the sake of our good queen, that she should suffer so when she has been so loyal to You." It made me shiver, that sudden thought, that loyalty could be so rewarded. It was said that Queen Catherine became a professed sister of the third order of St. Francis, even wearing a habit under her gown, though it was not known for certain if this were true. She was nothing but a gracious lady and generous queen. If she, in her piety and loyalty should suffer so, than what was our lot?

Father William told us that we are servants of God, and throughout the history of the Church, it was God's most loving servants who suffered the greatest: all the apostles, St. Paul, St. Catherine, and so many other martyrs. He said it kindly to me, and kindly did I take it, but after a time, it was not so much a compliment. If only true servants suffer in order to come into the glory of God, then perhaps we have not served the Lord as we should, for our lot was neither great nor suffering. Poverty is not so much if there is enough to eat with shelter above our heads, even if that shelter leaks from the rain.

For not the first time, I contemplated the nails piercing our Lord's precious body on the crucifix. He, too, suffered for our many and continuous sins. "Your greatest servant, Lord," I whispered to God the Father. Why should we enjoy such prosperity while others suffered? I thought selfishly of myself, and dismissed it. This was not true suffering. Though Thomas still plagued my thoughts at odd times, it was a foolish obsession, as foolish as his was now for me. Or did he outgrow his childishness? It pleased me to think he might have done, but almost with the same breath, I found myself unhappy. The prospect that he could finally devote himself to his wife should gladden my heart. But I, in my utter pride, still wanted a keepsake of him, a portion of his love to prove that it was possible. I was the same Isabella outwardly, tall, slim, plain if not plainer by the etching of fine lines across my forehead and at the edge of my mouth. But I was somehow made finer by the fact of Thomas' love.

"How you sin, Isabella," I admonished myself before the witness of the crucifix. "How you sin with dishonesty. Can you never be washed clean of it? Will I die with this upon my conscience and my soul?"

"Surely *you* do not sin, Isabella."

I whirled, appalled. "Thomas!"

THOMAS GIFFARD
SUMMER, 1531
Blackladies

XX

Oh thrice and four times happy those who plant cabbages!
—François Rabelais, 1548

I saw her kneeling when I entered the chapel. Though the shadows were smoky by means of snuffling wicks, and the light from the windows was dim from clouds, I knew it was her, for there was no other nun as tall nor as rigid as Isabella. She was praying aloud, and with her words, I experienced an intimacy with her that I had no right to feel. After all, she was not speaking to me, and would not have said as much had she known I was there. But when she spoke of sin, I could not—seeing her as I did, as I always did in my dreams with perfect graciousness—imagine her capable of sin!

"Surely *you* do not sin, Isabella," I said aloud.

Plainly, I had startled her. She leapt up and stared at Thomas the Ghost, for she had not seen me in the flesh for some years now.

"Thomas!"

"Forgive me, Lady. I did not mean to frighten you so. As you see, I have crossed your forbidden threshold again. In truth, it was a miracle." I strolled forward, narrowing the gap between us.

"'Today,' I told myself, 'I will go to Blackladies, and I will beg to be let in. I will humble myself with sackcloth and ashes, and the doors will open.' And so. 'Twas true. Without the ashes or sackcloth."

"How?"

"Cristabell was at the gate. She said nothing to me, asked nothing of me, and opened the portal. Did *you* tell her?"

"No," she said, turning away. "But I think…it was her way of telling *me*." She smiled secretly and turned, measuring me with those hazel eyes. "But since you are here at last, I welcome you back. It *is* good to see you. Enough time has passed, I think. You have been sorely missed here, Thomas. The others often ask about you."

I chuckled at her blush. "The 'others'? Shame on you, Prioress, for sinning with a lie."

Her blush turned to a furious crimson. "It is *not* a lie! They *have* asked after you… Well, Dame Alice, at any rate. Cristabell is, well…"

"Cristabell is Cristabell." We shared a laugh, and I warmed to see her smile. The years fell away, and it was as if we never parted. She appeared no different, except for perhaps a harder complexion. "I have so missed you," I whispered, ducking my head so as not to frighten her with my emotion.

She did not shy from me, but she did walk a few paces to put the font between us. "Please, Thomas. Now that you are here… There has been so much transpiring at court, and so little trustworthy news reaches us. Will you tell me? We must know."

"This…is not what I have come for, Isabella," I said softly.

"Please, Thomas…"

I ran my hand along the font's rim. Its coldness awakened me to its solid nature, its permanence. Court matters did occupy me, as they did all the nobles, but with her I wanted to think of court no more. "Very well. If ill-rumor you heard, then all I can tell you is that it is all true. The king desires to put aside his queen and marry that Boleyn woman. He wants sons, and to that end he convinced himself—with the help of that carp Cromwell—that he is not, nor has he ever been, lawfully wed to Queen Catherine."

"But how can such a thing even be entertained?"

"My dear, he is the king. He will not be naysaid when his mind is made up on the matter. He will have his whore and his sons."

"Thomas…" She lifted her head to the crucifix behind her, and I absently becrossed myself in contrition for my infelicitous words.

"Even the king's own confessor as well as Thomas More cannot seem to intercede," I said.

"But as chancellor, cannot More appeal to Parliament to vouchsafe for the marriage?"

"These are complicated matters, Isabella. It is more than Parliament can undertake, or even wishes to. It is more a matter for the Church."

"The pope, then. Will he not intercede?"

"The pope." I eased against a pillar, toying with the laces of my dark blue doublet. I made the effort to keep disdain from my voice. "How can I explain this to you so that you will understand? It is not so much that the king's conscience is injured—though it may well be treason for me to utter so to the contrary." I glanced behind reflexively, searching for any prying shadows. "The king fancies he is in love, and he does so because he needs an heir, and what more pleasant way to beget one than within the disguising of courtly love? The politics of an heir is seen as an English matter, not for Rome, not for the Emperor, not even for Parliament, and no longer for the good queen, who is well past her prime. It is a matter between Henry and his realm. It is power, Isabella. Can you see that? The pope, too, is a prince, and he, too, must invoke his own power, or fear to lose it. Such a chess game is played, Isabella! Oh, you are blessed to be a woman, and free from such disguisings!"

Pushing away from the pillar, I walked slowly down the nave and stood at the foot of the crucifix, looking up at its crude carving. "For his part, the pope abhors what is being done in England in the name of conscience, but I fear more than that. Isabella, you know I am no friend to religion. I think this game of cloisters is oft too self-serving." Her brow changed, and she opened her mouth to speak, when I raised a hand and bowed to her. "Present company excluded, Lady Prioress. I have always scorned the Church's politics and its heavy hand in enforcing it. But, I am a true believer and dearly love the sacraments, for I know they were instituted by Christ for His Church on earth, and that this same Church we call Catholic is the very same to whom Jesus gave unto Peter, and all the popes who followed—be they villain or saint."

"It cheers my heart to hear you confess it—no matter how mischievous. You do not know how much!"

Her face glowed with honest euphoria, and it gave me pause. "Does it?" Her smile unsettled me, and I frowned. "Then be warned, Isabella. This selfsame Church, which I grudgingly admit I love and in which you have put much store, is under siege."

"What? Thomas, truly your histrionics are getting the better of you."

"Listen to me!" I grabbed her arms and shook her. "It is not histrionics! There is too much to explain. You know not what I know, what I have seen, what I have heard. I cannot see into the future, but I like not what I see now."

She asked no more. Indeed, I could tell her no more. She only nodded, eyes blinking. Gazing at her thus, my collar grew too tight, and I released her to loosen it. I stepped back, nervous for the first time in her presence. I eased my palm over my sword hilt. "And so. As I said, I have other matters to discuss with you." She pushed back her distress behind a radiant smile. How lovely she looked, veiled and virginal. Lovely in her own way. As of old, my heart fluttered.

"Isabella," I whispered. "My tidings…well." My gaze wandered up into the rafters of the little chapel, following the sway of cobwebs and the play of light and shadow. When I lowered my eyes, they fell upon Isabella's sedate, gray irises, their dark flecks as enthralling as the glints in an opal. "Six months ago, Dorothy...my wife...fell ill. A long illness. To each of us such things must happen. At the end of it, God chose to take her."

"Oh, Thomas!" Her instinct propelled her toward me, and she laid her long fingers upon my arm. I looked down at their reddened joints and tapered nails.

"Yes. I grieved for her. It took some years, but we did become comfortable together, despite our differences. Afterwards...well, it was a lonely time."

"May God have mercy on her soul."

"Amen." I becrossed myself and moved away from the rood again, kicking softly at the tiled floor. "So. For six months, you see, I have been a widower, perplexed at my next move. My fellows urged me to remarry. It has been some fifteen years since I was free to do so."

"Free at last from your father's choice? Yes, Thomas. I suppose there is no sin in that reckoning."

"Yes. Free. To marry whom I choose. Isabella..." I took up her hand, pressing it between my own before bringing her fingers to my lips. Gazing into her hazel eyes, I rested that precious hand at last to my breast. "I am a very wealthy man, heir also to my father's estates. I have no more need for alliances and dowries. All that is past. Today is a different day. Isabella, at long last...I am free to choose *you*."

Her eyes, so kind, so gentle before, all at once sprung wide. "What?"

"Isabella, my heart, my beloved. I am free. There is no more impediment. I told you I would find a way without sin. Marry me! Be my wife. Be Lady Giffard. Imagine it, Isabella. *Lady Giffard!*"

Before she could speak, I dragged her forward and grasped her body against mine. I lowered my mouth over her dainty lips before they could open to object. I wanted to press my case to her first, to convince by these deeds of love before she could deride me with words. Where did words get us before? Now was the time for passionate deeds, for wooing, for kissing.

To hold her! To touch her thus! I was afire! My flesh awakened, and I crushed her closer, kissing her mouth deeply, tasting her lips' sweetness. I breathed my passion upon her open mouth. "Isabella. My love." I kissed them again, those swollen lips, savoring so intimate a touch. I kissed her cheeks, her eyes, her forehead—but I was confounded by that damned wimple, and with both hands I pushed it back, running my fingers through her hair—

"Isabella, your hair!"

Her face was opened in horror, her wet mouth askew and trembling. But it was her hair from which I could not tear my eyes. Her long hair had been bluntly sheared, right up to the bottom of her ears: her maiden's sacrifice to Christ. Unprepared for the sight of it, I stumbled back, aghast.

Like a soldier who lost a limb in battle, she grasped clumsily for the lost wimple and veil behind her back, trying to retrieve the missing. Distressed at the sight, I knelt myself to reclaim it for her. She affixed the wimple unsteadily, but held tightly to the veil, her long fingers white with fear.

Her face contorted. It was the face of maidens ravished after battles. It was the torn and sundered witness of the weakest and most vulnerable. I recognized it from my youth in France, from my carousing days. Never did it accost me as it had at this moment.

May God forgive me. I did not realize how selfish, how boorish I was in my arrogant assumptions. There might still be the kind of love I desired behind those frightened eyes, but more likely I would find horror at my actions. I prayed she would not be revolted, that she would not banish me again as I was for all those years for this same conceit.

All at once, I fell to my knees before her and wept like a child, for the lost years, for the lost hope, for the Thomas Giffard that could never be again, and the Isabella I refused to recognize. "Forgive me, Isabella. Forgive me!"

For so long, she said nothing, at last wiping a tear from her stoic face. "I forgive you, Thomas. Please. Arise."

I shook my head. Too miserable was I. "We are tied together, you and I," I said feebly, choking on my tears. "Some invisible binding hangs between us. In my foolishness, I could not help but feel we were divined for one another."

"Thomas," she sighed, managing a forced laugh before kneeling to pick me up. "*Divined?* That, I do not know. Perhaps not as spouses, eh? Thomas." Her brow creased again in consternation. "How I would have welcomed those words fifteen years ago! But how much has happened since. This is my life now. I had hoped you would have realized it."

"You are truly happy?"

"You ask it with such disdainful disbelief! That one *could* be happy behind cloister walls in this habit. Is that such a foreign notion? That one's life could be happily directed toward God alone?"

"You know my mind on cloisters. It is bad enough you reject me twice, but for this place!"

"Yes, I do." She looked down at the veil in her hands. Mended, patched, she treated it more like samite than the rag it was. No, I could not understand her sentiments. I could not see her giving up so much to stay in such a place, giving up that for which I knew she longed.

"If you love me still," I said—such a young man's voice from such an old man, "then will you consider it? We can go to the bishop…"

"No, Thomas." The kindness that glowed in her features shut down, replaced by that of the stern prioress. "You must stop this foolishness. I have been wed to Christ for fifteen years. *I* cannot be widowed. I have made my vows, and I have every intention of living out my days in this convent. Is that clear enough at last, Lord Giffard?"

It was the final turn of the bodkin in my gut, the *coup de gras*, bleeding my heart dry of every ounce of blood, every pulse. Dead. I felt as much. "So much I wanted to do for you, to make up for all the years. So much I wanted to give you…"

"Your friendship!" she cried, clutching my arms again. "Your friendship has always been my heart's lightness, my sunshine! Be my friend, Thomas. Put the other thoughts to rest. Marry again, by all means. You should not be alone. You *should* marry. But just…not me."

I breathed, but could taste no breath of flower, though their fragrance had been heavy in the air only moments ago. The ether was stale as if it were closeted. I could smell nothing, taste nothing, not even the vestiges of our kiss.

I wiped my tears away with my sleeve. "With your permission, may I return again to see you?"

"With all my heart, Thomas, do I give it."

"Then…fare you well, Lady Prioress. I cannot stay today. My heart is too heavy."

"I am so sorry, Thomas. But someday you will see the wisdom of it. Look at me." She spread out her skirts. Her wimple was torn from my vigor, and it smoothed down and hid what was left of the hair on her head, making her resemble a bald man. The veil hung from her hands. A pitiful spectacle. "How could *I* ever be Lady Giffard?"

I raised my hand to wipe away the memory, and with it my shame. "There is no need. It is our planning, Dame. When you are night, I am day. When you would sleep, I awaken. We are not so much mismatched as mistimed." I tried to smile, knowing not if I succeeded. "I will be back. God keep you."

"And you, Thomas."

I left her. I would not return for months, and by then I was wed again.

ISABELLA LAUNDER
OCTOBER, 1534
Blackladies

XXI

The less prudent the prince, the more his deeds oppress.
—Proverbs 28:16

When I received the missive—so long ago now—that Thomas Giffard of Caverswall Castle and Stretton, was wed to Ursula Throckmorton, I studied that writing with great interest. He married her three months after asking me. Apparently she was the sister of his close friend, and by all opinion, they were well matched. It must be so, for his much longed-for son and heir, John, was born to him two years later, followed by another son Edward. The Giffard dynasty was assured, and I said many prayers for them, lit many candles, for which the Giffards paid. I looked at those candles even now, their black smoke rising in ribboning wisps, their beeswax scent so much more genteel in the chapel's space than that of the tallow tapers, whose heft and substance burned with an earthy breath throughout the cloister.

Layered candle smoke darkened the rafters of the chapel. For years, candles burned and smudged the dark beams to a darker hue. How years can change a room, and matters of all kinds.

Change has been the hallmark of all our days, for the king's "Great Matter" became that of the realm's, insinuating itself even into the Church. He succeeded in divorcing the queen when all the clergy of the world voiced against it…but did nothing. He called his own daughter a bastard, and declared himself the Supreme Head of the Church and Clergy of England, though Parliament at least feared for their own souls and refused to ratify such a heretical title. The pope excommunicated King Henry for so long as he refused to take back Queen Catherine as his lawful wife. Still he refused, and married Anne Boleyn anyway. And then His Majesty ordered the submission of all the clergy in England to him, and Thomas More resigned his office of chancellor the very next day.

We sisters of Blackladies shuddered to hear that Thomas Cranmer—the king's priest and councilor—was made Archbishop of Canterbury, the primate of all England's clergy. It came as no surprise when Cranmer pronounced King Henry's marriage to Queen Catherine invalid. One could only imagine how the pope fumed at this, but an act of Parliament closed the doors forever on Rome by declaring England an empire, and therefore not obliged to comply with the Holy See's questions in marital affairs.

It was a roaring tempest of events, whorling in a terrifying frenzy. We kept the doors shut tight to Blackladies, hoping the storm would pass us by, listening with frightened hearts to all the faint rumblings in the distance. The storm was far away. In London. In Canterbury. In Rome. We feared it might reach us.

And just as we thought a glimmer of sun peered through the clouds, darkness converged again. The king's wife—for I could not in good conscience call her queen—bore not the longed-for son, but a daughter, the Princess Elizabeth.

The tempest brooded on.

Thomas was naturally busy at court. I prayed for him. These were difficult times. Though not a man for church matters, I knew he was a man of conscience and a great admirer of Thomas More. I wondered how Thomas fared, and I worried his opinions would undo him. Yet he was older now, surely more mature in his dealings at court, and not prone to foolishness. He was becoming a great man in Staffordshire, with sons. There was no need to worry over him Yet I did. I worried that we did not see him, and I worried what that might mean.

"Prioress?"

Father William peered at me in the gloom. We were short of candles again, which did nothing to help his failing eyesight. The years paid their respects to him, and he was an old man, hard of hearing, near-sighted, and used a cane now to get about.

Rising, I straightened my gown. "Yes, Father. It is Dame Isabella."

"Child, why do you stay so long in the dark?"

"I have become used to it." I took his arm, allowing him to lean upon me. "Will you bide in the chapel?"

"No, Dame. Take me to your splendid garden. In the chapel I see only poverty, but your garden, even in autumn, it has a regal splendor about it."

I shook my head at his words, but escorted him out of the shade of the passage and into the sunny cloister garden. The roses had given up the last of their blooms a month before, and they now stood prickly and empty, pruned down to their skeletal remains. Some of the hedges would remain green even under a frosting of snow, but the flowers were all spent, all gone to seed, to sleep until another spring. The naked trees opened to the sky offering a meager portion of sun. Looking up, I felt the sun's warmth on my chapped cheeks. I prayed it would be a mild winter, but our faithful horse had already grown a long coat, prophesying a cold season ahead.

Father William eased onto a bench and sighed, stretching his neck over his ruffled collar. "How long have you been prioress now, Isabella?" he asked quietly.

I ticked off the years in my head. "Thirteen years, Father."

Nodding, his ermine hair softly swayed. "I have been a priest for over fifty years. Fifty years. I have seen two prioresses here at Blackladies. I am feeling old, Madam. My bones creak and barely uphold me." He raised his chin and watched two finches chase one another in the topmost branches of the empty beech tree, complaining to one another about the scarcity of berries.

I studied Father William's sunken cheek, the glitter still evident in his yellowed eyes, the dry lips puckered slightly with age lines. I knew much about my nuns, working and living side by side as we did. I knew of their lives and their families. But in this quiet and pensive moment, I realized I did not know much about the man beside me, who consecrated the Body and Blood of Christ for us each day, who listened with a gentle heart to our confessions year after year. He was Father William to us, growing greyer and more stooped as the years tolled. I never thought of him as a man, as a son, as a child once. Strange how we image a person who seems more role than reality.

"I am not a philosopher," he said, still eyeing the birds at their quibbling. "Nor am I much of a theologian." He leaned back and flopped his hands up and then down in a gesture of bafflement. "I am only a convent priest. And I love my God." He turned and rested those mature eyes upon me. "Never before in all these years as a simple priest did I fear. But now, Isabella, I do."

"Fear what, Father William?"

"Satan walks the earth, child. He walks the verdant paths of England. And he would destroy us. Already he has seized the Germans in their own land by the mouth of Martin Luther."

"I have heard ill of him. But I must admit, I do not understand what he preaches, or why it is so dangerous."

"The foundations of the Church go very deep," he said patting my hand with his own spotted fingers. "They go to the very feet of the rock of Peter, our first pope. By the grace of God, the Church has held the wisdom of the apostles handed down to them by Christ Himself. Wild-eyed priests, renegades like Martin Luther, think they know what is best for the Church. They seek to rise against her, question her after all her years and all she has gained."

"Yet, I have heard that he seeks to reform. Surely there is need of it. Am I in error in this?"

"He defies the sacraments. He picks and chooses that which conforms to his philosophy, and there are so many willing to follow any wax philosopher that they cleave to him, forsaking their place in Heaven for whimsy today. But that is only the skin on the custard, Isabella. I remember when the pope called King Henry the Defender of the Faith for upholding the Catholic Church against her enemies by refuting this same Luther in a much-treasured book of the king's own devising, *Assertio Septem Sacramentorum*. I have that book, Dame, penned by the king's own hand. But now…"

"Now what? What more could there be?"

"There is more. I have heard from the bishop, from other priests. The king's commissioners will come to exact oaths."

"Oaths? We make our oaths to the Church. What oaths does he need that we have not already made to the bishop?"

"The bishop has no authority in this. That, too, has been taken by the king."

"The pope—"

"The Bishop of Rome, Dame. Remember that. Since he excommunicated His Majesty, he is the 'Bishop of Rome' only. The king no longer recognizes what he calls papist titles." His fingers rested on his cassock-covered thighs, and he drew them back and forth over the woolens, leaving gray streaks on the worn black cloth. "Corruption there is. I am not that sheltered a priest, nor am I a fool. Some men take their vows very lightly—not like you, Madam. Yes, there are terrible things. Terrible misuse of funds. Though these events are in the minority they are an obvious minority. Englishmen have needed little excuse, I fear, for finding a way to cut the ties of Rome. But dammit!" His hand came down sharply on his leg, but it was his curse that startled me more. "Our Blessed Lord chose Peter, a fallible man, to be our pope. He told him to 'feed My sheep.' He chose Peter to show us that humility is our teacher, for even those chosen among us to lead have their foibles. Priests, bishops, archbishops. They are men, prone to men's sins."

"I hear that some have stood for the Church, even against the king."

"How much longer do you think they will be able to do so?"

There was no answer, only to watch my own breath rise in griseous clouds. "What are these oaths?" I asked slowly.

"I know not. I am still unsure of all of it. I wish Thomas Giffard would make an appearance. He will tell us true what there is to know."

We never spoke openly of Thomas Giffard, and though in confession I acknowledged my feelings, Father William kept to his seal of the confessional. But I knew he respected Thomas as a patron, and I also knew that Father William kept good watch of me when Thomas was nigh, not as a gaoler, but as a father would.

"I only hope he is well," he said quietly.

For a moment I could not speak. "Why do you say that?"

"Because he has a reputation for making his pleasure openly known at court, and, as you know, that could be dangerous."

"I, too, pray he is well," I said softly.

"I have written to the bishop," he said. "I pray that he can give us counsel. I know not what to expect. I am too old a man to contend with this."

"Yes, Father. You should have peace in these years."

He patted my hand. "Isabella, I have great admiration for you. You have done Blackladies proud. Now you must take even greater steps. Talk to your sisters. Warn them."

"Of what?"

"Of what I told you. Warn them that a storm is brewing and that they must prepare."

I stared at him awaiting further explanation, but I knew by the shift in his eyes and the tremble of his lip that there would be none.

I clutched at my rosary and rose even as the bells called me to prayer. Mechanically, my legs carried me hence, and I succumbed to the resonance of recited prayer, though I confess, I heard little of it.

When the prayers were over and we all returned to the hall, my gaze swept them, from the fawn-like movements of Dame Alice, to the assured but careful strokes of the spoon into the porridger from Dame Cristabell, to Dame Felicia's ardent gnawing of her bread.

"My sisters," I pronounced aloud, unaccustomed to the sound of any other voice at meals except that of a reader.

Three pairs of eyes scrutinized me, chewing halted, spoons held high, dripping with golden droplets. "My sisters," I said again, resting my hands upon the cloth-covered table. My hand smoothed over the diligent repairs, over the rough stitches from our dear departed Dame Elizabeth, *requiescat in pace*. "For many years now, we have made our prayers for Queen Catherine, and always for England and its people. As the Lord wills, we have endured the troubles in our kingdom. The bishop of Rome, indeed, seems very far away. We who serve God cannot communicate so easily with his Holiness in times of trouble."

"What trouble, Madam, do you speak of?" asked Felicia.

Her eyes were clear. She always held her head high, a posture for which I was unaccustomed, feeling myself already too tall for those about me. "The trouble, Dame Felicia, is the king's commissioners. Very soon, I understand, they are to make a visit."

Scandalized, Cristabell broke her accustomed silence. "Will they come here?"

"I am assured of this by Father William. They are under the king's auspices and we are obliged to admit them. We are obliged to admit all travelers, at any rate, in compliance with the rule of St. Benet, hospitality being utmost."

"The king?" cried Felicia. "I see Cromwell's hand in this!"

"Dame, I do not know the politics. But I know they will come."

"What do they want?" asked Alice timidly.

A sigh welled up in me. "There are oaths to be taken. I understand not what those are."

"When should we expect them?" asked Alice.

"I know not. Soon, perhaps."

Cristabell raised her head. "What oaths would the king want? Is this not the bishop's responsibility to exact oaths of us?"

"Yes. But the bishop...it seems... Oh, sisters. Father William intimated that the bishop has little to say on the matter. It is, instead, a matter for the king."

Such silent, wondering eyes they turned to me. I knew their thoughts. Had we not endured enough? Instructed to say special prayers for Queen Anne when we knew she was not the king's lawful wife, we nevertheless bowed our heads and obeyed, because the king is our sovereign and because our bishop told us we must. We obeyed when we were told that the pope must no longer be called so. That he is the Bishop of Rome, as if he were only the head of a country parish. And we were told this, too, by the king's word, and we obeyed, because he is our king. And now he would send his commissioners to exact oaths, the nature of which we knew not.

But again we would obey. We must. I trusted in God and His mercy and I prayed the king's men were sent for a Godly purpose.

THOMAS GIFFARD
NOVEMBER, 1534
Stretton, Staffordshire

XXII

*"...as touching the oath, the causes for which I refused it,
no man wotteth what they be, for they be secret in mine
own conscience..."*

–Thomas More, 1534

We took residence in our home in Stretton not too long ago.
The estates were well kept and Ursula favored them, as did I. It was
only two miles from Brewood.

I stood looking out the window, each fluid diamond pane
revealing a November-wet view through its modulating surface.

Ursula swept down the stairs, eyeing me as she was wont to
do with those stern, dark eyes. She was tall and her features were
much like Isabella's only sculpted with a more genteel hand. I
would say that Ursula was more beautiful than Isabella, and
different in other ways as well.

She moved to stand beside me, easily slipping her arm in mine
with the familiarity of intimately shared years. I did not mind, and I
even turned to press a kiss upon the cheek she obligingly angled
toward me. With child again, Ursula was never weakened by her
pregnancies, but seemed revitalized. Her face glowed with health
and her hair even seemed thicker, its dark tresses heavy, like the

mane of a horse. She was not the shrew dear Dorothy had become in that earlier marriage. Ursula was instead a good and faithful wife, one who knew her place in my society and who fostered contentment at home.

Contentment was a much-needed commodity now, for court was becoming a battleground. On the one side were those who remained faithful to the Church of Rome, and on the other, those who would follow the king's minions even into Hell. I spoke no treason, I made no man my enemy. But I saw that even loyal men were being imprisoned for their thoughts, even as Buckingham had been executed all those years ago for harboring private thoughts of treason.

From the window I could see the distant road, its amber ribbon breaking over the slope of green hills. There was a long string of people traveling along it, and I knew they were pilgrims setting off to see the relics in a nearby monastery.

Ursula clutched my arm before pulling me away from the window. "You spend much time at this view, husband. What of court? You have not been there in many weeks, almost a month. Will you not be missed? Does not the king require you?"

I patted her hand before I disengaged from her. "I am not missed by the king, for he has many ushers and grooms to attend to him, men who do not have papist sympathies."

She glanced toward the door, a habit we of a sudden cultivated, fearful of our own servants. There was not a nobleman who did not take that backward glance when deciding to fervidly speak his mind. "Yet you took the oath. As did we all."

"To save our lives, my dear. But I do not like this secular meddling in divine affairs. It has the off taste of meat left too long in the sun."

"Why do you gaze out the window?"

"I am looking at nothing," I confessed. "Except today. Pilgrims."

"They go to the abbey to revere the relics. They do not think they will be there tomorrow."

"I have never seen this many pilgrims along the road. Even during plague times."

"These are plague times," she said quietly. She moved to the casement, touching the glass delicately with her long fingers, the white ruffles of her sleeve falling past her wrist. "You have never been a religious man, Thomas. Why is it so important to you now?"

I chuckled and moved to stand behind her, wrapping my arms affectionately about her enlarging waist. "Age, Ursula. I am getting old. And when a man gets old he begins to think about greater things than himself."

"Your soul, Thomas? I thought you encased it for safekeeping long ago in a chest, for seldom did you take it out to amuse yourself with it."

"I take my soul very seriously, indeed," I said, my voice muffled by her headdress' veil. "And...my honor."

If a man could not speak his mind—nay, even think in his mind a private thought—then there was little honor to be gained by being at court. With Ursula heavy with a babe, I was excused. But I did fear, though I said nothing to Ursula. In the past, I dueled, I fought in battles, I looked honorable death in the face, but now I feared. I feared men like Cromwell, the likes of which were not fit to wipe the dung from my shoes. That I—a Giffard—should fear his like! *Take Breath and Pull Strong?* It would take more than a steady hand and a long bow to do the work in this realm that needed the doing.

My hand reached to my doublet and fondled that pendant that lay beneath it. I took to wearing a crucifix. I felt, in these times, I needed it close to my skin.

"Perhaps you, too, should go to the abbey," she said, picking up her sewing from where she left it on the casement. "Ease your soul on the veneration of a martyr's bones."

"Most likely they are the bones of a rabbit." I smoothed my doublet over the cross, thinking of relics and of waste. "I know too many places encasing wax blood and pig's skin for saint's flesh."

"Oh. You do not like this trafficking in saint's wares? You sound very like Cromwell and his ilk."

"Foolish, greedy men take coin from the innocent and naïve for one look at these relics. A bishop will tell you it does no harm to the people, but I say it wrongs them terribly."

"Do you not believe in relics, Thomas?"

"I believe in few of them."

"There is the old saw that if you took every piece of the true cross encased in reliquaries it would build an army of crosses."

"So it is said."

"And yet I myself have seen a splinter of the cross..." Her voice changed, softened, and I turned to look at her. "I was very moved by it. I shall never forget it, in fact. I prayed when I saw it, Thomas. I prayed with a fervency I have seldom possessed. I gave myself to God, dedicated my works to Him, however feeble they may be, through the sight of that single object. If it were not the cross of our Lord, it might as well have been."

I bent toward her, touching her cheek with the tips of my fingers. "A sobering statement," I said softly. "Full of all my own arguments." Straightening, I happened to glance to the window again, and noted a rider kicking up mud along the path, scattering the pilgrims as he rode. Soon it was apparent that he was wont for our gates. I thought I recognized the sodden colors, but he was soon hidden behind the hedges and trees. My pulse hammered at what this visitation might mean, for surely this was a rider from court.

We were told George Throckmorton arrived and we received him at once.

"Dear George!" cried Ursula, rushing to greet him. She kissed her brother upon the cheek, and he stretched his arms to look at her.

"So it is true. You are with child again." He smiled up at me. "Did I not say this would be a good match?"

I nodded. "And I am ever grateful for your prodding on the subject," I answered. He continued to smile at his sister until his thoughts intruded on his features, which were spattered with mud from his ride.

"My manners," I said, gesturing to a servant to bring wine and a bowl for him to wash himself. I tried to make light of weighty matters, for I sensed this was no social call. "George, please sit. Groom yourself, if you will."

He first washed his face and dried it quickly with the towel before gratefully accepting the wine. Sitting back, he appeared agitated as the servant hovered.

"Joseph," I said to the servant, "you may withdraw. Leave the jug."

George watched Joseph depart and spoke only when the door was firmly shut and an interval passed between the last click and the faint footsteps of Joseph's egression. "I have news, Thomas," he said sitting forward. He cupped the goblet's bowl between his hands, fingers curled and anxious. "Cromwell is sending his commissioners to the abbeys, forcing the religious to take the oath of succession."

"What nonsense is this, George? Is he insane?"

"Husband!" Ursula clutched my arm, but I ignored her. Let the damned servants hear me! Let them know what their king is doing.

"It is already happening. Most are taking the oath, but those who have refused…"

"What, George?" she asked. "Who have refused?"

"Monks. Priests. They are being burned for treason."

Ursula put a pale hand to her mouth and leaned against the wall. "Monks and priests?" she whispered. "What harm are they to the kingdom?"

George turned to look at her, his long, red-gold beard almost a part of his jerkin's breast. "Anyone who does not swear to the invalidity of the king's marriage with Queen Catherine—I mean, the Princess Dowager—must be made an example of. Even be they monks and priests, for they are becoming the most dangerous of all to King Henry. Any who are under the auspices of the pope—" He closed his eyes in frustration. "I mean the bishop of Rome—are His Majesty's greatest foes. It is this influence the king fears. If priests bark from the pulpit about adultery and blasphemy, he cannot stand against it."

"Then why do not more of them do so, George?"

"Because, my dear sister, they are being imprisoned for so doing, and then executed. It is a stony path to follow, opposing the king to side with the bishop of Rome."

I scowled. To hear, in my own home, that a brother-in-law of mine must correct himself on matters provoking the king's anxiety... "The pope," I said boldly, "found for Queen Catherine in her suit. Little good it does her now. And little good the king's hurried marriage to that Bullen woman did him when she produced another girl."

George took a quick gulp of his wine while staring at me with his olive eyes. "It is all a tailless cat chasing its tail. Thomas More himself was imprisoned because of it," he said to Ursula, "because he would not take the oath and would not say why."

I slapped my thigh. "A man's conscience again! Can a man not follow God's law without fear of prison or worse?"

"The king is the supreme head of the church in England. If he wants an oath he will get his oath."

"Even from poor clerics," I rasped.

"Especially from poor clerics."

"Even from nuns," Ursula said softly.

I stared at her. I did not realize it until she said it, but they, too, were in danger. Involuntarily, my lips mouthed, "Isabella."

I heard George's voice vaguely through my clouded thoughts. "I tell you, Thomas, I do not know my own countrymen any longer. And where court was once merry, it reeks of fear and discontent. Brave men cower when Cromwell walks the halls. They fear him. Faith! I admit I fear him, too! What's to be done?"

"What is there to do?" I muttered behind my hand. I smoothed down my mustache and worried at my beard.

"There is talk…"

"Speak not of treasonous talk, George. Not in my house. Would you widow your sister?"

"I am loyal to the king. But I am not loyal to his minions who teach him heresy."

"Cromwell."

"Yes."

I shook my head. "He has too many spies. No. I can be patient. Like Wolsey, he will hang himself by missteps and vanity."

"Can we wait that long?"

"It may not be all that long."

"But these oaths—"

"—must be taken." Yet even so, I imagined Isabella in all her boldness standing up to these men and leading her sisters to certain doom.

A servant arrived with a tray of meats and dried fruit, and George ate gratefully while Ursula ministered to him. I stood again at the window, listening to their talk with half an ear. My mind was on monasteries and just how quickly I could get myself to Blackladies.

It was not long until George obliged me by retiring for an afternoon rest. Ursula watched me steadily as I called for my horse to be readied.

"Where do you go, husband?"

"Brewood. I have business there."

Ursula moved closer and measured me. "Thomas, I have never asked you. I have respected and honored you as my husband and my lord. But today—especially today when so much is in turmoil—I must risk your wrath. I have wondered these many years what it is that so intrigues you in Brewood."

I stiffened. I was no adulterer, though it was true that I sinned in my heart for another. "I have told you before. My father and I are patrons to Blackladies. It is only a small priory, and very poor."

"Priory." She strode away from the window, and as gracefully as her girth would allow, sat upon a chair. The gown draped about her like furling crests of waves. It engulfed her being with their deep, raven reflections. She clutched her sewing in the white fist of one hand, its needle dangling from a crimson thread. "I have heard the rumors, but I was loath to believe them; that you spent your time at the priory…because of the prioress."

My gaze grew steady upon her. "Yes, madam. It is true. We were childhood friends, you see. She was the daughter of a yeoman farmer near our lands."

She settled back, a matronly smile on her face. "I see. You go to warn them, then. Go, Thomas. Do warn them." Here her smile dispersed. "Save them, if you can."

My heart grew within me, and I knelt to her, taking her hand and pressing a lover's kiss upon it. She could never know how grateful I was for her confidence and her concern. I also knew then, that I was unworthy of such a wife.

I left Stretton at breakneck speed without thinking further of so estimable a wife…God forgive me. I thought only of nuns, of one in particular. Horse and rider clattered over the roads until the church spire of Brewood appeared above the black nettles of naked trees. I skirted the town and tore along the Ladies Brook to the outer walls of Blackladies, its stone and timber not as impenetrable as the nuns would think. There are so many chinks in a stone wall, after all, so many places where a foundation can be worn away without the owner's knowledge, that a sudden storm could loosen it, toppling the whole affair.

I trotted along the vine-draped wall, its ivy browned from an early frost. Absently I rubbed the stallion's velvety black neck, his piquant odor rising as his muscles rippled. We came to a low spot along the wall and I gazed outward to Blackladies' fields. The barley and wheat in all but one field was harvested down to stubble. Goats moved along the sloping fields, nibbling their share of the crop. The last of the wheat in a far field was golden, running up the slopes in blurred amber like a fire rushing a hill. Rooks bedeviled the seed heads and, like the rooks, the nuns in their black habits walked the fields along with the fieldworkers, waving distractedly at the vandalizing birds. Some of the servants brandished scythes and smote the stalks as if sending the Devil himself back to Hell.

There she was, standing near the center of the empty field, a black tower of a creature among the milling gray bodies of muddy goats. The sun wore on the landscape today, gilding the brown-leafed thickets, but the air was still cold.

Another nun—I could not tell which—stood at the far end of the field with an older man, a crook in his hand. Three motley goatherds.

I spurred the stallion and he cleared the wall before we soberly galloped up to her. She noticed my arrival in a spatter of straw-speckled mud. Her astonishment would have been charming if there had been time to consider it. But there was no time. I slid unsteadily from my horse, tossing the reins behind me.

"I need to speak with you. Now."

She did not question me as I took her by the arm. I could not even excuse myself for roughly handling her, but neither could we stay within view of the others, for they had noticed my inauspicious arrival. Instead, I led her back through the fields to the gate, and under its hiding shade. I stopped and glared at her, yet still she waited for whatever dread thing I wished to announce. If I could only trust her to be obedient, I would have nothing to fear. But I knew her superiors would not instruct her in this.

"It is important I talk with you about this, Isabella. Very soon, the king's commissioners will come and make you swear an oath."

"I know, Thomas. Though I know not the nature of this oath. What is it exactly? I knew you would know." Her face was white, drained of even the faint blue veins that oft smudged her lids. A sprig of straw clung to her veil, waving gently with each of my desperate breaths.

"Earlier this month, Parliament passed the Act of Succession. In it are several points. Point one, that the heirs of the king and Queen Anne are lawful. Two, that the marriage between His Majesty and the Princess Dowager—"

"Queen Catherine!"

"The Princess Dowager! You must now call her that. That the marriage between His Majesty and the Princess Dowager was never valid and that the issue from that marriage is a bastard."

"Oh Thomas! How can I?"

"There is more. Three, that any foreign authority, prince or potentate, may not exercise any authority over those subjects in this realm." I let the last stew in her, watching for understanding to bud upon her face. When it did at last, I clutched her arms, silencing her protests. "You must take this oath, Isabella. There can be no nonsense about it."

"I certainly will not! You are asking me to swear that I shall no longer be obedient to the pope—"

"The bishop of Rome," I corrected.

"That I shall no longer be obedient to the *pope!*" she sneered. "And that the poor Princess Mary is to be called a bastard by the very same subjects who lauded her as heir to the throne!"

"That is precisely what I am telling you to do."

"I will write to the bishop at once. He can counsel us. He can speak to the king..."

I released her and moved to lean against the arch. The stone warmed in the burnishing sun, invoking an earthy aroma of clay and of meadows long dead. My gaze fell to the trees edging the borders of Blackladies, to its surrounding low sloping hills meandering toward the sleepy village, a village innocent of courtly ways, of such schemes plodding inescapably closer.

"Do you not smell that in the wind, Isabella? It is the stench of unprincipled men and clerics, the offal of Englishmen drinking from the cup of Luther."

"But, Thomas. I do not understand."

"Do you think the king will stop with this? He no longer fears the pope. Why should he? He is the anointed of God. Defender of the Faith...and now supreme head of the Church in England. King Hal is now our pope and he is looking long and hard at these monasteries and at the monks and nuns within them. If Hal is the pope, why do you then swear your loyalty to a distant monarch? If he is to have his religion as he desires it, you need be *his* servants. Smell the wind, Isabella, and see which way it blows. It blows away from the direction of Rome."

"Even so. I cannot say this oath."

My Isabella, strong and determined. Yes, she could have run the Giffard estates without suffering any mischief. She could have governed with an iron hand but been beloved by all beneath her, for she possessed the talent of winning hearts to her reasoning. But now was not the time for such vainglory. Now was the time for submission. Christ's blood! How I wish she was my wife and bound to obedience to me! "You must. It is treason to disobey."

"But an oath must be taken in conscience. We can choose not to take it."

"Like Thomas More? He languishes in prison even now for refusing to say such an oath, or for saying why he refused. Even his lawyer's clever mind could not find the way to save himself. This is no game, Isabella. Do you know what it is to die a traitor's death? Do you? A nobleman is allowed decapitation, though his head is mounted on a pike so that the ravens may peck out the traitor's eyes and then his traitorous tongue—"

She held her hand up, her cheek even paler. "Stop…"

"But not for you, Isabella. It would be fire for you. Burning hot like the flames of Hell, to purge you, your skin peeling off, sizzling up like a pig's!"

"Stop, Thomas!"

"Or hanged, struggling, choking on knotted rope, your bowels emptying on the scaffold. Is that what you want?"

"Oh God, help us!" she cried, crumpling to the ground.

My heart seized within me, and I, too, fell, grasping and rocking her, laying my head against hers.

"Hush, sweeting, hush. I will never let them take you. Never."

She wept. I held her a long time, relishing her weight against me, inhaling the scent of meadow clinging to her worn wool gown.

At last I used all my courage to release her, helping her to her feet. But I could not resist wiping her tears away with my fingers.

She lifted her head. Her eyes were reddened but just as bold as before. "You said so yourself. Thomas More would not take the oath."

"Dammit, woman! You are not Thomas More! You are just a woman, and no one will rise up at your death... No one except me."

Her hazel eyes searched mine. "Have you taken the oath?"

I nodded briskly, shame spotting my cheeks. "Yes. I did. I spoke it loud."

"Why, Thomas? How?"

"Because I am loyal to the king, and I believe this madness will pass. But while it rides this wave, those of us loyal to the true Church must survive. If we are all gone, who will restore it when this time is done?"

"But the king's heirs. When the king's wife delivers up another child, surely that child will be raised in heresy."

"It may be so...but there is the Princess Mary."

"But you yourself have said that she was declared a bastard."

"Other bastards were considered for the throne before this one. And much can happen between now and that time."

"It is madness, Thomas."

"It is all madness." Standing before her with a softened expression, I gently lifted her chin with a finger. "That is why clear heads must remain on their shoulders. The king likes the Giffards," I assured, and let her chin go. "As you show by example, so, too, shall I by mine. The Catholic Church *is* the Church, and His Majesty shall know it by my actions. Were I in prison, it would mean nothing to him."

"Thomas, I am frightened."

"Do not fear. God is with us." We fell silent, listening to the breeze rustle through the fields, and goats braying softly on the wind. "I will teach you the oath. You must find a way to swear it."

She shook her stubborn head again. "I cannot. How can I be God's servant and deny that which I know is true?"

"Then lie."

"Thomas!"

"Lie, Isabella. All of your sisters must lie for their own sakes. They will execute you if you do not."

"I cannot deny my faith."

"Then we will find a way to satisfy both. In your heart, you can reason a solution to all they ask you."

She raised her head, eyes shadowed under her veil. "When I stand before God, how shall I answer Him? Shall I save my life only to lose it?"

"Promise me, Isabella. Swear on the cross you will take the oath."

"Thomas! No!"

I dug into my doublet, ripping buttons from their threads. I pulled forth the silver crucifix and plunged it into her dirty hands. I closed my hand painfully over hers. "Swear, Isabella! Swear!"

Desperately she tried wrenching her hand free. She grimaced at my harsh strength, even as I surely impressed the figure of Christ into the flesh of her palm. Futilely she struggled, until my vigor wearied her and she surrendered with a weakened, "I...I...swear, Thomas. I...promise." Satisfied, I released her, pulling the cross from the imprisonment of her hand. "Why did you do that?" she accused. I cringed under the assault of those eyes, burning with rancor.

"I will not let you die, you stubborn woman. There are better ways to fight them than martyrdom."

"I am weak," she lamented, her whole body sagging. "I could have refused you."

"They need you. Your nuns. You. Do not desert them. Guide them."

"How?"

"I will show you. Will you trust me?"

Her tender words rose gently from her whitened lips. "With my life."

"And always," I said as tenderly, "my heart is likewise in your hands."

ISABELLA LAUNDER
NOVEMBER, 1534
Blackladies, Brewood

XXIII

I will speak openly your decrees without fear even before kings.
—Psalm 119:46

Vespers was done, and I should have risen to lead my sisters to the hall and to a well-earned supper, but I could not make my legs move. Thomas had left soon after he made a disgrace of me, and I went to the chapel to pray until the office, to ask forgiveness for succumbing to his insistent pleas.

Were it any other man, would I have succumbed so easily?

The sisters were patient and did not stir. I sat, merely looking at their feet from across the narrow aisle. Frayed shoes, frayed hems, frayed women. The four of us, so small amid the larger world. What harm could we do with our aging faces and scratchy voices? Who were we, but women, nuns? We were so small and so poor a house that we needed monthly stipends from the Giffards to put enough food upon our tables. How often did we go to bed with bellies growling in order to feed our dear servants, whose features showed their weariness but whose voices were silent on it?

Men went into battle to die for the king. Who would battle for our like?

The time passed, and still I did not rise. They shuffled, stifling a cough behind a hand in case I was asleep and needed a gentle reminder. But I raised my head to show I was fully awake before breaking the silence of the chapel and of the sanctity of our office. "My sisters. I cannot lead you to your supper. Not yet. Not when my heart is so heavy."

Their solemn faces, like brushstrokes of white upon the swath of black that was their veils, awaited my explanation. And what was I to say to them? Was I to say, "Come sisters, it is time to toss away your vows. You must lay your hand upon the precious word of God…and lie"?

"Thomas Giffard was here today," I announced unnecessarily. "He brought very grave tidings. Soon, the king's commissioners will come to exact the oath of succession from each of us."

"What is this oath?" asked Alice. "Did he tell you?"

"Yes. I wrote it down." From within my scapular, I brought forth the wrinkled page. I unfolded it and smoothed it out upon my lap. "It is in four parts. With our hand upon a Bible, they will ask us each in turn." I squinted at the page in the dim candlelight. "'Do you acknowledge our gracious sovereign as supreme head on earth of the Church in England?'"

I glanced up from the paper to study their faces. Cristabell's was stony, while Alice twisted her lower lip between her teeth. Felicia raised a brow, but listened attentively. I cleared my throat and began again. "'Do you allow the bishop of Rome, or any of his servants, to have any authority over you?'"

This time, Dame Felicia's scoffing irritation rumbled up from her throat, but I read on. "'Do you acknowledge the legality of our sovereign's marriage to Queen Anne?'"

"Ha!"

I looked up for only a moment to acknowledge Dame Felicia's brief commentary. She remained silent, her eyes fixed upon me.

"'Do you acknowledge the annulment of our sovereign's former union with the Lady Catherine…and the illegitimacy of its issue?'"

For a moment longer, I stared at my own scrawl on that hurried document before lowering it. "Sisters," I said, crushing the paper in my curled fingers. "This is the oath we will be asked to swear."

Cristabell threw back her head and noisily huffed her annoyance into the musty air. "How can we swear this oath?"

I could not look at her, so fearful was I that she could turn my course. But I had promised Thomas on the body of our precious Lord…

"If you do not swear it, it shall be considered treason and Lord Giffard assured me that you will hang or burn. He said that others have already done so." I folded my hands in my lap. "I will not order any one of you to swear it or not."

"What of the bishop?" asked Cristabell. "Will he not stop this?"

"The bishop can do nothing."

Alice raised trembling fingers to her cheeks, searching from face to face. "If the bishop has no power…then what if it is true? Perhaps we have been in error…"

"Do not be a fool, Alice," rasped Cristabell. She made a careless gesture with her hand in the air. No doubt she would rather have slapped Alice.

Felicia, thoughtful in her silence, offered at last, "I think we should make a decision and all abide by it."

"Stand together?" I asked, hopefully.

"Yes," she answered with a firm nod. "Or die together."

"I do not want to die!" cried Alice jumping to her feet.

"Hush, Alice." I moved to her and engulfed her in my arms, much as Thomas did for me. "None of us wants to die before our time. But to die for our faith…that is another matter."

Cristabell stared at me with her small, determined eyes, eyes that before had always glared at me with suspicion, but now looked with ill-deserved confidence. "What should we do, Prioress?"

Courage fading, I shook my head. "I know not. If the king—surely anointed by God—decides on this course, then who are we to dispute it?"

"The king is not the head of the Church," snorted Cristabell. "The pope is the head of the Church."

"The bishop of Rome, Cristabell. Say no other title." I stared thoughtfully a long moment at the crumpled paper betwixt my fingers. "Though let us consider," I said slowly, thoughtfully. "The king rules all in this land. It is he who chooses his archbishops and gives land to monasteries. He was so called the defender of the faith at one time."

"He is a heretic," Cristabell said.

"If we cannot agree…"

Felicia sat forward. "What will *you* do, Prioress?"

"I…I have made a promise that I will swear the oath." I lowered my face, crushing my lip so hard with my teeth that I tasted the flavor of steely blood on my tongue. "I know not whether God wishes me to die for this or to take up the quiet struggle in humility and modesty."

"How do you mean?"

I positioned myself forward, and without realizing it, the others did so, too, listening deeply to my conspiratorial tones. "If we took the oath, we would live and remain reminders of that power which is greater even than kings. We would be living proof of God's Church on earth through the passion of Christ. To see us, would be to envision Rome."

"I will abide by your say so, Prioress." I glanced at Cristabell, so sober, so confident. Too few years ago she would have happily seen me burn.

"S'trooth!" cried Felicia in her full-breathed gasp. "I will take this oath, and any other to keep the king's men off our backs!"

"Dame," I said, attempting to quiet her ardor. "Do you take your oaths so lightly? Men have died in consequence of keeping their conscience."

"If a choice is offered, Lady Prioress, I would keep my head, for a poor trophy it would be to the king. As for me, I will take the oath…if it be your will that we do so."

I looked to the others and they, too, nodded in agreement. I took courage from them, though my fists knotted tightly to the point of aching. "Then this is what we will do. The oath is the fiery furnace of Daniel, and we will walk through it unscathed. It is not that we must agree to that which we swear, but merely abide by it. We will swear to our king our loyalty, for indeed, as good English nuns, we do belong as subjects to him."

"I hope Cromwell himself comes," boomed Dame Felicia. "I will have an oath to give him!"

I chuckled with frightened giddiness. "Would that we all possessed Dame Felicia's courage!"

"Courage, Madam? I am scared half out of my wits! But I do not fear with you as our general."

"God is our general," I kindly corrected.

"Then you are His lieutenant. I can march proudly behind so appointed a soldier."

An unlikely soldier, I thought. But now the only one they had.

THOMAS GIFFARD
JULY, 1535
Hampton Court

XXIV

"There can be no better way to beat the King's authority into the heads of the rude people of the North than to show them that the King intends reformation and correction of religion…"
–Thomas Cromwell, 1535-6

With lips straight as a line and shut as tightly as a castle's keep, I watched my fellow courtier's comport on the dancing floor. Velvet gowns trimmed in fox fur and ermine spun with each turn, each step. Bejeweled hands grasped other bejeweled hands, their gold and precious stones glittering under flickering fireglow. The air smelled of ginger and mace, late of the cakes and dainties consumed and left in crumbling debris on the long tables in the banqueting hall. We feasted, did England's nobles…even as Thomas More's head moldered on a pike on London Bridge.

"You do not dance today, Lord Giffard?"

The voice startled me and I hoped he did not notice, but there was very little that escaped our vicar general and chancellor Thomas Cromwell. When I turned, there was a slight glimmer in his squinted eyes, while a tortured smile lifted one corner of his mouth. The man who prosecuted the late Thomas More. No, he missed nothing. "I took a fall from my horse last week, my lord, and I find my leg still aches me."

"Then sit, my lord. Sit, and we shall spend our lonely time in conversation."

He beckoned me to a chair, and though I was loath to sit with him, in truth, my leg did ache and I longed to rest it. I sat beside him and took the wine cup he offered me.

"Now this is better, is it not? I do not myself cavort in dances. His Majesty outshines us all, at any rate."

"Indeed," I answered, lifting my cup in salute to the king.

Cromwell held his cup but he did not drink from it. Either this was his way to keep his head clear while others quaffed and loosened their tongues…or he feared it might be poisoned. I drank nonetheless. The room was hot, my leg ached me, and I felt tired of running from that which was inevitable. I was pleased, though, that as I drank, I found the wine to be excellent, without the taint from any vicious liquor.

"You have been at court all your life, have you not, Lord Giffard?"

My gaze steadied on his. He was a commoner, and there were many who made it plain to him that he would always be so in their eyes—though this was done before he rose out of Wolsey's shadow and grew to be both the king's lap dog and advisor. I wondered, as I looked into those empty eyes, if I ever treated him ill. It was too late now, at any rate. "Yes, my lord. The Giffards have always been at the English court, to the best of my knowledge."

"I do not dispute it. A fine house is the house of Giffard. A strong line. With sons?" he queried, an eyebrow disappearing under the dark cap he was fond of wearing.

"Yes, my lord. Two sons at the moment. And a beautiful daughter."

"Ah, a family. Looking to you to teach them what is right, to love their king and their God."

"Not necessarily in that order."

"Ho! You jest with me, Lord Thomas. May I call you so? It seems I have known you a long time, but seldom have we conversed."

"No, my lord. To my regret."

"To your regret." He laughed, raising his cup, yet still he did not drink from it. "You need not use such fawning language with me, Lord Thomas," he said quietly. "I know I am not liked at court. A commoner who rose in the ranks and who now holds offices even above...say, you...for instance."

Eyeing the "s" chain of the office of chancellor lying across his chest, I nodded in acknowledgment, all the while trying to keep my face and my tone neutral. I tipped my cup again. The wine had a sour aftertaste. "Then why so anxious to talk with a nobody such as myself?"

He laughed again, and for a horrific moment, I thought he might slap me on the back like fellows in a tavern. I was relieved when he did not. "You are not a 'nobody', Lord Thomas. You are a man with many holdings, as is your father. A man who keeps significant holdings in this realm can hardly be termed a nobody." He snorted and turned again to the dancers, who at last bowed to one another when the music came to an end in its last strains. But a new song was taken up, and His Majesty called for another dance with Queen Ann, who had worn a sour countenance all evening.

"The queen dances tonight," he said casually, but I was on my guard, aware Cromwell never made a casual utterance.

"Should she not? She and the king always enjoyed such jovial dancing."

"It is said she is with child again. If I were she, I would take to my bed. But I suppose she fears the king will still dance...with another."

Impatient, I set the goblet down. "My lord—"

"You took the oath, did you not?"

I swallowed a raw lump, wishing the goblet were full again. Cromwell sensed my discomfort, for it was, after all, by his design, and he picked up the jug to pour me more. His brow rose again, though his squinted pig-eyes grew no larger.

"You know I did, my lord," I said. "Else I would not be sitting here beside you now."

"You are a great patron, nonetheless, of abbeys and such religious houses."

"Is it unlawful to donate to poor houses that do the work of God?"

"But so many do not do the work of God, as you call it. So many abuse what is given them. Ah!" He interrupted himself to welcome another man who made his way through the throng, a man who looked to be as common as Cromwell but decked himself as if he were the noblest of gentlemen. Though if gentleman he were, it was a recent provision. "Lord Thomas, have you met my secretary Thomas Legh?"

He looked familiar to me, as all of Cromwell's cronies somehow did, with their obsequious demeanors and overzealousness in dress. Legh bowed and sat beside me without a by-your-leave. "We have met, my Lord Cromwell," he said more to me than to him, though I could not remember such an encounter. He was small and corpulent, the fur on his gown's collar so thick it reached to his ears. Several gold chains hung over his gown and each of his fingers sported at least two rings. "We met some years ago, and you brushed me off as a dog brushes off a flea."

For the first time I smiled. "Surely not, Mr. Legh."

"He smiles," said Legh, good-naturedly…or mendaciously. It was difficult to tell when he wore his smiles as broad as he wore his gowns. "Perhaps he recollects."

"No, I do not recollect, but I must abide by your word that it was so. My apologies. My thoughts must have been otherwise occupied."

"'Tis true. You did not seem to be half listening to me. At that time, it was also true that I was only a secretary in the late Wolsey's employ, and now, as you see, I am a king's commissioner."

My gaze slid from one man to the other. Merciful God. What had they to do with me? Did not Cromwell just ask if I took the oath? God have mercy.

"But what was I saying?" said Cromwell unnecessarily. "Oh yes. We were speaking of oaths and of abbeys. And patronage."

"There are so many abuses by these clerics," said Legh, shaking his head. "If you knew the lasciviousness, the greed I have encountered, Lord Giffard, you would surely withdraw any and all patronage of these despicable houses."

"I have no doubt that such abuses occur," I said levelly, "for abuses transpire in all institutions. Greed, for instance, is apt to snare a man who has the best intentions. Even...a king's commissioner."

For a moment, Legh merely glared at me, his dark eyes sketching me in his mind. Then, he burst into ignoble laughter, catching the attention of those standing nearby.

Cromwell chuckled. "You are a man of wit, Lord Thomas. I wonder...are you a deeply religious man?"

"That depends. A man can be deeply religious sometimes only when he needs it the most. When he is in peril, for instance."

"Do you think you are in peril?" he asked in a quiet, unctuous voice. He enjoyed his role too much for my taste. I could not help but cringe in mild disgust.

"Am I?"

He laughed again, and Legh joined him. "My lord, you listen too much to wagging tongues at court. I am a harmless man, a simple man, from simple beginnings. As you see, I find my comfort in humble clothes and modest means."

"Are *you* a religious man, Lord Cromwell?" I could not help but ask.

His smile was fixed. "I am God's humble servant and also that of the king."

"I see you put it in proper order, Lord Chancellor." I rose. "And now...if you will excuse me."

"But my Lord Thomas, I am not done speaking with you."

I dreaded stopping, but he grabbed me by the sleeve. "Was there something you wanted, then?"

He put his hand to his chest and spoke to me with his head somewhat bowed from long practice with talking to the king. "I only ask about religion, Lord Thomas, because it is heavy on the king's mind, he being the Supreme Head of the Church in England."

"Yes, my lord." I said nothing more than was sufficient. It was becoming increasingly difficult to remain civil to him. Perhaps that was his design all along.

"His worry has been with the monasteries and with the display of relics for profit."

"Are those his words?"

Cromwell sucked his teeth for a moment. "Not his words precisely, my lord. But the gist of it was this: that he is most interested in discovering which monasteries are guilty of these grave offenses and to…clean them out."

I raised my voice. I did not wish to be supposed conspiring with the likes of Cromwell. "Clean them out? Ruination, my lord?"

Cromwell moved closer and spoke in lower tones. "Not ruination. Reformation. To rectify abuses and create uniformity of religion. He has appointed me to gather commissioners to examine the monasteries. My men have already begun their tasks."

"And so? What is it you want of me?"

"I would appoint you a commissioner, Lord Giffard. You would go to the monasteries within your demesnes and take inventory of their goods and property, and give a proper accounting to the king."

"Why does the king need an accounting of their goods and property?"

"To root out abuses, of course. Abbots have been known to sell off small parcels of the abbey lands for gain, I am afraid, Lord Thomas. And such commerce there is in relics! It would shame you to know."

"I see." I could little argue with what he said, for I, too, knew such abuses to be true, but I wondered what deeper thing was intended by these visits. The king wanted an accounting, eh? I dared not postulate what that implied.

"I thank you for your kind consideration of me, Lord Cromwell. Your confidence in my house is not without merit. But I must decline your commission, for I have many duties to attend to on my lands and at court."

Cromwell did not look surprised, but instead feigned his disappointment. "As I suspected, my lord, you are a busy man. And the king favors you and your kin. It is good to stay in the king's favor."

"That, my lord, I have always striven to do. It is good advice. I do not take it lightly." I bowed, and exited as swiftly as I could.

I met Ursula some time later at the other end of the hall. We watched as the king danced with one of the queen's ladies, one of the Seymour.

"My dear," I said to her quietly. "I was approached— cornered, I should say—by Cromwell. He had the gall to ask me to be one of his commissioners to inventory the abbeys in my demesnes."

"What did you say to him?"

"In all politeness, I refused."

She clutched my hand. Hers were pale. "Perhaps you should not have done that, husband."

"I will not be under Cromwell's thumb," I hissed. "Mark me. He, too, will fall, just like Wolsey. Though by Christ's blood, I did not ever think I would miss the days when Wolsey darkened the halls. For at least he loved the Church and would have preserved it. Ursula, I felt such dread when Cromwell spoke of the Church. He is a man with no love of clerics. I do not understand why the king tolerates his like."

"His Grace goes through clerics like a man consumes a meal," she said, shaking her head. "When he has his fill, he discards the course to start on another. But now it is the monasteries themselves. Have not all the religious taken the oath?"

We leaned our heads together for to speak as quietly as we could. "Those that did still live. Yet clerics are not half the problem. It is all very well and good to become one's own Church, to disinherit your daughter and heir, and to get you another wife before the first is dead, but the rest of Europe does not have to abide by it."

"You speak of the Princess Elizabeth."

"I do. Yesterday the king's advisors discussed using her betrothal to secure certain treaties, but the French ambassador already intimated to me and others that she is no bargaining tool for this realm. Not when the rest of the crowned heads consider *her* the bastard."

"Keep your voice low, husband."

"It is the truth."

"Just men have died for the truth before this. Witness Thomas More."

"I sicken when I think of that. I sicken to think that my king, the man I have respected and served... It must be the likes of Cromwell to turn his head. He is behind this venture into the monasteries and it holds nothing good. I do not like this turn at all, Ursula."

"You will want to return home to warn them at Blackladies, will you not?"

I did not look at her. How much did she truly suspect? How much did she know? "Yes, I will."

"Then let's away as soon as we might."

We departed the next day and arrived at Stretton with somber postures. All the while I was thinking of Isabella and what could be done, but as soon as I crossed the threshold of Stretton, I made straight for our private chapel.

Alone, I walked in under the solemn arch, glancing at the flame in the sanctuary light that signified God's presence in the tabernacle. I stood a long moment before the small altar, examining the golden crucifix, before I was compelled to kneel. My gaze fell upon the cross, its intricate carvings flickering in amber radiance from the candle flames. In that moment, I was suddenly fearful. Fearful of all that was and would not be again. Why did I lift no finger to stop it all? Is a man's earthly life so precious that he would do anything to keep it?

And then I thought of Thomas More, and my eyes burned.

I brooded over the crucifix a long time. No man would dare question my honor, and those who tried, fell to the point of my sword. But where was the honor in this? How was a man to be a man, serve his God, and serve his king, if he must put a lock on his conscience?

Before long my mind fell again upon Isabella and her decaying convent. No love had I for convents, especially Blackladies that kept her prisoner. But—God help me—it was the life she chose when no choices there were, and I was grateful for such a harbor for her.

What scheme was the king planning now that he needed accountings from such destitute places?

"Will you go, husband?"

Ursula's slim silhouette slashed the bright light of the doorway. If I squinted, if I looked at her at just the correct angle, she could almost be Isabella; tall, thin, a face worn from years and worries, of troubles far from her control.

I told her I would go, and moved to stride past her. Softly, her voice whispered in the sacred gloom, only a whisper. "Is it... Do you...love her?"

There was no anger in my heart, and none upon my face when I turned toward her. "Do you truly wish to know?"

Her composure vanished. Color bloomed in her cheek and her eyes lowered, blinking. "No. I find...I suddenly do not." Her eyes rose again, seizing mine fiercely, possessively.

Was it possible to love two women? I pressed my hand to hers with the impossibility of expression, before I left quickly for Blackladies.

ISABELLA LAUNDER
WINTER, 1535
Blackladies

XXV

...malicious and lying witnesses have risen against me.
                                                    –Psalm 27:12

When Thomas warned us all those months ago, I expected the commissioners to come over the hill at any moment. When they did not come, I contented myself that the commission was over, having found nothing amiss. But when the appointed commissioners did come at last, local men—Sir John Talbot, Walter Wrottesley, John Grosvenour… and Sir John Giffard—they took inventory of the entire household, including that in the cheeseloft and brewhouse. Embarrassed by our poverty and our piety, they soon went away again, apologies upon their lips and coins of offering left in the almsbox. I thought that was that, but foolish was I. For this simple inventory was not all there was to it. More commissioners were to come, men who were not local nor concerned for the monasteries in their midst. These were commissioners from court, and I was troubled by what they might want.

"No good at all," said Father William as he watched the three of us—Dame Felicia, Cristabell and I—prepare the evening repast.

Felicia chopped and peeled the garden roots and crumpled dried herbs into the cooking pot while I stirred it all with a large wooden spoon, its savory steam rising about me. I cast a glance to our salt cellar with its dwindling inventory. "They will come and look at our poor priory and sit in judgment," he went on. "These tradesmen and rustics. They, who have never spent a decent hour in prayer, will say to us we are wasting our time."

"We will do our best to show them otherwise."

"What is it they want this time, Lady Prioress?" asked Felicia.

"They seek abuses. Reform, not ruin, so it is said."

"But there are no abuses here," said Felicia. She leaned forward like an alewife, her forearm lying across the table. "Except, perhaps, for the continual presence of Thomas Giffard."

Silence followed her pronouncement, and I could not help but raise my eyes to Cristabell, doing her best to scrub the color from the wooden table.

"Do you credit these visits to be abuses, Dame Felicia?" I asked softly.

She twisted her lips, pulling her whole face with it rather like a rabbit's twitching nose. She glanced once at the prudent Father William. "You are prioress. If you do not deem it unseemly, then neither do I. He is our patron. He brings us news. Faith! I wish he would come today and tell us about all this foolery!"

"He has already warned us countless times. I only wonder how many more times we are to worry over such visits from court."

It was then I turned to the doorway. Still as death and just as pale, Dame Alice stood. At first I thought her to be ill, and I moved toward her, but she raised a hand and said in a roughened voice, "They are here, Dame. The commissioners are here."

No one moved at first. Father William braved the inevitable. "I will greet them," he said.

"No, Father," I heard myself say. "I am prioress. I will greet them."

I patted his hand in reassurance before walking forth with heavy steps. I untied the napron and flung it away from me. I gathered my confidence in the smoothing out of my gown, in affixing my rosary, and in straightening my veil, all motions I readily did on any given day out of practice. Today, my hands went through the motions as if I were a ghost on her nightly hauntings, mocking that which she did in life.

At length I reached the front gate and unlocked it, glancing at the round man at the portal and the taller man beside him. There were men in livery behind them. I wondered if they meant for all of them to enter as well.

"You are the Lady Prioress?" the first asked me.

"Yes, my lord. Prioress Isabella Launder."

"I am Dr. Legh. And this, my associate Dr. William Cavendish. Here, my brother Richard."

"My lords," I said to them, bowing. He caught my gaze flicking toward the other men, and a warped smile creased his face.

"My men can wait without. Too many men in a woman's cloister would not do, eh?"

With relief I bowed again. "Let me take you to the hall."

He spoke quietly to his brother who waited in the courtyard with the liveried men. I led the way with no further conversation. I felt their glare upon me, two sets of scrutinizing eyes, deciphering my very soul from beneath the folds of my gown.

Once in the hall, I gestured to the benches and retrieved two ceramic cups that I filled from a jug of beer. I apologized for the lack of wine and explained that we seldom served it at Blackladies.

They both glared into their cups as if they never saw the drink before, but after a moment, quaffed each in turn. I filled them again.

"You need not stand, Lady Prioress," said Dr. Legh. "Sit. We will talk. Certainly you are anxious. I mean to relieve you of your fears."

I reached behind for the seat and slowly lowered myself to the bench, sitting closest to Cavendish. His straw-colored hair reached almost to his shoulders and an equally light-hued beard, shot with streaks of gray, covered his chin. Dr. Legh was round and squat like a turnip, and his dark velvet gown only added to his girth. He wore a black furred hat with ear flaps. His nose was red and chapped from the weather.

We all watched each other's breath rise in soft white clouds. I stuffed my hands within my scapular for warmth. The fire had burned down to gray ash in the hearth. In order to conserve fuel, I ordered that no fire should burn in any room when no one was present.

"Madam," said Legh cordially, "we are here by the king's commission to discover whether abuses are transpiring. Many of the monasteries in this realm are flagrant in their abuses. We have seen much of it already." He paused as he pulled a black book from his scrip. Licking the end of his thumb, he leafed through it, until coming to the spot he desired. He withdrew a pencil and placed the pencil's tip to the page. "Now, Madam. You do acknowledge his gracious majesty as Supreme Head of the Church in England, do you not?"

"I have sworn the oath, my lord."

He looked up at me with expressionless eyes. "That I did not ask you, Madam. I asked if you acknowledged the king as the Supreme Head of the Church in England."

"The king rules England," I said soberly, "and he is the patron of the churches on English soil. Verily, King Henry is the head of the churches."

"*Church* of England," Legh corrected.

I shook my head, but did not raise it. "Church, churches. You put too fine a point on grammatical matters, Dr. Legh."

"And you obfuscate by them, Madam."

I felt light-headed, but crushed my nails into my palms to keep thoroughly alert. "But so. It goes without the saying."

"I am afraid, Madam, that it very much must be said. Tell me, how do you take the king?"

"I…take him as God and the Holy Church take him, as one hopes he takes himself."

Cavendish drew forward. "You must play no games with us, Madam. These are serious matters."

"Forgive me, sir," I said softly, but the Lord gave me strength within my outrage. "Forgive me for the slow creature I am, for I am but a woman and weak of mind. These concepts are hard learned by me. You say that the king is the head of the Church and that the bishop of Rome is no longer to have the title pope, and so I must attend to you. Is our king, then, now the apostle on the seat of Peter? For just England or all the Churches of the world?"

Cavendish blinked at me before casting a wary glance at Legh. "Well…His Majesty… he is… he sits in power over England's Church. No foreigner will dictate his authority here."

"I see. Then I thank you for setting us aright."

Legh scowled at Cavendish and waved his fusty hand. "That is all well, then. Let us go on." He consulted his book again. "How many sisters have you here?"

"Four, including myself."

"Four? Four keep this house?"

"Yes, my lord. And several servants. We could not do it without their generous help. We are blessed by such attendance."

"Indeed. And are they justly compensated?"

"As best we can. 'Pay the worker his wage,' Dr. Legh. We make certain the servants are paid before ever we use the funds. Oft there is scarce enough left."

"Enough left for what?"

I looked up at last. "For food, Dr. Legh."

He cleared his throat and swallowed more beer. He slid his cup toward the jug and made as if to take more, but he seemed to think better of it. "Show me your chapel, Lady Prioress."

"Anything, my lord." I rose and pulled my veil around me.

We reached the dim chapel and I reached into the font to sketch a cross over my forehead before bowing to the crucifix.

Both Legh and Cavendish hastily becrossed themselves and squinted at me. "Have you no candles, Lady?"

"We have the sanctuary light, Dr. Legh. We light no others unless we celebrate the mass. Beeswax candles are expensive. We use some of our own beeswax, but we sell most of it."

"You paint a gloomy picture, Prioress."

"Do I? I assure you, it is not gloomy here. We are all very happy, in fact."

"Indeed," said Cavendish. "According to this," and he consulted his own book, "the annual income of this house is £20 13*s* 4*d*. But come. I understand that your patron donates lavishly to this house. Where is it, Madam? Where do you put these donations? If not in candles, then where? Are they not given to the poor?"

"The donations are given to this house for the specific upkeep of the nuns and their welfare. May I remind you, Dr. Cavendish, that we are poor."

"You need not be," said Legh, squinting into the dimness. "You may go back to your homes, after all."

For the first time, I recognized in them something foreign, something malignant and tarry, stinking like peat. I heard in their voices, saw it in their eyes, a breath of evil. Oh, I knew it existed. From the truth of the scriptures, I knew it was in the world, but I never before encountered it myself. And now I feared, for I knew what these commissioners wanted. They wanted our destruction. They were not after reformation or to root out abuses, but to destroy God's Church. I finally understood that if the king were to rule a Church, it must be his own and not that of St. Peter's. I saw at last what brave Englishmen were afraid to utter, afraid to believe that their sovereign was capable of. Even Thomas, in all his veiled warnings, never suspected this. *Lord,* I prayed, *preserve me and my nuns from such malignancy. Help us to overcome your enemies. In Christ's precious name I beg.* "This is our home, Dr. Legh, Dr. Cavendish. We are holy sisters. We belong to God, as did the Holy Mother."

"This is not a proper home, Madam. A proper home has a man at its head, with a woman to wife and children."

"A home can be in many forms. We are God's handmaids. We toil for Him."

"Toil? At what, Madam? Poverty?"

"We pray, Dr. Legh. For all mankind. And we do so in our poverty as Christ Jesus did on this earth. I can best serve God by possessing great compassion for His creatures...Even for you, Dr. Legh."

He snorted and hitched up his belt over his considerable middle. "Prayers, Madam, are not a worthy occupation for young women who can better suit the realm by begetting children for the king's army."

I frowned. "You are indelicate, sir."

"I am no more indelicate that the supposition that your playacting at poverty can do the world at large any shred of good."

"If no good then no harm, at least. And we do serve the poor. How much in your capacity as a king's commissioner do you do so, my lords?"

He ignored the last and puffed bigger, a cockerel in a barnyard. "And yet there are still poor in this parish, Madam."

"As I said. We are poor ourselves. We cannot alleviate all the poverty in this land alone."

"We are not here to discuss the doings of your charitable acts. I am instructed by the crown to question you and your nuns."

I bristled and straightened to my full height, which was taller than Legh. "Then ask your questions."

He consulted his book again, but found he could not read it in the dim light. He stepped out onto the porch and expected me to follow. I did so slowly in my due time, my skirts gliding across the stone floor in ripples.

After a pause, he raised his head. "Are you chaste, Madam?"

Involuntarily, I turned my shoulder toward him as if to fend off the blows of his words. "I object most strenuously to such a question! You insult me!"

"By no means, Madam." Without change to his expression, he looked at his book, and then again at me. "I am instructed to ask you and to ask your nuns about you—whether any immorality of any kind goes on here."

"I shall answer nothing without my confessor present."

"That will do you no good, Lady. I am instructed to obtain an answer from you or suppose a conspiracy of silence. Silence condemns as easily as confession."

"By your reasoning, how can anyone be innocent?"

"Come, come, Lady. I see you have a fondness for dramatics. Let us not have a disguising here. Now answer. Are you chaste?"

Looking him in the eye did no good. I have heard of the king's torturers. Rumor had it that they were deaf to the pleas of their victims. There was no mercy in this man's eyes. He wanted his answer, and like the torturer, he would extract it by any means. "I came to this priory a virgin twenty years ago," I said softly, "and I remain so to this day, as God is my witness."

"Is that so?"

"What proof do you require, my lord?"

He smiled that warped expression again. "Your word, Madam. And that of your ladies. Now. How are your funds distributed?"

I screwed up my fists. "I have accounting books which you may look through. As I said, our servants are paid first, and then our bishop, and then to Rome."

"The crown, Madam? What of the crown?"

"The…the bishop sees to that, Dr. Legh."

He huffed a clouded breath into the cold afternoon and consulted his book. "Where is the plate and good stuffs?"

"Plate, my lord?"

"Yes, yes. The plate. The gold. Surely there are vestry items."

"Gold? There is no gold. The communion cup that resides back in the chapel is silver. There is no plate."

"Surely you have stores of the Church's riches, Madam."

Was the man incapable of understanding? Or did he think me a liar? "Dr. Legh, I beg you to look around you. We have no riches. These poor gowns are all we have."

"Do you trifle with me, Madam? Do you expect me to believe—"

"Yes, sir! I do expect you to believe when I say so. This is a house of God, and I respect my position even if you do not."

His expression laid bare his soul. The Devil showed his hand at last. "I find very little to respect here, Madam. You forget, I have been through most of England, and I have seen deceits and immoralities that would cause a blush to your cheek. Scandal aplenty, Madam. Spare me your sermons. Do not speak to me of respect. Respect is earned."

"And what have I done to deny it?"

"It must be earned, Madam. And a fool does not earn my respect, for only a fool would chose to live in poverty for an ideal that cannot be met."

"You are a most ungodly man!"

"Perhaps. I have no stomach for clerics." He stepped closer, his shade Cavendish glaring at me from behind his wispy brows. "Why do you persist in these useless antiquated rituals? You are a sensible woman."

"It is precisely because I am a sensible woman that I persist in what you deem 'useless ritual'. Oh, how I feel for you. Yes, we are under a yoke, but obedience to God and His word is a most pleasant yoke. The world is large, and sometimes frightening. We know what it is to be a child of God. A child obeys or is crushed by such a world. But a child also learns. A child lives within the framework of her family. The Church is my family. No matter how fragmented or how distant its members, I will know them by the covenant they keep. I will always know them."

"Pleasant speeches, Madam, do not change the subject. The king is displeased with papist practices that traffic in relics and graven images."

I strode back down the chapel of St. Mary, my feet surely never before making such a cacophony across those sacred stones. I gestured to the statue of Our Lady with a trembling hand. A small candle burned at her feet. She rose out of that glow into the gloom of the chapel, but her face was sedate, serene in the turmoil around her. A little cracked from the years and the damp, paint peeling slightly, she was still regal in her niche, still mild as her lowered lids kindly regarded those at her feet. "Is this a graven image? Is it? Do you think I *worship* this? This is merely a portrait of our dear Mother. Do you think me a fool? I know it is not she, any more than that image carved by artisans on the cross to be our Lord. Papists are not fools, my lords. We are merely devout. We want the tangible. We want to look into the face of God, peer into Heaven only to know it better. For in that, we hope to find our path there through the narrow gate." I purposely glared up and down the corpulent Legh. "And it is a very *narrow* gate, my lords."

Cavendish coughed into his hand, but Legh did not stray his gaze from mine. "This we will see. Call in your sisters. We would question them as well."

He turned and made back for the hall. I won nothing. There was nothing to win. I did not know what would happen, but I did know that no matter what was said here, we had lost. The Church had lost, for the decision was made far before these men passed our threshold.

I hurried to the kitchen. Startled by my arrival, my nuns bolted to their feet, faces as white as their wimples. I took a deep breath. "Sisters, you are to come now. These commissioners will ask you questions."

"What kind of questions?" asked a breathless Alice.

I shook my head, unable to believe it all. "Terrible questions. Insolent and discourteous questions. And you will answer them, because the king demands it and we are his servants."

"I will go with you," said Father William, pushing himself to his feet with his cane. I could not object. I could no longer speak. I led my nuns in prayer first, and then I preceded them all to the hall.

We entered and faced our judges. We stood while they sat upon our benches, drinking our beer from our few cups.

"We have asked questions of your prioress," said Legh, consulting his wretched black book, "and now we will ask you nuns. Who will be first?"

None of them moved. I could hardly blame them. I trembled, though I could not tell if it were more from fear or outrage. At last, one moved forward and I raised my eyes in surprise to Cristabell.

"And you are?" asked Legh.

She stood stiffly but erect. A woman to reckon with was our Cristabell. "Dame Cristabell Smith," she answered, voice steady as a rock.

"Very well, Dame," he said, making note in his book. "How many nuns are you here?"

"We are four, as our bishop charged. He said there are to be no more than four at Blackladies, and no more there are."

"And so. Do you and your sisters regularly perform your Divine Office as proscribed by your order?"

"We do."

Legh pursed his lips. "Do you live according to the Rule of your order, following its statutes without straying?"

"We do."

"The sick, Dame. Are they treated well?"

"Yes."

"And travelers. Are they given safe haven and hospitality as is mete?"

"Yes."

Legh tapped his fingers on the table with irritation. "Do you have anything to add to your terse comments, Dame?"

Cristabell blinked once. "No."

"One thing more. Besides your servants and your priest here, are men allowed within the precincts of the convent?"

Cristabell looked at them steadily, seeming to measure their worth by the gold about their necks and the fur on their gowns. "But men are not allowed in the cloister."

Legh sat back, fingering the gilt belt buckle at his waist. "I have been told, Dame, that your patron Thomas Giffard often comes to the priory. Is that correct?"

Though my own breath left me, Cristabell's was steady. I saw her shoulders rise and fall evenly, and the fog spin from her nostrils from the cold. "Yes. He is patron, as you said."

"Does Lord Giffard come within the precincts of the cloister?"

As steady as I have ever seen her, she even leaned closer to Legh when she said, "That would be forbidden, my lord."

"Indeed. But you did not answer the question. Does Lord Giffard come within the precincts of this cloister?"

"Lord Giffard is, and always has been, a gentleman of the highest rank. He well knows the rules as do we."

"And yet you did not answer me straight, Dame."

"She answered you," said Father William.

"Indeed, sir, she did not. Answer me, Dame. For I see a conspiracy of the worst kind forming."

"Lord Giffard would take a horsewhip to you both, my lords," barked Dame Felicia, "were you to dare utter such in his presence."

Legh glared at her. "And who are you?"

"I am Dame Felicia Bagshawe. F-e-l-i-c-i-a—"

"I have it, Dame," he muttered, scratching it down.

"And further, Dr. Legh," she went on, "that you should plainly ignore all the good we do in order to satisfy your salacious appetites—"

Legh bolted to his feet. "Prioress! Silence your nun!"

"Dame Felicia. Your answer has sufficed."

"As you will, Lady Prioress." She bowed her head to me, and stepped back with the others.

Legh's face blushed red. Stuffed as it was in its furred collar, it resembled a crabapple bursting up from a peat bog. Flustered, he shuffled the many gold chains over his gown and slowly sat, resting his nubbin fingers upon the table. Cavendish leaned toward him and whispered something. Legh nodded, his cheeks returning to their tawny hue.

"I am compelled to tell you that all who wish to leave this convent may do so immediately without censure and without punishment."

"What of our vows?" cried Felicia.

Legh turned his eye to her, his jowl sagging with a sneer. "What of them, Madam? The king instructed me to inform you that you are not bound by the dictates of foreign princes. You therefore owe no vows to anyone save the king."

"And God!" said Father William.

"That is so," said Legh with a curt bow to his head. "All who wish to, may go. Indeed, if any of you are under twenty-four years of age you are compelled to go. The vicar general insists. Dame. You. The young one. What is your name?"

Alice moved forward tentatively, clutching at the hem of her veil. "D-Dame Alice Beche, my lord."

"Are you under twenty-four?"

"No, my lord. I am two and thirty."

"It matters not. You may still leave this convent, if you wish. Though I remind you that you are all still bound by your vow of chastity."

"Lest we breed more papists?"

"My Lady Prioress!" he said, in feigned shock. "Who is being indelicate now?"

"Little good it should do a young nun released from the convent if she cannot find solace in a husband! Come, come. This is absurd."

"You call the king's commands absurd?"

"I call you absurd! This interview is over."

"No, my Lady Prioress. It is not over. Further, we have more demands to make. One, that there be no displaying of relics for gain, and that you, Lady Prioress, are confined to the precincts of the priory. If stay you will, there shall be no wandering about."

"Is that all, Dr. Legh?"

"All, Lady?" He smiled, nodding toward Cavendish. "Yes, Lady. That is all. For now."

I closed my eyes, summoning the peace of Christ. By obfuscation—may God forgive us—we saved ourselves. But for how long? I raised my lids and calmly gazed at our guests, for guests—no matter how despicable—they were. "Then, may I offer you the hospitality of our house? The supper is almost ready and we can accommodate you in our lodgings. We sisters will set up hay on the floor in here while you may take our room."

Legh's expression of triumph faltered as he scanned the hall, its chipped paint and draughty windows. He must have smelt the faint aroma of our poor vegetable pottage as its steam arose from the kitchen fires, planting not hunger in his belly, but revulsion. I was reminded of his liveried men as he smoothed out his gown with bejeweled fingers. "No, thank you, Lady Prioress. We will find accommodations in the village." He rose. "We will return again tomorrow to inspect the premises."

Dame Felicia offered to escort them to the door, and Dr. Legh warily acknowledged her. Never was there a time we were more pleased to lock the gates behind a soul who visited us.

When Felicia returned, we glanced worriedly at one another. "And that is what comes from having King Hal as our pope!" she trumpeted.

THOMAS GIFFARD
NOVEMBER, 1537
Hampton Court

XXVI

" ...I have never read in any doctor approved by the Church that a secular prince can or ought to be the head over things spiritual."

–Thomas More, 1 July 1535

At the wedding of King Henry and Anne Boleyn, it was remarked how apt were their initials carved onto the new doors of the palace, and embroidered on banners and robes. "HA" it read. "HA, HA" all over London. What a grand jest, indeed, it was to be perpetrated upon the English people. They refused to laud her as queen because she unlawfully supplanted our good Queen Catherine, and there were many who would have thrown more than garlands. It was said that townsfolk were paid to cheer her on the streets, but even those were sparse.

They laughed in earnest, when years later, her head rolled off her neck under the facility of a French swordsman.

Though she was no more guilty of a conspiracy of adultery than our good Queen Catherine was of not being the king's legal consort, Anne Bullen helped instigate this calamity which struck down the Church as we knew it. No tears were shed for Mistress Anne Bullen, dead now over a year.

It was not long after that the king's bastard son, Henry Fitzroy, a lad of seventeen years, died. The king consoled himself with yet another bride, indisputably lawful as both former wives were dead. Mistress Seymour became the king's consort, and in time delivered a legitimate and much-longed-for son, Edward. The child lived where so many before him died, but Queen Jane was not as fortunate. A kind and meek woman—such a stark contrast to that of Anne—died not long after her son was christened.

So much had happened in so little time. I sat with Philip Draycot and George Throckmorton in my apartments at Hampton Court, and we, like three old men, purged our morose thoughts at the bottom of a goblet.

"Prince Edward thrives, praise God," Draycot said, perhaps thinking of his own son Richard, ill with a fever.

"Praise God?" I echoed. "But *where* should I praise Him? I do not recognize this Protestant service nor these supposed priests."

Draycot cast a wine-soaked glance at me. "Do you still rankle at the surrender of the smaller monasteries, Thomas? The report stated how these were dwellings of corruption, where abuses of the worst sort were discharged with regularity."

"A report made by Cromwell. Do you take his word over that of a monk?"

Throckmorton snorted into the bowl of his goblet, slurping the last of it. "How pious you have become over time, Thomas. For years you have disdained these very houses as evil places, succoring the ignorant and irreligious."

I glared at him, my own fingers strangling the goblet's stem. "Can a man not change his mind on these matters, George? That these poor houses—so small they cannot possibly do the harm for which they are accused—should be shut down, their doors closed, their occupants turned out. What is to become of them? The nuns and their servants must shift for themselves, eh?"

"Some will go into the larger houses, I imagine," said Draycot. He rose and poured himself more wine from the flagon the servant left for us. He picked over a plate of sliced chicken, congealing under its glaze of honey and nuts.

I stared at him, turning my incredulous expression to encompass Throckmorton as well. "Are you both fools? Do you think the king will stop with a few houses worth less than £200? Why do you think inventory was taken and accounting books gone through? Was it to make certain the money was spent on the poor, or was it to see what value the king could demand once he sold these properties—these properties belonging to the pope!"

"God's blood, Thomas!" Throckmorton shot toward the archway, pressing his ear to the door. He cast me a glare of reproof. "Keep your voice down, if you must speak this way!"

"The plot is large, my friends," I said to them. "If you think he will stop with the smaller houses, then you are fools. The tools of the pope must be annihilated, consumed back into the populace as if they never occurred."

Draycot peeled himself from his chair and stood above the fire, raising his curled knuckles to the warming blaze. He stared into the flames as he spoke. "The uprising in Lincolnshire last year did not last a month, Thomas. Many were killed. Mostly the poor, naturally, those who were dependent on monastery lands for sustenance. Their 'pilgrimage of grace' did not stir His Majesty, and they were all put down. There has been no whimper from the rest of the country."

"Are you saying that we welcome this dissolution, that these abbeys and convents are just as well destroyed?"

Draycot leaned his arm against the mantle, his fist opening and closing. "I mean that men have new feelings about their faith they never dared have before. And that we wish to see what may come of this."

"Have they no love for their religion?"

"Like you, Thomas?" spat Throckmorton. "You, who have always remonstrated these very houses you now canonize! You, to whom religion was an inconvenience! What is it, Thomas? What is it that has changed your heart?"

I drew my finger under my mustache, toying with the bristly ends. "Are you not afraid?" I whispered. "Do you not fear this? Is this reform? Or is it greed? Is it Hal's revenge at a pope who would not lie for him, would not give him a divorce?" I shook my head at the enormity of it. "This reformation of monasteries. Did monks and nuns spring forth from our heads only yesterday? Or was this an institution long held, long honored, since before even Saint Benet? Where is the precedence for such an acquittal?"

I shut my lips. I could say no more, and no more could they think to say to that. I knew Draycot and Throckmorton celebrated private masses in their homes as did the Giffards, as we would continue to do.

Blackladies—so small and of so little consequence—was one of the many slated for suppression. Not by any ill they found there, but precisely because it was of no consequence. I bought an exemption for them, but I soon found such an exemption to be of even less significance. Last month I was informed by Dr. Legh that this exemption was now forfeit and the doors would be closed forthwith. He seemed particularly pleased in the telling of it, but I could do nothing in retaliation to the king's commissioner, though there was much I would have been pleased to do.

"What will you do?" asked Draycot. The both of them knew my outward struggle with Blackladies, though not the inner struggle that kept my interest so piqued.

"The priory will go on the block," I said. "There is little to be done…but to buy it myself."

"Buy it? I see at last!" Throckmorton moved toward me. "Such protestations! And in the end you will do them the service of buying their precious priory. How many will your father buy?"

"George!" warned Draycot.

"No doubt he has chosen a few to covet," I admitted. "I only want the one."

"But why, Thomas? Why such singular interest in that little nothing of a priory in Brewood, for God's sake?"

"I have my reasons," I muttered.

"It could not be that the rumors are true, could it?"

"George…" Draycot seized Throckmorton by the arm, but George shook him off. "This is not the time, George…"

"Of course it is. My brother-in-law intends to purchase this priory. To live in the place it is rumored he has a mistress. Is it true, Thomas? Do you forsake my good sister for some nun?"

I should have shrugged it off, but I was incapable. I lunged from my seat, gripping George's throat and stilling his words with the strength of my fingers.

He stumbled backwards and we rolled along the floor as Draycot shouted at the both of us to stop. George managed to place his boot against my thigh and push himself away from me. Panting in a corner, he raised an accusatory finger. "It *is* true!"

"She is not my mistress! How dare you! You know her not! You know me not! You cannot know what I have endured—"

And then, I unmanned myself with weeping. Throckmorton stormed from my rooms, but Draycot knelt beside me and lifted me to my feet.

"I did not believe this rumor…before now," he said softly. "He is naturally outraged. His own sister is your wife. But a nun, Thomas!"

"She was not a nun when I met her." I wiped the tears from my face, but my relief was in the saying of something so long suppressed. "It seems I have known her all my life. And when I married Dorothy, she went to the convent. I did not realize that I loved her until I discovered where she went. By then, it was too late."

"But after Dorothy died—"

"I went to her. I begged her to marry me, though she was completely unfit. She is the daughter of a yeoman farmer, after all. Unschooled, unlearned. Completely unfit. But I wanted her, Philip. I want her now. But I cannot have her."

"And…what of her?"

"She loves me. I know it. But she is stronger in her vows than I am in mine. But now, what's to become of her?"

"You have kept this secret dear, Thomas, but I do not envy you your dilemma. What will you do?"

"I will buy Blackladies and keep it for her and her sisters until this foolishness is over."

"What if the king will not grant it to you?"

"He must!"

"You must talk to him of it at once, then. For I fear this Dr. Legh has a grudge against you, and may turn the king's course."

I patted his arm. "You are right, Philip. I thank you for this advice and for…for not judging me."

"You need to seek out George. Explain it to him as best you can. He is a man. Perhaps a man first and a brother second."

I agreed with Draycot, and I moved to the door to do as he suggested without pause. Outside my rooms, Throckmorton paced the gallery. I approached him cautiously and waited for him to acknowledge me.

"Well," he said. "I apologize for making such a fool of myself."

"There is no need," I said with relief. "George." My hand fell gently upon his shoulder. "I *have* been faithful to your sister, my wife. In body, if not in my heart. But these matters conspired long before I met her. I am only sorry they continue. I am a weak man with a romantic heart. I cannot seem to change that which is embedded in me. But I assure you, I have done no wrong, and I shall not shame my family. You see, I love Ursula, too, for her understanding that there can be layers to a man which she cannot be privy to. Where no one can be. No one but his maker. I would give anything not to feel this cold fear, but it is not only for this chaste nun, George. You celebrate the mass, as do I. Would you ever give it up on the word of a secular prince?"

George studied me an excruciatingly long time, before he slowly shook his head. "By God, I would not!"

"I do it to protect more than a woman, but an ideal. I will not see it perish from this land."

He clutched my arm, frowning. "Would that we could do more, Thomas."

"We will all do what we can…within the law."

I left him, feeling better that we mended the fences between us. I held him in no ill will, for he was a man of much honor and tenderness. What would I do if my sisters Dorothy or Cassandra came to me weeping of similar misdeeds from their spouses, I wondered?

I waited outside the king's apartments until a servant came with wine. I took the tray from him and sent him off, taking it in myself. The king was in the company of Cromwell and Archbishop Cranmer. His majesty was glowering at a paper and booming to the ceiling, "These are not enough! You promised me more, Cromwell!"

"The houses so far suppressed, sire, only bring in so much. Soon there will be—" He noticed me, and turned pointedly in my direction whilst drawing silent.

The king turned as well, and waved his hand. "It's only Giffard."

"Your grace," said Cromwell, leaning toward the king to speak privately. But Henry would have none of it. He got to his feet as fast as his bulk would allow.

"Out! Out with you, Cromwell. I'll talk no more of this today."

Cranmer moved forward. "But your grace must discuss—"

"My Lord Cranmer, do not speak for my chancellor, for he knows more words than a serpent to beguile me. Off! Both of you. I would be alone with my usher, here."

Cromwell hesitated, and for a brief moment, I thought he would argue with the king. Eyeing me, he thought better of it, and signaled to Cranmer. The both of them left with a bow, while I stood mutely in the shadows, a flagon in my hand. What did I come here for? To mete out the same to the king?

I had played a safe game for too long. It was time to make an unexpected move.

"Your grace, if I may beg your indulgence…"

"Oh, not you too, Thomas. You were my excuse to rid myself of them and their damnable prattling." His expression softened. "Very well. What is it?"

I set the flagon down. "Your grace, I have just been made aware of a priory in the vicinity of my lands that is to be suppressed…"

"And you want it excused."

"I have already paid for its exemption, your grace, but now it is to be suppressed anyway. My desire is to be able to purchase it."

He took a long moment to study me sidelong.

"It is only a small convent, your grace. A little property outside of Chillington Hall in Brewood."

The edge of a smile formed on his face. "Why do you want this poor little priory so badly, Thomas? Hmm?"

"It has memories for me, your grace. Precious ones."

"Precious memories? You sound as if you are mourning a lost love."

I swallowed hard. Would he understand? As the man he was, as the man I knew, could he not see into the depth of my heart and comprehend? Softly, I answered, "Yes, your grace. I am."

"One of the sisters you mean? Damnable!" He twisted quickly and unexpectedly for his size. After the death of Queen Jane, he ate to excess, growing larger until he was almost unmanageable, and the ulcers in his leg caused him to limp, decreasing further his mobility. He raised his staff, thrusting it in the air in anger. I stepped back out of the way. "That is precisely why I must lance this canker out of England, these faithless whores in nun's weeds!"

I must have been blinded by his words, out of my mind far worse than with George, for I pulled by blade partway from its sheath before realizing who it was I threatened.

Too late I slapped the blade back in its scabbard. He drew himself up to his full height, tall, broad, altogether forbidding. "Do you draw your sword upon me, Giffard? ME?"

At his shriek, two guards rumbled into the room, their halberds lowered toward me. I stared at them in horror. They grasped me each by an arm and I expected to be dragged forthwith to a dungeon cell.

With his fist, the king clouted me hard upon my shoulder, and then my head. He rained his blows upon me, and I could do nothing in my own defense. Indeed, I knew all was lost, for how could I escape this room alive now that I had drawn my sword on my sovereign?

I fell to my knees.

For a long moment I sat there panting, aching from his blows. It took another long moment for him to wave off his guards. They protested, but he insisted, shouting to the rafters. More courtiers crowded the passageway, but the king bellowed for all to retreat. At last, reluctantly, the guards left the room, ushering the others away from the door. His Majesty stood glowering over me, fists punched into his hips.

With my head bowed I implored with my hands. "Forgive me, your grace. If you only knew how faithful a servant this woman is to God and to the crown, you would not speak so. It is only because I have such respect for her that I did so imprudent a thing…"

"And for this one you draw your sword on the king! God's wounds, Thomas! This is not the Roundtable!"

"I beg forgiveness and mercy, your grace."

I waited on my knees, my head bowed. I expected at any moment for him to hew it off himself. Not only did I ruin myself, but my course. Blackladies was now lost.

"So much you would sacrifice for this little scrap of land. You could have lied about it. You could have made up a story to satisfy me."

"I…am not in the habit of lying to you, your grace."

"Nor of drawing your weapon, I hope."

"No, your grace."

"You are a bold man, Giffard," he huffed. "Stubborn and mayhap unwise. But chivalrous, and that I have always admired." Energized, he seemed to want to pace but his leg prevented it. He rocked instead. "I have never had cause to mistrust the Giffards. Must I now?"

"No, your grace. We are ever loyal to the crown. Ask any man."

"Yes. How many men can swear to that, to 'ask any man'? I'll wager a bitter few can rely upon it. Yet I know I can ask any man about you, and hear each and every one to speak of your integrity and your character." Henry measured me. "I know you are a pope-Catholic, Thomas. What is your intention with this priory, eh? I will not have it continue as it is in its vicious living."

"I am not making of it a new priory, sire. As your grace has proclaimed, these properties must be remade into proper houses. A new residence for myself and my wife. No intention further than that, my lord."

"How many children have you, Thomas?"

His ire abated, but well I knew him, and suspected that his rage was only held at a distance, easily conjured again. Still on my knees and cautious, I said, "Four, your grace."

"And how many of them sons?"

"Two, Majesty."

"And your wife. Is she fruitful?"

"Your grace?"

"Don't be coy, Thomas. Is she pregnant again? Always you are away from court because your wife is lying in. Do you think I do not know the doings of my ushers?"

"I pray you, sire."

"Answer me."

"Yes, your grace. She is."

His cheek trembled and he shook his head. How brilliantly copper were those locks once. How bright the beard. Now they were dulled with gray, his skin textured with creases. Yet my beard was still as dark as ebony, and he and I were both forty-six. "You who sires so many children, with yet another on the way. And I, who had three wives, could only beget three children, and only one a son. It does not signify that you should also covet in convents."

"My lord, it is not as you think. I only want the property so that no other creature should defile it."

"It's to be a home, Thomas." His voice rose again, warning me of distant thunder.

"There are vile homes," I said steadily, "just as there are vile monasteries, sire."

He ticked his head at me as a nurse does to her charge. "Thomas, Thomas… Yes, so there are." He stood over me, laying his hand tenderly on the shoulder he lately clouted. At length, he sighed, patted my bruised shoulder, and dropped his hand away. "This is the love from afar?" I said nothing, amazed he remembered our conversation from so long ago. "I will do you this favor, Thomas. I will consider your request because I owe you for your years of service and loyalty. But hear me; henceforth, if I choose to insult your own mother's virtue, you will leave your blade where it lies. Is that understood?"

"With my heart, your grace."

"Then get up. It makes me knees ache to see you thus. And don't make me angry again, Thomas. I have so few men at court I genuinely like. Make no enemy of me."

He helped me to my feet, and held my arm affectionately. "Never, your grace. I shall always be your man."

"Good, good." He patted my arm. With uncertain relief, I helped him back to his chair.

ISABELLA LAUNDER
16 OCTOBER, 1538
Blackladies

XXVII

Woe to the shepherds who mislead
and scatter the flock of my pasture, says the Lord.
*–*Jeremiah 23:1

I knelt in the chapel for perhaps the last time. By the king's order—despite the reprieve given us by a generous donor—Blackladies was to close its doors. We were called wantons and wastrels, such vile names we did not earn.

Stunned, I knelt alone in the dusty gloom. What was to become of us? We who dedicated our lives in the service of God, who gave their maidenhood to God's house, who were now shriveled and too old to bear children, we were to be thrust into the world. Even the younger ones, still able to be espoused, were held by their vow of chastity, and could find no consolation there. We were to be given pensions to live on, as if this lucre was compensation for the destruction of our lives and for the looting of God's Church.

But it must be so. For we are mere women and loyal to our king.

"But surely the king will come to our aid," I had said to Father William when the notice arrived days ago with Sir John and the others to take a final inventory.

"Child," he had replied to me, "do you not know it is the king who is seizing them?"

Seizing? Such a harsh word when describing houses of God, of holy men and women. I heard the rumors, as such they were. There were always those places where greed, or gluttony, or lust could overtake the good people who started their lives there with good intentions. But these situations were not frequent, else how could the houses have helped so many in so many places in England? Our own house boasted of its poverty, and we did as much as we could for our poor, and they were grateful. But a word such as "seize." A word used when speaking of battles and of assault. Did the king mean to assault the monasteries?

"Why would he do that?" I had asked.

Father William could not answer, for he did not know. Thomas had warned us, and I saw the Devil in the likes of Dr. Legh and Dr. Cavendish, and felt the coldness of their intent in the pit of my belly, but I could somehow not truly believe it.

"A last prayer?"

I turned to see Cristabell framed in the doorway. Clutching the altar rail, I pulled myself to my feet. Suddenly, I felt ages old. "Not a last prayer. Surely not my last."

"No. Of course not. You possessed more faith than all of us. If God does not listen to you—"

"No, Cristabell, do not say it. I am the worst of sinners. Never have I let go of my desire for Thomas Giffard, and I fear it has ruined us."

"You think God thinks so little of the rest of us that he would punish all the Church in England for your lack? You have a narrow view of the Almighty. Or an inflated one of yourself."

I measured her, with her hands buried deep within her scapular, her chin creased and doubled with time and weariness. "I do not know what to think any longer."

"There is always hope. God gave us that. I have lived in hope all my life. Especially here, though the wrong kind. It is only in the last ten years that I hoped in the right kind, mostly because of your prayers for me." In silence we contemplated the crucifix. Quietly, she asked, "Will God abandon us, do you think?"

"I know not. Who could have thought such things would come to pass. No one could have planned it or prepared."

"I am somehow relieved Thomas Giffard will possess Blackladies. It has the ring of justice."

"Perhaps."

"Where will you go?"

"I have written to my sister Agnes, and though she complained bitterly at such an inconvenience, she vowed she would take in both me and Alice, but... It is a dream, Cristabell. A living nightmare. Isolated from all that is familiar and cherished, we walk into the unknown. Why should such a thing befall us?"

She shook her head, her mouth stiff with emotion. She swallowed and turned her head, raising her chin. "I have a cousin who has agreed to take me in. But what of the others, the old ones?"

"Yes. I worry over them. No pension will sustain them alone. And many of their families have long since died."

"Do you suppose the king made provision for them?"

"Hush, Cristabell. No more anger. Anger has brought us here to this day. I do not blame the king. Not really. In truth, I blame his councilors who have lied on his behalf. To what end? Could it all be greed for power?"

"Discontent as well. Englishmen have not liked the strictures of the Church and pope."

"If reform they wanted, then why did they not reform? This is not reform. This is death."

"Do you know when?"

"No. Like a prisoner in the tower, I await my executioner."

And just as a bell tolls for the condemned, so, too, did our gate bell suddenly chime, startling the both of us. Together we went to see about it, encountering Dame Alice and Dame Felicia

251

coming from opposite directions. "Sisters," I said, greeting them all. "How is it we are all assigned the job of porter?"

"You have neglected your duty, then, Prioress, in assigning it to no one," said Felicia good-naturedly.

I felt warmth in my cheeks and smiled in my shyness. "Well, then. Let us all go together to greet whoever it is at the door."

And so we walked together, and when we turned the corner we were glad we did. Dr. Legh and Dr. Cavendish waited by the bell rope, surprised themselves to see us all approach. "How now? What display is this?"

"A display of community, Dr. Legh," I answered him. I was determined to be a proper nun to the last moment...which seemed to have arrived.

"Open the gate, Prioress. I have here a bill of surrender for this priory."

My heart lurched painfully, and I becrossed myself before going to the gate. With each action my treacherous mind ran the narrative: *This shall be the last time I open the gate for a visitor. And this the last time I welcome them to our hospitality.*

"*Deo Gratias,*" I said with a bow.

No sooner did he pass through the gate did he begin his own narrative. "This bill of surrender puts the property under the crown. You, your servants, and your nuns are to vacate the property immediately. I have brought proper attire for all of you so that you may not be further encumbered with these habits."

I was unprepared for his boorishness, though I do not know why I should have been. "May we not continue to wear our habits, Dr. Legh?"

"No, indeed. The vicar general has declared it... and the king as well."

Dark muslins and woolens were bundled under his servant's arms. This time he made no play at courtesy, and allowed his men to enter the precincts. Somehow, because he declared it so, it was no longer sacred ground. At least not to him. I shuddered, but said nothing. Instead, I led them to the hall, where I instructed my nuns to light the hearth. A roaring fire I told them. Our guests will be comfortable.

We entered to a warm room. The fire was smoky, but its toasted aromas lent the chill air a scrap of consolation, and I turned at last to face my judges. Dr. Legh was determined that I should look at his paper, for he thrust it into my face.

I took it solemnly, but did not read it. "Are we to sign it?"

"No. That has been accounted for."

Glancing at the bottom of the page I saw that it was, indeed, attended to. All the nuns' names were affixed to the bottom, looking for all the world like signatures. "Dr. Legh, this has an appearance that we have signed this document."

"It matters not, Lady. It is done and it is legal."

"That is a matter for a greater judge," I said quietly, handing it back.

"Have you made arrangements to vacate the premises?" he asked, ignoring my words. He did not need to heed them now. Now we were only an inconvenience to be dispensed with.

"Yes. We have. Though it will take some days for messages to arrive and for our families to come. If we had known ahead of time—"

"But you must vacate today."

"Dr. Legh! Would you have us in the streets?"

"In truth, Madam, I care very little if you do. It is my commission to make certain you vacate the property in due order."

Tight-lipped, I stared at this little man, growing even smaller in my eyes. "Very well. There must be an inn in the village. I am certain they will be charitable to us for a few nights. If not, there are always their stables. If it was good enough for our Lord, it shall be good enough for us."

Cavendish grasped Legh's arm and whispered something into his ear. Impatiently, Legh listened, his face mirroring his every chafing thought. At last, he sighed elaborately and bowed his head. "Dr. Cavendish points out that a few days will matter very little.

You may stay while your messages are sent, but you must put on these clothes in the interim."

The holy saints of England must have bolstered me, for I stepped forward, glared down at Legh, and said in a most stern voice, "We will do no such thing while in this house. For as long as we inhabit here, it is holy ground, and we will comport ourselves as holy sisters in the garb of holy sisters. You shall have to strip me naked yourself if you wish for me to wear those detestable clothes one moment earlier than I must."

Legh took a step back and, flustered, pulled at the fur trim of his gown. "Very well, Madam," he muttered. "I...I will leave this for another time."

They retired to Brewood, while we awaited our caretakers to come for us and take us away, though I could see Legh's men in their ostentatious livery walking the edges of the grounds as if he expected our resistance, a castle in a siege. I wanted to send a message to Thomas, knowing it would arrive in an hour's time. I imagined in my mind's eye his leaping onto his charger and rumbling over the rise as would any gallant knight, as he used to do when he visited me on my father's farm. Though this time, the dragon was too large to slay, and it would be only enough time to save the maidens.

Yet save us for what?

I did not send the message, knowing that Thomas would certainly be informed that his property was vacated and awaiting his pleasure.

The servants, however, made ready to leave, and that afternoon, they stood at the gate with their meager bundles, ready to bid their farewells to us.

I unlocked the cloister gate and allowed them to enter. Tearfully, Meg hugged each one of us. "Now, Meg. No tears. All of you," I said, opening my arms to them. "Surely you are blessed for such good and loyal service."

"Will all be well with you, Lady Prioress?" asked Philip Duffelde.

"All will be well. God is watching over us. He has not forgotten us."

The men bowed to us with their hats in their hands while Meg and Kat raised their naprons to their noses. Now I would never know if Meg succeeded in landing old Tom Smith. I would simply have to pray for its outcome.

Now truly alone, we nuns felt the loss as the cloister somehow pulled in on itself. The birds did not seem to sing as they did, nor was the sunlight as merry upon her old walls.

We celebrated the Divine Office and spent much time in private prayer and in the good company of each other, clinging to the last moments of our society. After prayers, Cristabell and I walked together, once old enemies, now true sisters, soon to part for all time. I little believed I would see Cristabell again. We were to quit for distant parishes, distant lives. Would the Divine Office play in her head as it would in mine? I was filled with such despair, I did not notice the garden as we walked through it, its blooms now spent, its leaves deadening and gnarled. "Look," she said, and I raised my head to where her hand pointed. A single rose yet bloomed, dark red like blood. It was tucked deep within the nearly black leaves of the bush, protected from the chill winds and driving rains. I brushed forward and leaned over to press my nose to the petals, inhaling its remarkable perfume. The moment of it made me smile, if only briefly.

"It remains," she said, surprised.

"Do not underestimate the tenacity of a rose in bloom."

"They are sturdy plants. Year after year I watched you prune them to nothing. I always thought you were too harsh with them. Yet each year they would return the stronger, even more lush than the year before."

"Let us take our lesson from the rose." I caught her eye, but I saw doubt in her soft expression.

"Will he keep the garden, do you think?"

He. It was always "he." It shall ever be "he" and we will always know who is meant. Since the day Blackladies went on the block—God have mercy—we heard that two gentlemen sued to buy it: Edward Littleton of Phillaton, and one Thomas Giffard of Stretton. Even the abhorrent Dr. Cavendish maneuvered to buy the property. But the king—in perhaps his last act of kindness toward the old convent—granted it to Thomas. I was angered when I first heard of it, but not for long. I understood his pain, which was almost as deep as my own.

"I do not know if Lord Giffard will keep the garden. Indeed, it shall no doubt be in the hands of Lady Giffard, I should think."

"Shall I tell you something, Lady Prioress?"

"Please." We walked solemnly, softly on the sacred grounds.

"Even though I am witness to its end, even though I shall leave this convent at last, I am grateful I stayed. After all my earlier protestations I would now give the world to stay to my death. And I have you to thank for it. We were adversaries once, and it was my fault. How you found the compassion to forgive me my many sins, I will never know. But I am glad you were chosen prioress. I am glad for Kat Alate and meddling Meg. I am glad for doddering Father William. And I am even glad for Jane and Mary, wherever they may be. And most of all, for Thomas Giffard. He proved a man can have integrity even in the face of the greatest disadvantage."

I could not help but glance back at the rose. "Yes. There is much to be said for tenacity."

THOMAS GIFFARD
END OF OCTOBER, 1538
Stretton

XXVIII

"I am rather inclined to believe that this is the land God gave to Cain."
—Jacques Cartier, 1491-1557

Alone in my rooms, I read the inventory, tenderly compiled by my father and his friends. Such a solemn list. Such a poor list, and such feeble sums I paid for it all. The hall: two tables and a bench, 12*d*. The prioress' parlor: one folding table, one bench, one chair, one cupboard and the hangings of painted cloth, 2*s*. The nun's chamber: one featherbed, two old coverlets, one old blanket, one tester of white linen, two bedsteads, two benches, one cupboard, one joint chair, two old coffers, one bolster, two pillows and four pairs of sheets, 10*s*. The bailiff's chamber: one mattress, one coverlet and one ax, 12*d*. The buttery: two ale tubs, one old chest, one board, one tablecloth and two candlesticks, 12*d*. The kitchen: two dressing boards, two stools, one bench, one ladder, 1 ½ bushels of salt, four porridgers of pewter, four platters, two saucers and two brass pots, 5*s*. The larder: one great chest, one trough and two little barrels, 6*s*. The brewhouse: five tubs, one keeler, one old tub, one old table, one old wheel and one cheese press, 16*d*. The gyling house: three cooling leads, two brass pans and seven old tubs, 8*d*. The cheese loft: two little tubs, two cheese racks, two churns, one little wheel and two shelves, 8*d*. The kilhouse: one hair cloth, and one ladder hanging on the wall of the said house, 11*d*. Also sold was grain, 18*s*, one horse, 4*s*, one wain and one dung cart, 16*d*, and ten loads of hay, 15*s*. To George Warren was sold the chalice and three spoons for 26*s* 8*d*.

This was the house of iniquity that must be suppressed. This pitiful convent, its riches only in the golden prayers offered up like incense, its pride only in its gaggle of sparse nuns with all their foibles and dispositions. If any error they made, it was in trusting too naïvely the courage of Englishmen in defending their faith, for I believe that the people care for nothing except war and taxes.

At any moment I expected to hear that Blackladies was surrendered, and it was only for me to take ownership. I chuckled airlessly. Ownership. I? Of a monastery? Such blasphemy. Yet amid all the greater blasphemies to come, it was perhaps a lesser sin. I saw the day when His Majesty would somehow desecrate the shrine of Thomas Becket, that saint most revered in the land. A pilgrimage to Canterbury was as common as the same to an alehouse. How long would the king endure a shrine to a bishop who stood against *his* king? This was not a banner to wave to the populace, yet did he have the stomach to do away with such a glaring beacon? I prophesied that he would, at least with Cromwell egging him on.

It put me of a mind to contemplate my own soul's depth, and to wonder if I had done enough. Should I have gone against my king in support of my faith? Should I have refused to take the oath? Lesser men had done so: Fischer and More, and so many others. Yet the banner of the Giffards has flown high. The Giffards had stood beside the first Norman king on the battlefield of Hastings, and we have walked within the shadow of the crown ever since. Whichever way the banner blows, that is how a Giffard sways. If outwardly he must seem a Lutheran, than it must be so to honor his sovereign. But inwardly, the Giffard mantle wears a Catholic heart, and always shall. I will have a proper priest for my masses and in the pope's Latin. None of these tainted Bibles in common tongues.

"Oh, Isabella! What have they done? What will you do?"

It occurred to me that I might ask her to live on our estates. She would be comfortable and even find the life useful. What would she say to such an offer? I blushed in the thinking of it. What would Ursula say? It need not be at Stretton. Certainly it could be Chillington, or even…

My thoughts had been to purchase Blackladies, but they went no further. Did I intend to live there? I knew Ursula wondered as well, but never did she ask me. It was not a topic easily discussed between us. Though now, with my head drowsy with the warmth from the fire and from a belly full of wine, I sat back in my chair and considered.

She lived there for twenty-three years. Might I do as much? My mind raced toward fluid arches and diamond pane windows set aglow with beeswax tapers. Polished oak paneling to warm the walls, and brickwork to ornament its exterior. I would change the entrance and expand the drive to encompass a park. The stewpond and the mill may stay as they are. Yes. I could see it all in my mind's eye. How it might come alive in its renewal. Alive with the voices of children and families. Alive, too, with the mass in its chapel. Alive and not gone completely.

Snapping open my eyes, my gaze fell upon a tapestry with just such an idyllic setting, and my spirits fell. Would I ever be able to forget that the stones beneath my feet were sacred, that their walls housed prayers and sacrifice? Would I ever be as worthy to live within those walls as Isabella surely was?

"My lord…"

My servant William entered tentatively, knowing my mood of late. "There is a messenger from the king's commissioners, my lord. From Brewood."

So it came at last. Blackladies' surrender. Would it be prudent to make a visit, or would it be unwelcome to those who must be dispossessed? There is nothing quite as loathsome as the presence of a landlord when the tenants are turned out.

"Bring him in, William," I said.

After a few moments, the liveried man entered, bowed, and handed me the missive. It was from that horrible Legh. In his obsequious hand, I read that Blackladies surrendered on the 16th and that they only awaited the nuns to vacate. No doubt they awaited their relatives to spirit them away. Perhaps it was time I did pay a call on Blackladies…while it was still Blackladies.

ISABELLA LAUNDER
NOVEMBER, 1539
Blackladies

XXIX
Remove not the ancient landmark which your fathers set up.
                                                    —Proverbs 22:28

"Are you ready?"

I heard Thomas speaking and yet I did not recognize him at all. He stood behind me in the haze of my remembrance, for all my thoughts were of memories now. I felt my veil flapping outward, reaching for him like a desperate hand. I tugged on it. It behaved like a sail, and I longed to let it fly, with myself flying away with it.

"Isabella, are you ready?" he said again.

Surely this was what an executioner says before he takes you to the gallows. And of course, at that moment, you are never ready. I considered Sir Thomas More. I heard he was a noble gentleman as he walked to his death, speaking no treason even unto the last. Beheaded. Martyred. *Good God.* "Will they take the roof, do you think?" I asked dazed, thinking of beheadings.

"It must be so. The king's commissioners have declared it…so that it shall henceforth be uninhabitable to its former occupants."

I heard the sneer in his voice, but the cry of a hawk caught my attention, and I shielded my eyes with my hand to watch. For a long time it winged in effortless, illimitable circles, always

261

searching. "You make no sound," I told the bird. Thomas twisted his head to observe the soaring blade of wings. "You are Death," I whispered. "Death makes no sound as he swoops down upon his hapless prey. Soundless talons grasp and rip, tearing the creature from the safety of earth." Its shadow passed over me and I shivered before turning to Thomas. The dark, bearded chin raised upward, and the stubble on his throat rose as he swallowed. "Are *you* Death, Thomas? Have you come to rip us free of our safe place?"

"I am offering you an opportunity to preserve what you have."

"What I have is in God's hands, not yours!" My raw fingers covered my mouth and helplessly I shook my head. "How can you know?"

He moved to stand beside me, reassuring with his mere presence. How splendid he looked! How splendid he always looked. Shoulders broad and flanked by the wide borders of a fur collar over an embroidered skirted jerkin. There was gold in a cumbersome chain on his chest, gold on each of his fingers, gold on a broach on his feathered hat.

I sighed, thinking of Blackladies. "I will miss it, this ramshackle bag of bones. They will not need to pull down the walls. They will fall of their own accord." We chuckled. It felt good to hear the both of us, yet it was too soon replaced by the wearying eloquence of a frown. "Yes, I will miss it. But more than that. This life cultivated within these walls. How can that be duplicated? I cannot understand, Thomas, what drove our own countrymen to forsake their Church. Were these pagan idols that they thought it necessary to bring down the very walls? Do they still call themselves Christians, Thomas, who turn out those given to God, allowing a desecrated king to dictate what is 'church' and what is not?"

"Yes," he said. "They have that self-righteous mantle about them, like a younger generation wagging a finger disrespectfully to their elders. They think we poor papists have been misguided fools. They see now the profit in having a king as pope."

"Is it because we believe the bishop of Rome to be the one ambassador of Christ from that long line of apostles back to Saint Peter himself? Is it because we believe that the Holy Mother deserves her rightful place of veneration in our chapels, because she gave her very body to be used as the ark of God? Is it because we hold that our Lord meant for all the world to be under the one roof, a *Catholic* roof, Thomas? And now they tear the roof away."

"But you must admit"—he faced me, a gold encrusted fist digging into his hip—"there *was* corruption and misdeeds. Yes, even in monasteries and convents. Some would say especially those places."

"But why break the pot because the wine is bad? Find the corruption, and fix it."

"Oh, they fixed it right enough," he said, shaking his head so that the feathers swayed. "And replaced them with their own corruptions. Someday Cromwell and his minions will be found out—"

"Hush, Thomas!" My fingers covered his mouth and I felt his warm breath on my nails, the bristly mustache on my fingertips. Slowly I withdrew my hand and stuffed it with the other within my scapular. "I would not have you speak treason. Somehow, I feel the wilderness can hear you."

"Thomas Giffard is no traitor. All the court knows it."

"And they knew it of Thomas More as well." Falling silent, we both listened to the churning wind as it rushed through the yellowed beech leaves, tangling each spindly branch. Suddenly, it cried out in such lonely tones that I was overwhelmed with incomprehensible grief. Long held in, I, too, cried out my despair, "How am I to bear it? I made a vow!"

He clutched for my hands and dragged them out of their nest, crushing them in his warm fingers. "And you keep them as dear as the day you made them, Isabella. I am testimony to that. I will stand before God Himself and declare your virtues."

I used my arm to smite a rivulet on my cheek, for Thomas still held my hands. I pulled them free, tugged my veil about me one last time, and turned from the priory. "Thank you, Thomas. That is the dearest utterance you have ever made to me."

"The dearest, eh?" He chuckled ruefully. "Very well. I mean it... Ah Isabella," he said with a forlorn sigh. "If there was ever a time when a man felt he outlived his usefulness..."

This was not the Thomas Giffard I knew. His voice was almost as desolate as mine. "No, Thomas. Not you. There is more for you to do, I am certain. It is I who was cast out of the nest by the cuckoo. I had a home and now it is no more. Now you are lord of this...this manor, such as it is. At first I was angered at the news until I realized the reasons behind it."

"The reasons?"

"Yes. Your father was to purchase it, was he not?"

He smiled. "Yes. You have found me out. He had his plans... And I have mine."

"Will you...will you live here, Thomas?"

He turned to me with as solemn an expression as Thomas Giffard was ever capable. "I will."

It was not for me to divine his motives, but I was pleased that he would be its caretaker. It would no longer be the Blackladies we knew, and yet it might retain a flavor of what it was under Thomas' stewardship. The foundations were set with blessings, after all.

"Do you..." He cleared his throat and began anew. "Isabella. You need not go to your sister's home to live. I have been thinking on this. The Giffard estates are many. Even my father...that is, we have agreed that you...that any one of your sisters are welcomed to reside there. You need not work as hard as you have. You can still devote your time to prayer and such like."

He could not bear to let me go. Poor Thomas. If I possessed one whit less of strength, I would have flung myself into his arms and taken the sympathy he was prepared to mete out. Praise God I was strong enough to resist such an urge. For there was little doubt I loved Thomas with all the heart of a woman. But there was also little doubt in my mind—for it was the saving grace of my life—that I loved God more.

"It…is a generous offer, Thomas. But I cannot make use of such a thing. So much rumor abounds about us as it is. It would not be well for either of us."

"Can I not do this one thing for you, beloved?"

Biting my lip, I turned, the veil shielding me from him. "You have not called me that for over twenty years."

"Yet each day I thought it. You are still my beloved, my Isabella. But I have also never forgotten that you are Prioress. I make this offer to you with all courtesy, Madam. As much as it may appear, there are no motives behind it."

"Still, I cannot accept. Though Alice may be pleased to make a home on one of your estates. She and her mother are always at odds. Will you do me this favor and take Alice? At least for a little while."

"Anything, Prioress," he said.

We grew silent. We both gazed at Blackladies, its moss-stained lime, its louse-eaten timbers, its stern eyes now dark. We looked with glazed and lovelorn eyes. "Do you think someday this madness will be lifted from England and this house may be restored to its more useful purpose, Thomas? Might that happen?"

"If it does, you may be certain, Madam, that I shall happily return it to its original state. Well…perhaps *without* the leaky roof."

"Then I can be satisfied." Yet even as I uttered it, the uncertainty of my present existence weighed heavily. I clutched the scapular, the very same my predecessor wore and the prioress before her. How many grave ladies have worn this armor of black before me, and how many more were destined for its future on English soil? I would not don the plain woolens and headdress Legh and Cavendish brought for us to wear. That was for later. I would leave Blackladies as a nun.

"Shall I collect Dame Alice, then, if she is willing?" he said.

I nodded, still gazing at Blackladies, her timbers and stone. "It was kind of you to offer to come for us, Thomas. I shall await my brother-in-law."

He stopped and gazed at me. I did not deign to look, for I knew his expression was not fitting to our situation. But I did see him solemnly bow, as any courtier would to a great lady.

"Madam," he said softly, and slowly withdrew.

THOMAS GIFFARD
MARCH, 1540
Swynnerton

XXX

Nay, tempt me not to love again: There was a time when love was sweet;
Dear Nea! had I known thee then, Our souls had not been slow to meet!
But oh! this weary heart hath run so many a time the rounds of pain,
Not even for thee, thou lovely one! Would I endure such pangs again.
                                                            —Thomas More

The bundle lay tight against my chest as I made the long walk to the entrance. A porter ran out to meet me and I belatedly realized that it was the master of the house, William Beche.

"My Lord Giffard. You honor us. Let me help you." He offered to take the bundle, but I wanted to present it myself to Isabella, for I longed to see her and how she fared in her new life.

"Is the Prioress...I mean, is Isabella at home?"

His brows rose over his ruddy forehead. "She is ever here, my lord. She never leaves the grounds. Not even to go to market. It is most unnatural."

"She is used to walls."

"Yes, but she is not locked up here, my lord. Here she has the freedom of the grange to do as she likes. No one hinders her. Yet she will not go beyond the garden and fields."

"Will you take me to her?"

"Surely I can offer you our hospitality first, my lord. In the parlor. My wife will fetch her for you."

"No, thank you. You need not fetch her. I will go to her." *As I have ever done*, I thought.

Shaking his head, he nevertheless took me through a gate and into the grounds. Agnes, his frowzy wife and Isabella's sister, accosted us. I remember her in her younger days as a slight creature with a roving eye, but now she was plump and red-cheeked, the folds at her eyes scratched with lines. "My lord," she said with a curtsey before shooting her husband a warning glare. "I did not know you had arrived."

"Madam," I said with a nod.

"You must take refreshment, Lord Giffard. Let me call a servant—"

"There is no need, madam. I do not wish to inconvenience you. I only brought this for your sister."

I proffered the bundle in its sack. Spindly, claw-like, it was one of the rose bushes salvaged from Blackladies. The gardener dug it up for me and packaged it. I assumed Isabella would know what to do with it. "It is a rose bush," I said to her.

"Oh, my lord, she does not tend the garden anymore."

"Oh? I am most distressed to hear that. She took particular fondness in tending the gardens at Blackladies and at home in Beech."

"Yes. It was her favorite occupation. And yet here she does not even ask to do it, and as you can see, Lord Giffard, it can use her touch."

Around us were the drooping attempts to coax spring from the fledgling garden. Weeds crept into beds, and a birdbath was muddy and soiled with droppings and feathers. "Perhaps this will bring her comfort and she will start anew."

"Let us hope so. Oh. There she is."

I raised my head and saw a stately lady all in black, walking slowly and aimlessly in the field beyond the garden. Her head was down and the headdress' veil blew out behind her. Not quite as I remembered her. She looked more drawn and more fragile in her commoner's clothes. Strange how I could not recall her wearing anything other than a habit.

"She does not wear her nun's clothes," I remarked more to myself than to them.

"Yes. She would if allowed," said Agnes. "Faith, my lord, it does not signify. Why she persists in this melancholy display—"

"Custom, madam. She was a nun a long time. She hopes to be so again."

Agnes drew silent, and her husband beside her seemed uncomfortable in his own quietude. Finally, he asked, "How is our Alice, my lord? We have not heard from her for a month now."

"Dame Alice is well…"

"Just 'Alice', my lord," Agnes interrupted. "Only a daughter now."

I smiled ruefully. "She will always be *Dame* Alice to me. She is happy in her retirement. She enjoys my children as a governess."

"Certainly you might wish to have Isabella serve in your household as well, Lord Giffard?"

I glared at her. "What is the matter, madam? Is not her pension enough to keep her under your roof?"

"She isn't happy here, my lord. I meant no offense."

"She will not come," I said, tight-lipped. "There is no need to ask again. She will stay here."

"Then let me call her, my lord, and tell her you are here."

At that moment, it did not seem wise, this visit. To look into her forlorn eyes and be able to do nothing was a heartache I could not bear. Her solitary figure moved more like a spirit along the greening fields, the mist becoming part of her like some pagan image from an old fable. But missing the opportunity to speak with her would be a greater heartache, and so I nodded to her sister as she went to fetch Isabella's shade.

She looked up toward me as her sister spoke to her, and I moved slowly across the windswept field to meet her halfway. Agnes departed as I approached.

I planted a smile upon my face, though Isabella did not return the expression.

"Thomas," she said softly, vaguely. She looked at me almost without recognition, and then turned again to the surrounding vista as if looking for something.

"Isabella, I am glad to see you. It has been many months."

"Has it? I am uncertain these days of the passage of time."

"Perhaps you would be more aware if you returned to your garden. I understand you no longer toil there. Why?"

"It is full of such life and living things. I do not feel I belong there anymore."

"Among the living? But you are alive, my dear. And you have such skill in this. Look. See what I have brought you."

Slowly, she turned her eyes to the bundle, and she smiled at last. "Is it a rose bush?"

"Yes. From Blackladies."

The mention of the word made her frown and she turned away from it, pulling her headdress' veil around her as she was wont to do with her habit's veil. "Take it away. It does not belong to me."

I took her arm, grasping harder than I meant to do. "It is yours. I am giving it to you. And I want you to cultivate it and care for it as you have done for so many years. Do you care nothing for my gifts?"

She turned and gazed at it, reaching a hand out to touch its gnarled trunk. "You…salvaged it?"

"For you, lady."

She raised her eyes and looked at me fondly, shaking her head. "Do you love me still, Thomas? Look how old we are. I am fifty-two, long past that first summer. Surely I am no longer lovable."

I softened my hold on her arm, caressing with my thumb. At fifty-two she was at last a handsome woman. Still slim and tall, the years filled in the face that was long and boyish. Her eyes, always kind and somewhat mischievous, were still the same as I remembered. "Always lovable," I said. "No matter how wrinkled and gray we become. I feel as if we are an old married couple. We seem to know each other's moods so well. We know what the other is thinking, even when many miles separate us."

She smiled. "An 'old married couple' indeed!" She chuckled and hid her yellowed teeth behind her hand. "We are what we are, Thomas, wrinkled and gray."

I straightened and pulled at my doublet. "Speak for yourself!"

She laughed, and her pain seemed to give way at last. Like a baby chick tearing through the membrane of shell and nest, Isabella's eyes took in the world as if for the first time. She even deeply inhaled, taking in something new and restorative. Perhaps her old self.

I placed the bundle into her hands. Its soil sprinkled across my jerkin. "Plant this. Do not doubt that I will check on it from time to time to make certain you are properly caring for my gift. I do not give gifts lightly, madam."

"Nor do I accept them lightly." She nodded courteously.

"You were always a strong woman, Isabella," I said looking out past the fields. "Come back like these roses. It tears my heart to see you so sad. Restore that garden. Keep the memory of Blackladies alive, as I shall make it alive."

She raised her face to me. "I do have a way with roses...and with gardens." She looked at the spindly bundle tucked in her arm. "Roses are tenacious things."

With relief I hugged her shoulders and sighed, wondering what the spying eyes of her sister were reading from this encounter. "Tell me, Isabella, is it so very difficult, this new life?"

She rocked her head against mine for a moment—like old friends—and she sighed. "Not difficult. Just...different. And lonely."

"Lonely? But you are with your own kin."

She shook her head and pressed her lips together. "I think of Dame Alice and Dame Cristabell and Dame Felicia as my kin now, Thomas. Odd that my own family seem like strangers to me."

"Yes," I said, squeezing her shoulders once more before letting her go. "I can see how that can be."

"How fares Alice?"

"She is well and content in my household. I fear I shared with her many memories of you." Isabella blushed and I laughed to see it. "Yes. You remember."

"I recall some stories about *you*, Lord Giffard, but I am too much of a lady to share them with anyone."

"And I thank you for that," I said with a bow.

We gazed silently across the fields just as the mist lifted. Green buds speckled the dark soil as far as our eyes could see.

"How is Blackladies?" she asked suddenly.

"Strange you should ask. Tomorrow I go to see to its...its rebuilding."

"You need not spare me. You mean they are going to tear it down."

I flicked my gaze at her and saw her eyes were dry. "Yes, Madam," I said soberly.

Her hoarse laugh startled me and I looked at her. "I am imagining Thomas Giffard living on the same stones as generations of nuns. I can't help but laugh at such a thing."

I chuckled nervously. "Faith, Madam! I never had that thought in my head...until now. Do you think I will be haunted?"

Her eyes—as always—pierced through mine. "Not by them, I think."

"Only one," I agreed.

She seemed to wear a satisfied grin and I turned my gaze back to the countryside and its sky clouding up in gray puffs. "Isabella," I said softly, "I have news for you. I have a new daughter. She...she is christened...Isabel."

She flattened her expression, but it was one I knew well. It seemed to say to me, "Incautious, Thomas." Then she turned to me and examined my face as if memorizing each contour, from my proud nose to the wrinkles at my eyes. "I am glad you came. It was as if I was in a dream. Nothing seemed real."

"I have awakened you."

"Yes, Thomas." She did not cease her scrutiny of my face until her eyes took on a devilish glint—a look I have not seen her wear in thirty years. "*You* are a terribly handsome man, Thomas Giffard."

My eyes widened at such bold words. For a moment, I was speechless. "Isabella!" I sputtered. "I...I am...flattered."

"It was not meant to flatter. It was to tell you true what I have always known. And I think...I shall kiss you."

Before I could speak, she reached up and with her free hand on my cheek, she planted a firm kiss on my lips. It was not a lover's kiss—not such as I would have liked to have given her—but it was instead the kiss of a longtime friend.

There was a playful jaunt to her mouth when she released me, and it echoed my own. "Why Isabella! What would your sisters say to that?"

Her boldness faded, replaced by a blush. She clutched the rose bush tightly. "I do not know. There would be words, that much is certain." She glanced back at the house. "I have scandalized Agnes again, no doubt."

She was merry, and it was a balm to see it. I risked it all by running my hand around her waist. "Then let her be thoroughly scandalized with this." She did not shy this time. She raised her face boldly to mine. My mouth dipped to caress hers and lingered gently, tenderly. It was both ardent and chaste. We were lovers who were not lovers, and so we kissed like those in a dream.

When I withdrew from her she smiled at me. "Shame, Thomas," she said, though she had no look of shame in her eyes.

"Perhaps I should go," I said. I stepped back and bowed formally before straightening. "Will I be welcomed back, Lady Prioress?"

My question, an echo of one asked so many years ago, also made her smile. "If it is your will, Lord Giffard. How can I ever stop you?"

I said nothing more as I swiftly left the grounds. I do not give my gifts lightly.

❖

I left Swynnerton and arrived at Blackladies the next day for the unpleasant task of watching them tear down the roof. No nestlings shall return to the roost, so it was declared. The roof must go before any new construction was to take place. And so, as an Usher of the King's Chamber, I was obligated to follow the letter of the law, lest His Majesty turn the priory over to a less worthy man.

I watched from the edge of a copse as they pulled the rafters down. A great cloud of dust billowed as wood and stone filled the courtyard. Only when the dust dispersed did I urge my stallion closer. He picked with his heavy hoofs over the new rubble, and I tried to envision the place remade into my new residence.

The rubble was deep, and so I dismounted and climbed it, ignoring the workmen as they bowed and doffed their caps. Did they know what damage they truly inflicted? Did they realize how irreparable were these walls once pulled down? More than stone and wood. Much more.

I had done my best to salve Isabella's heart, but this scene of destruction pulled at my own soul. I was glad she was not here to see it.

The garden was unrecognizable. And though as a man I should never have been privy to the interior of the nun's cloister, I had enjoyed a singular privilege that could not be explained in a court document or to a dispassionate inquisitor.

It was lovely, her garden, a creature of Isabella's own devising. A place of refuge and beauty. Of peace.

And now it was rubble. The foliage was gray with dust as if some unholy snow storm had blown through. One beam had fallen across the garden, crushing her proud rose bushes beneath them. Red petals scattered like blood on a battlefield. Rosewood limbs lay broken and vanquished. I was saddened to see the roof come down, but I was far more affected by the sight of her slain roses.

I knelt beside them, lifting a limp bloom in my palm. Their fragrance was still pungent in the air, still strong and full of the promise that only a rose can give. How much they had weathered, and now how little remained. It would certainly take a cataclysm such as this to destroy them utterly, for they never before surrendered. Proud, they were. Their faces always toward the sun.

I let the bloom fall from my hand, its fragrance still permeating the flesh. Truly a death worth mourning.

Still, a rose is a hearty thing. Pruned down to nothing, it surprises its gardener with the tenacity of its blooms. And a rose possesses that singular ability to be grafted to stronger stock, to push out its roots, hold on, and live again.

AUTHOR'S AFTERWORD

Prior to 1540, there were some eight thousand men and women serving in England in over eight hundred religious communities. By 1540, none remained. Besides the evicted monks and nuns, it is believed that as much as ten times that population was also turned out of the dissolved monasteries and convents. These people were either servants dependent on religious houses to make a living, or they were older persons reliant on the monks and nuns for their retirement care.

Once dissolved, the monastery buildings were sold, the churches were stripped of their riches, and in some cases burned, their empty shells still standing today as silent testimony to Henry VIII's division with Rome.

Ironically, the fall of the monasteries was also the fall of the chief instigator of their destruction, Thomas Cromwell. By this time, King Henry was married to his fourth wife Anne of Cleeves, forming an alliance with Lutheran Germany, but the reasons for the alliance were quickly slipping away. Not wishing any more enmity with the emperor (which Henry incurred by his fight to divorce Catherine of Aragon) and losing interest almost immediately in his new wife, the marriage was quickly dissolved— and so was confidence in Cromwell who machined the match. Cromwell was imprisoned and subsequently executed for treason.

The character of Thomas Legh is well documented in the papers of the time. He was as detestable—if not more so—as depicted.

As for Thomas Giffard, he did rebuild Blackladies and resided there until 1559, a year before he died, leasing it in that last year to his son Humphrey. He remained Catholic, as did many in the town of Brewood (pronounced "brood" by contemporary locals), and he is even mentioned in documents as one being fined for recusancy or "tarrying at home" instead of attending the king's Protestant services. No doubt, he celebrated private masses in his own home.

Despite this religious difference, he maintained unusual favor at court. He was appointed sheriff twice, and served as bailiff and custodian for a deer park in Bishop's Wood. Once Queen Mary came to power, restoring Catholicism to England, Thomas was knighted at her coronation, and served as an honored member of Parliament during her unfortunate reign.

His father lived to a ripe old age of 90 years, and Thomas himself died at 69, with seventeen children, ten surviving. In his will, he left to "Dame Alice" the amount of 40*s* and a black gown. Dame Alice apparently went on to live a comfortable life under the surviving Ursula Giffard. She was made godmother of George Giffard, one of Thomas' grandchildren, and perhaps later lived under the care of Thomas' daughter Isabel who married Francis Biddolph. They had a son named Humphrey, whom Alice named as executor of her will. Many of the items in her will look suspiciously like the inventory from Blackladies.

Thomas was entombed in his family church in Brewood, the Church of St. Mary the Virgin and St. Chad. In a twist of cruel irony, the man who defended the Catholic faith with secret masses now finds himself buried not in a Catholic church, but in one now entrusted to the Church of England.

Isabella Launder received 40*s* when they closed Blackladies. Her nuns each received 20*s*. They were all granted pensions for life. Isabella's was 66*s* 8*d* a year, and the others received their yearly stipend of 33*s* 4*d*

Isabella lived with her sister Agnes in Swynnerton until she died in March of 1551. It is not known how old she actually was. According to documents, only two nuns survived her: Cristabell

Smith and Isabella's niece, Alice Beche. Another niece married Christopher Alate, a former tenant at Blackladies, and was most likely a relation to Catherine Alate, one of the priory's servants.

Isabella was laid to rest in the parish of Stone not far from Beech on April 28, 1551.

GLOSSARY

ANGELUS A noon ringing of bells as a reminder of specific prayers to the Virgin Mary.

BOLTING HOUSE A place for storing flour.

DIVINE OFFICE They were first used for monastics, denoting the specific hours of the day for certain prayers. Also called the canonical hours, these soon became how the laity could divide the day, since the monks and nuns rang bells to call their community to prayer. It was a precursor to clocks, and the occupants of village and city alike, knew what specific time of the day it was by the ringing of the bells. They were divided roughly like this:

Matins (during the night, usually midnight, sometimes called Vigils)

Lauds (at dawn or 3:00 a.m.)

Prime (first hour, 6:00 a.m.)

Terce (third hour, 9:00 a.m.)

Sext (sixth hour, noon)

None (ninth hour, 3:00 p.m.)

Vespers (6:00 p.m.)

Compline (9:00 p.m.)

GYLING HOUSE Gyle is wort in the process of fermentation, so a gyling house is another place in the long process for the brewing of beer.

KEELER A shallow tub for cooling liquids.

KILHOUSE A place for drying grain. Also "Kilnhouse".

SKEP Woven beehive, where we get the shape of a beehive hair-do.

STEWPOND A pond for keeping fish for eating.

WAIN A horse-drawn wagon.

ABOUT THE AUTHOR

Los Angeles native and award-winning author **Jeri Westerson** writes the critically acclaimed Crispin Guest Medieval Noir mysteries and historical novels. Her mysteries have garnered nominations for the Shamus, the Macavity, the Agatha, Romantic Times Reviewer's Choice, and the Bruce Alexander Historical Mystery Award. When not writing, Jeri dabbles in beekeeping, gourmet cooking, fine wines, cheap chocolate, and swoons over anything British. **JeriWesterson.com**

Photography Craig Westerson

Made in the USA
Lexington, KY
11 July 2015